The Steffan Legacy.

Guy Trevelyan-Martin has asserted his rights under the Copyright, Designs and Patents Act 1986 to be identified as the author of this work.

This novel is a work of fiction albeit based on contemporary times, places and people. The names, characters and incidents are all the work of the author's imagination. Any resemblance to any places, incidents or people, living or dead, is purely coincidental except for the media presenters who may let me know if they object to being named.

Copyright Guy Trevelyan-Martin 2016

To Poppet for not letting me stop.

The Steffan Legacy

Chapter 1

Mrs Sandy Quigley

I just couldn't be doing with the bollocks of it all anymore. And forgive me if I waffle. I get wound up.

It came to me like a smack in the head. I hadn't really been dwelling on it. But this idea flashed into my head and wouldn't let go. Like a dog with a bone it hung on and gnawed at me. What was pre-occupying me was the pressures of work, I'm a stress test engineer testing all kinds of materials for all kinds of uses and, ironically, it has been quite stressful recently, but I was sitting at home with Joe, glass of wine in hand, as usual, watching the television. I can't remember what we were watching at the time. I think I was reading a magazine as well but the detail has all faded after the brouhaha you are about to read of. The Prime Minister, announced that we were basically a Christian country and this was pretty much the last straw. I think there had been some kind of religious or race inspired something that had agitated him and he needed a response to settle his mainly white, mainly male, mainly upper or middle-class constituency. I'm afraid the detail of it has been left behind such was its lack of importance in the grand scheme of things.

I know, I should breathe sometimes when I'm talking about this but the whirlwind has been intense. I said to Joe that I really couldn't be doing with all this bollocks any more. I know, I swear, I work in a male dominated industry and you just have to put up with it. It gets to you, you swear as well. Joe told me off and asked what it was that was getting to me. Now we both shout at the telly quite a lot, more so as we get older. So, I told him, The Prime Minister and his Christian country, putting a badge on it, defining it as one thing excluding as many people as he thinks he is including.

Me and Joe are atheists. We were both brought up to believe in God but we lapsed and now you might describe us as pretty fundamentalist atheists. Some people at work talk of there being a higher power; that there must be someone or something responsible for our existence. I believe we are all responsible for ourselves and we should just get on with it. If something happens, good or bad take the credit or take responsibility, don't blame fate or the gods, or coincidence. JFDI.

(There was one time when I had to sign something for the probate on my mother's will when I had to swear an oath on the bible and I couldn't. I said to Charlie, our solicitor, that it was no good, swearing on a bible wasn't swearing at all. There has to be another way and there was. It was called an affirmation which all goes to show that we don't have to swear to a God that we don't believe in.)

Neither Joe nor I are really political; we vote, I know how he votes and he knows how I vote. Last time I went Green which was unusual. We take an interest, we listen to the discussion, read papers, listen to the Today programme on the way to work, but we are fairly set in our ways. Not for one second did I think what we were about to do would lead to what it did. Little old us. But I don't think it was us that caused the problems. I don't want to say it was everybody else but maybe it was laws of unintended consequences. You know, a butterfly flaps its wings and so on. Or am I being too charitable. Perhaps I am but over the centuries we have seen faith groups at each other's throats claiming credit for the good things and blaming all and sundry for the bad.

So Joe asked me what I was going to do about it. About what? I asked, about being a Christian country. I had rather moved on. "I don't know", I told him. I hadn't really thought it through. I had thought about it, briefly, on the way to work, in the shower, but not made a plan for anything. I thought it was just another shout at the telly opportunity every time a religious leader appeared.

When I was younger and been taken to church, I had read the lesson for my proudly proud mother and an adoring congregation, standing like a little poppet in front of the lectern placed in the centre of the aisle. Every Saturday I would rehearse with my mother, making her heart swell at the prospect of the plaudits the next day. I don't want to be too mean about my mother in case my girls get the idea that it is okay to be disrespectful about your parents, and in print as well.

We've learned about the pagan Romans trying to suppress the enlightened Christians, The first installation in the Jesus story and then the crusades, Christians at war with Muslims, we studied Henry the Eighth and his legacy, the Spanish Armada, Catholics against Protestants, Protestants against Catholics, Missionaries going into the jungle to try and tame the uncivilised natives (We had Albert Schweitzer drummed into us at Primary school) and virtually since we were born the Northern Irish Protestants and Catholics shooting each other, bombing each other. Now we've got Sunni Muslims and Shias and I don't know which is which running amok in the Middle-east. I don't know which lot of these ISIS people or the Taliban or Daesh or Al-Qaeda are which. There's the Kurds, Peshmerga I've read about, PKK, either being blown up or blowing up in Turkey. Assad's lot with the Russians and the Turks against the Kurds against ISIS. I really had lost the will to understand because I don't know if they are on the same side, or opposing sides, what their aims are and who they are targeting. I decided I didn't want their religion or any religion to be a part of my life. Take a breath. The upshot is that they are killing each other by the hundreds or thousands all in the name of a God or the interpretation of what a God is said to have said in whatever version of the bible, the Quran, the Torah or whatever it is you read. Breathe. How on earth can you watch the news and believe these people believe they have an ounce of good or right or justice in their bodies. Look at what the ISIS lot were doing to the Yazidis and tell me it was driven by faith in a God. Insecure blokes with small dicks if you ask me. Glass of wine please.

I turned the page on my magazine and forgot all about it for a while. I have so many mags and web sites to refer to in work that sometimes I struggle to keep up. I think we were watching old DVD's of the West Wing, there's not much on the telly we watched in those days, mainly films and boxed sets. Bartlett was such a good

President and I liked Josh best. Joe, as you'd expect fancied the blonde girl, Donna. Sorry, rabbiting on but it might help you to understand where we were coming from in all this.

We went to bed. We have a routine, wash up the wine glasses, put things away, jim-jams on, brush our teeth. You might think this is silly but we refurbished the house a couple of years ago and had the fourth bedroom turned into an en-suite with two sinks and we invariably brush our teeth at the same time. (Those who brush together, stay together?) Off with the electric blanket, read a bit and then go to sleep. (You didn't really need to know we called them jim-jams, did you?) That night, I struggled to get to sleep. You'd think the wine would do its job but it didn't. Joe had challenged me, I thought, what was I going to do about this Christian country stuff? Normally I sleep soundly; I turn off the light, have a kiss and a hug with Joe and go out like a light. That night, I tossed and turned in a kind of unexpected, unanticipated, turmoil. I'd look at the alarm clock and see that it had moved on forty minutes or so and wondered if I had slept or just dozed and I did this most of the night.

At three twenty-seven, I remember the time well, it's like it's the darkest hour, I shook Joe awake. "Joe, Joe, I've got it."

"What?" It takes a good shove and a kick to wake Joe. I've haven't had to do it too often, a couple of times when there were strange noises in the house, but often enough to know it takes a bit of effort. He gets off really easily and mumbles, farts, snores and occasionally shouts, especially after too much red, until the alarm goes off.

"Sandyland, what do you think?"

"I don't know." He sat up. "What am I supposed to be thinking about?" He rolled over to face me and mumbled at me. "There I was with Cameron Diaz on that beach at La Marina, in Spain, naked, nothing sexual, chatting about leading, good grief, chatting about workplace conditions, smokers, air conditioning. How weird."

"No, listen, you perv" I said back to him, I'm surprised it was Cameron Diaz and not Donna from West Wing, "Sandyland. We're going to declare this house and garden a nation state. What do you think?"

"And name it after a caravan park by the sea. You can do better than that. Come on, get back to sleep, we've got to be up for work in two and a half hours."

"I haven't slept, Joe, this is really coming together".

"You know I've supported all that you've done for the best part of the last forty odd years."

"Oh yes."

"But can we talk about it in the morning. Please. I'll never get back to that beach now."

He was right. I did manage to get to sleep. It was as though I had purged the thoughts in my head. I also knew it wasn't a satisfactory solution, Joe was right about it being a caravan park name, but I was on my way. And then when the alarm went off at six we got up. Usual routine. I didn't want Joe to worry too much so we did the usual. He didn't mention the conversation in the night. Perhaps he had forgotten it, perhaps he had ignored it, perhaps Cameron Diaz on a naturist beach in Spain was more interesting. Anyway, he likes a bath, I have a shower. He likes eggs and bacon, I like muesli, he has too much coffee and I drink camomile tea.

The usual routine until he went off to work as per but I phoned Charlie, our Solicitor, to see if I could get to see him. I had this idea swirling around in my head like a big fat bumble bee trapped in a glass jar buzzing and knocking at the sides as a new thought emerges. You must know what I mean, something you can't let go of. You either sort it out or let it go. I had to sort it out.

I got an appointment with Charlie and phoned work to let them know I wouldn't be in. We were testing the elasticity of some new polymers coming in from China for use in the next generation of food packaging. I thought that could wait for a day. Work calls it a duvet day. Very inspired.

Chapter 2

Charlie, the Solicitor

Good morning. It was slightly odd getting that call from Sandy. I haven't done any professional work for them for years, not since their wills were drafted. But as friends we probably have each other over a couple of times a year, we meet at parties at Christmas and in the pub sometimes. Our kids are the same sort of age and my wife met Sandy outside the school gates donkey's years ago, got chatting, had coffees and so on and we stayed friends.

She sounded very excitable which isn't uncommon. She's always been, shall we say, energetic, in her approach to many things. She was less energetic when I asked her out when we were teenagers. She was gorgeous, still is very attractive, not at all mumsy. Badminton and swimming have kept her in shape and she works hard doing something I don't understand. I try not to regard women by their looks, don't get me wrong but when you are first attracted to someone it is usually what they look like the prompts you and then how you get on with them. My problem with Sandy is that I never got past first looks. Never mind, she's been with Joe for way over thirty, nearly forty years, nearly as long as Kate and me.

At ten thirty she engulfed my office with her enthusiasm for an idea that apparently had kept her up all night. You wouldn't have been able to tell that she hadn't slept well. She always looks fresh as a daisy. She wanted to declare hers and Joe's house and garden an independent state. Now I have spent years doing conveyancing, the odd divorce, petty thefts, wills and leases and this was quite a turn up for the books. I must tell you, it stretched me somewhat. I've made a decent living over the years. I belong to the golf club, the Rotarians amongst other organisations. Kate and I, I think, are well respected in town. I have a small suite of offices in the High Street. I employ one other solicitor and we share a receptionist come secretary, Judith. We are a typically dull, suburban practice and will never set the world on fire. I have no ambition to sit on the woolsack, just earn well enough to support a middle-class lifestyle. Long-haul and skiing once a year, second home in Normandy and an E Class Mercedes. Enough about me. I'm largely irrelevant after it all started except I do re-appear towards the end.

As I was saying, Sandy burst into the office, explained about The Prime Minister, what he'd said and what she wanted to do about it. I said I didn't think there was any precedent but in my increasingly dim and distant memory I seemed to recall one of those old forts, out in the English Channel, that the owner declared independent. Sealand, he'd called it. There was, indeed, no precedent in English law but we googled it and very soon became aware of how it had formed and the problems that had arisen. Something about permanent occupation and having a proper constitution. I had a few appointments that day so Sandy was popping in and out of my office. I sent her off to the library to see what she could find out there but she was back, full of ideas.

One of the key things for both of us, in anticipation of her explaining to Joe what was going on, was about membership of the

European Union. We both felt that with free movement of people, capital and free trade that the impact of Sandy and Joe declaring independence would be minimal, barely noticeable in the grand scheme of things. There had been a referendum when the vote was to leave the European Union but the increasingly viable proposition was the continued free movement of people and money and there was going to be a two-year hiatus when article 50 was invoked and the negotiations began. Not top of mind at that very moment. We both also felt they would be able to continue banking with their banks and that their pension pot would be safe, access to healthcare would be as per the EU rules and regulations and, it bears repetition, because this was all going to be of no consequence; no one was going to notice.

Sandy explained it was just intended to be a bit of fun, a childish, petulant snub to the establishment. At about half past six we finally called it a day. I asked her if she'd like to pop out for a drink, a swift half, but she said she had to get back to Joe. Lucky man.

Chapter 3.

Mr Joe Quigley

If you saw me on the street, you would ignore me. I am average height, have stayed the same weight for most of my life for which I thank a higher metabolic rate for coping with the amount of wine we both get through. I shop for clothes in Marks and Spencer, shoes in Clarks, haircut once every couple of months and no distinguishing features. Male pattern baldness, jowly cheeks, a bit of bagginess under the eyes but not unfit. I use the double negative because we play badminton once a week and swim often, particularly with the grandchildren on Saturday mornings when we look after them. I guess this limited exercise helps the liver cope with the alcohol.

I get back from work before Sandy and I usually put dinner on. That day, I had some nice Aberdeen Angus 28 day hung fillet steak and some chunky oven chips. We buy a lot of food from specialists over the internet. There is a butcher up in Scotland who does this fantastic beef, another in the Shetlands does lamb that grazes on salt marshes and we get fish direct from the fisherman in Cornwall. Vegetables are delivered once a week and we treat ourselves to organic. I don't really know if they are any better for you but we do give a toss about the environment, what with the grandchildren and so on.

I work locally in what they now call Facilities Management, that's corporate talk for Office Manager, but in a large manufacturing business on the edge of town. I've been with them for twenty plus years, enjoyed a bit of promotion and, as time passed by, jobs passed me by. No regrets. I didn't think I wanted to or needed to put up with the pressures of doing more senior things and, you know that Peter principal thing, where people get promoted to a level of incompetence, well, I didn't fancy that. I wanted to stay in a comfort zone. Who needs the grief? I earned well enough, as did Sandy and I only had four years to go to retirement, as did Sandy.

As I was telling you, steak and chips. I put the chips in the oven, confident that Sandy would be home at the same time as usual, cut some rocket lettuce and a few spinach and beetroot leaves from the garden, picked a cucumber and some tomatoes from the greenhouse, tossed them in a vinaigrette of balsamic, mustard and extra virgin olive oil. You can tell I like to cook. It is something I have done for years and we both like good ingredients. Now the kids have gone and are settled and we are earning decent money with the mortgage paid off, we can afford some of the nicer things. We put a lot into the pensions as well because we both fancy a bit of travel when we retire.

Ten minutes before Sandy was due I poured out two glasses of red, took a hearty swig from one and put the steaks under the grill. Bit of sea salt and black pepper. (I don't want you to get the impression we have a problem with alcohol or that we are in denial. We are a part of that group, I think they call it a demographic, of white middle-aged, middle-class boozers who drink too much.

Should know better, but we feel we deserve a glass or two, or three, after a hard day at work.)

You can set your clock by Sandy getting home from work. If she's going to be late, she'll call. If there's traffic, she'll call me from her car. She holds on to her youth by driving a mini. This time it is a convertible. It does have Bluetooth so she isn't breaking the law. I checked my phone, there was nothing, no missed calls, no unread texts, no emails. I began to worry and took the steaks out from under the grill and the chips out of the oven.

I called her. "Sorry love," she said to me. "I'll be home in ten minutes. Let me gather my thoughts and I'll tell you all about what I've been up to."

I trust her completely. I've never had reason to doubt her but I did ask her where she'd been. It wasn't an intrusion or me lacking trust, I was genuinely concerned for her. "I'll tell you all about it when I get home," she insisted.

I put the steaks back on and had another slurp remembering breakfast television that morning when they had had another pop at the over fifties drinking too much. I felt a little guilty but hey ho. We've survived so far on a diet based on what we fancy not on health grounds and generally we have consumed more wine than a joyless teetotal doctor would recommend. I know, self-delusion is a part of the issue. To tell you the truth, we probably do a couples of bottles an evening between us, shared evenly. We have a trip to France every couple of months to stock up. Have done for years. Am I going on too much about the booze?

Now usually, and you might guess this if you have known and been with the same person for well over forty years but there is little that's new to talk about. We've covered money, work, keeping each other happy, sex, friends, family, people at her work that I know and the few times I talk to her about my work. It isn't very interesting making sure things do what they are supposed to and the windows get cleaned, the buildings get repaired or repainted. That evening she came in, full of beans and looking more excited than I had seen her for years which is, as you might guess, unusual. "I'll tell you all about it when I've eaten," she said and drank a large part of her large glass of red.

I was impatient to know but didn't press her. I know better than to do that. I finished cooking the steaks, served the chips and salad and we ate and drank the red wine.

She told me that she hadn't been to work, had taken what they apparently call a duvet day and had been with Charlie, the solicitor. He's a bit of a rogue. We've known him for donkey's years and he's always had a thing for Sandy.

She spent the next hour telling me all about Sealand, the EU, the free movement of capital and people and she emphasised this last part. Charlie had told her no one would notice. All Charlie had said we should do is write to the Prime Minister, the Home Secretary, the Foreign Secretary, the Local Authority and perhaps put an advertisement, a public notice, in the local paper. It seemed a bit over the top but Sandy said "come on, be up for it. It's a bit of fun and when did we last have fun? When did we last cock a snook at authority?" She was, of course, right. We had become dull.

When we met outside the US Embassy protesting about Vietnam it was a thrill. Shouting, chanting, singing the old Joan Baez number, "We will overcome". We were going to change the world. We both smoked a bit of dope, we had both tripped, we were political, we were angry, we were part of the generation that were the first to rebel against what our parents and their generation felt and did. In our torn levis, desert boots, her in a very smelly Afghan coat, me and my Levis jacket (I know, double denim my daughters would say, reminding them of that Clarkson man on the telly). We were never a danger, never arrested, but we did feel like the world was ours to change. We wanted to make it a better place for everyone and I think we were the last generation that gave a toss. I don't think punks did, they were more anarchic. Until we got caught up in children, mortgages, bills, school uniforms and so on.

We had become settled and normal and lost most of our rebellion. All people age that way. There must be a law about it. We hadn't smoked any cannabis for about ten years and if the girls ever found out that we had that would be it, I'm sure. They would replace our late parents as the formal tellers off and wag their righteous fingers at us. Somebody once said something about rebelling against your parents by having the same attitudes as your grandparents did, but what's the benefit of being head of the family if you worry all the time about what your kids will think if you transgress? (Forgive me, I sometimes just go on a bit too, like Sandy).

"We need to permanently occupy the house, which we do, and have a formal constitution. Now this is the good bit." She had some momentum going now. "We can say we have the same constitution as England or Great Britain or whatever, because it is unwritten, but we can disestablish the church, which is what we want."

I was impressed by what she had gone though. She had really done some thinking and she asked me if I was up for it. "Come on," she said, "let's have some fun".

"It can't be that simple."

"It won't be that simple but it will be a bit of fun. Are you up for a bit of fun, like before, like before we got old and get older. We're both past sixty, let's not fade away like an old Rolling Stone, gathering no moss".

"I see what you've done there. Give me some more details".

"I don't have many, but here's a few thoughts. We declare our borders to be the same as the Land Registry for the house and garden. We've got a fence and front gate already. We continue to work and pay our taxes and our council tax, national insurance, car tax and so on. Then we work out a name and finally we get a flag made and plant it in the ground."

I am a little less high-spirited than Sandy. I do like to contemplate issues for at least a little while. "Are we going to get looked after when we are demented and infirm. You know I'll look after you and I know you'll look after me, but we both know there comes a time". As you get older the idea that you might become infirm with that slow decline to a death that may or may not be swift grows and the need for the security blanket of care as you wither away always nudges at your thinking.

"If we pay in, I'm sure, within the EU, we'll be okay. If we do end up leaving the EU and the rule's change, then we may have to reconsider."

She was very convincing. "Sounds daft. But yep, I'm game. Now pour me a glass of wine." I was surprised I had gone against character. It was her infectious positivity that lead me to make the decision to agree. And I do not regret it for a moment.

"We need to sort out a process." She added. I got the impression she had really been working at this. "I've been looking at the Scottish Nationalists question for their referendum; you remember, 2014. We should have a referendum to give it some official stuff, and the question they had was "Should Scotland be an Independent Country?" Not complicated at all."

"Do you think anyone is going to give a toss about what we do?" What I really enjoyed was that we were both getting excited by the idea. We hadn't exchanged this many words with each other in one evening for as long as I could remember. Shout at the telly, yes, but this was like a long and enthusiastic conversation, like being young again. It all bode well. In the sixties, we would have said it was a 'gas'.

"No, but we might as well. If we're going to do it, we should do it properly or as properly as we can. A name, a name, come on, let's get a name sorted out. Think!"

"Sandy and Joe land".

"No, you were right last night, it sounds like a holiday camp, something a bit more serious."

"It should end in 'land', like England, Scotland, Ireland is that a land of 'ire', it wouldn't surprise me, Holland. Switzerland. Germany is Deutschland, Poundland?"

"Very droll. But not all. We're not restricted to 'land', think Spain, France, Italy, all those Scandinavian countries, except Finland I suppose".

"This is worse than naming a dog, or a child, at least you have names you can discount like for a dog or a cat or a goldfish, because you used to know someone at school with that name and they were not the cool kid, same with a baby I guess." I was rambling with enthusiasm now. She had really got to me.

"Remember the trouble we had with Daisy and Bec's names".

"All too well. Your mum. My mum, grans, aunties all had to be remembered to exclude them in a show of no favouritism. Take away the uncool kids, the friends' dogs, any biblical reference and all you're left with is a narrow choice".

"You compromised with Bec, short for Rebecca."

"But we agreed on Bec. Now, come on, let's think. Get this thing going".

"Is there a hurry?"

"No, but there is a will."

We to'd and fro'd names all evening. Names from the television, names from the books we were reading, names from the books we had recently read and the result was nothing we could agree on. We went to bed. This evening we were both worn out by this flurry of thinking and conversation. I was getting as excited as she was.

Chapter 4

Sandy

In the morning things got silly. "Deuxbassins" piped up Joe when he and I were brushing our teeth.

"Taisezvous," was my response to the silly idea. I felt Joe wasn't taking it seriously. It was fun though. During the day, we texted each other with ideas, silly and otherwise. "Nogod" came through from Joe and I responded with "Keinegott". Funny how they all have a European basis to them. Then Joe called me. "I've got one," he said.

"Go on, out with it."

"Salivar" he said with pride.

"What's 'Salivar'?"

"I thought it sounded national, a little part of Europe and it rolls nicely of the tongue".

"You're a prat, but I quite like it".

That evening we spent thinking about a name, each with a glass of red and another glass of red. My brain was fizzing again and I had to dull it with a few more glasses. On the television that evening I remember there was a Rabbi and an Imam discussing the assertion that we lived in a basically Christian country. Neither of them cared for the idea and both asked for tolerance and understanding fearing they would be marginalised. It was like two wind bags fighting over a fart. Neither Joe nor I could be bothered. We had our own plan. We turned the channels over, nothing, so it was back to Josh, Donna and President Bartlett on West Wing.

(You might also remember this was the year that Hillary Clinton and Donald Trump were standing for President. If only Bartlett had been real or Aaron Sorkin was a Presidential advisor not a screenwriter.)

We had watched West Wing all the way through a couple of times and I, as the kids would say, rather zoned out. My mind wandered back to the conversation I had had with my parents when I told them I didn't want to go to church any longer. I remember them sitting in their armchairs, my mother with her feet up on the staple of British furniture, the pouffe and my father lazily smoking a cigarette.

I told them that I couldn't believe in the concept of the virgin birth and had upset my mother when I said I thought Mary must have been having an affair. I know this is teenage stuff but I was a teenager at the time. "Imagine," I blurted out like that all-knowing kid I was, "your husband comes home from spending time away at work, building a trireme or some such for the pagan Romans and you tell him you're pregnant knowing you haven't had sex with each other for ages. And then you make up a story about an angel, called Gabriel of all names, how he visited you one night from heaven of all places, when your husband was away and now you're pregnant. It would take some very gullible bloke to fall for that one and then take her to Jerusalem to give birth to the child, in a stable. Come on!" We'd had a sex education class in school as part of biology and I thought I knew it all. I read "Jackie" when I was younger and that taught me all a teenager needed to know about boys and kissing and sex and relationships.

My Dad was funnier though. Every Sunday, my mum took me and my sister to church and then to the parish breakfast of warm rolls and marmalade with the handsome, earnest vicar and his charming if plump wife while my dad had a lie-in and wandered around in his pants and read the papers. This was his "me time" and he objected, saying that it would be spoiled if I were home. I had to confess a lie to them. On Saturday nights, they thought I was going to the roller disco with my friends but the reality was that I had been going to the pub, to the Long and the Short Arm with my mates. It was where I first noticed Joe, a couple of years older than me with his long hair and teenage attempts at a moustache. With his Led Zepplin denim jacket, Levis of course, he was the coolest thing I'd ever seen. "I'd like a lie-in on Sunday morning as well. I won't get in your way". My dad recognising that he would have to wear more than his pants gave in. My mum chose to agree fearing that her once well-spoken lesson-reading daughter might publicly object to being spruced up for church every Sunday and in a teenage tantrum say something unsuitable from the lectern.

"Can't you wait until after your confirmation dear. It will help when you want to get married in the future."

"And about the loaves and fishes. Is it a parable I don't understand or a story coz if it's a story then it's just as much crap as..."?

"You've made your point dear" said mum.

Chapter 5

Joe

We made love that night. We still had a reasonably active sex life. It was like a rekindling. I remember it well because it was the night I came up with the name. At half past two in the morning. After sex, I normally go straight to sleep. She's probably told you. Sandy doesn't complain any longer, as I said before, in a long-term relationship things tend to slip. We used to have a cuddle and chat, but I rolled over and, she told me next morning, I was snoring like a drain. But then I snapped awake with this idea. I thought it through a while wanting to make sure it worked on every level it needed to and nudged Sandy. She woke up saying, "wha? wha? whass going on?

I said "Hendrix. Hendrix is the name for our country".

"Hold on a minute. Let me wake up". She took a sip of water from her bedside glass. "How d'you get that?".

"You remember when we met again at the embassy?"

"Uh-huh".

"We both loved Jimi Hendrix."

"Uh-huh."

"We can't call this place Sandyland."

"Come on, get to the point."

"Nearly there. Electric Ladyland. Now I don't want to live in Ladyland, I am in touch with my feminine side but…"

"And."

"You're electric. That Oasis number you liked when you still listened to Radio 1, so Electric Ladyland, Hendrix. What do you reckon?"

"I'll sleep on it."

She did and in the morning she said, "yes, I like it."

I felt like opening a bottle of champagne. I was beginning to like the idea. It was a kind of release, a freedom. Convention be blowed. We had no intention of leading any different kind of life but the whole name thing brought back memories of when we were young, when we were rebellious, when we hadn't conformed long before the mortgage and the kids and the sense of responsibility. I had some old, but perfect classis Levi 501's with the orange label, the flares, tucked away up in the loft. I was the same weight as I was at twenty so I thought they'd fit. I decided I was going to get them down that evening and write some letters. A bit pathetic I know but a little bit of rebellion when you're past sixty is the same as a lot of rebellion when you're a teenager.

We both went to work that day and neither of us could wait for the working day to end. I ordered a takeaway that evening because I couldn't be bothered cooking. This shows how big a deal this was, me not being bothered to cook, the decision made easier because and we have a very good Thai restaurant nearby. I got the Levis down and was happy that I could squeeze into them. I did look a bit of a berk though. Flared levis should team up with a Ché moustache, fresh skin, a wispy beard and a cheesecloth shirt. Not my pallid exterior, the bags under my eyes and a Marks and Spencer white shirt. Sandy found her old Afghan coat, wrapped in polythene and put that on. If only we had had a bottle of Sainsbury's Carafino we could have re-created life all those years ago. As it was we had a bottle of Moet tucked away in the fridge so we popped that.

We'd had a couple of glasses and I went in search of a second bottle when the phone rang. It was Bec's day to call and catch up.

Chapter 6

Bec

You know when like, you've known your parents forever and they've never done anything out of the ordinary except be parents and put a roof over your head, feed you, clothe you and set an example. Like what me and Steve are trying to do with our kids, Nathan and Bradley. It isn't always easy, I've found that out for myself but the idea, the idea that you nurture them is built in, isn't it?

Well it's a hell of a shock to find them, your folks, your olds, doing something like this. They'd never been very political, I thought, always voted but weren't active in politics. I didn't think they had ever been on a march except the Thatcher milk snatcher one or so they told us. They voted; I don't know who for, they would never tell us. They said we had to make our own minds up not do what they did because of who they were.

When I called Mum and Dad to see how they were, they sounded like they'd been on the wine again. They drink a bit, Steve and I are virtually teetotal, never too much or not that I've ever noticed but that evening I could hardly make sense of what they were saying.

I call them a couple of times a week to check up on them make sure they are okay and it's usually not much more than, "how are you? How are the kids? What have you been up to," maybe something about my job, or Steve. Never anything, like, deep and maybe catch up on something that had been on the news. This one was a shocker.

She came straight out with it and told me they were declaring independence, wanting to live in a place that didn't have someone in favour of religion as Prime Minister and a view that we all live in a Christian country. She told me about various Prime Ministers, one of them supposedly taking up Catholicism because his wife was Catholic and there might be votes in it. I knew they were atheists but I didn't know it had got as bad as that. I don't mean bad like it's a bad thing, you know what I mean. I called Daisy straightaway, she called them to be told they had opened a bottle of champagne. She got confused, thought they were looking for independent living which she took to mean they wanted a carer not to go into a care home. I think it was their booze and her panic made her get the wrong end of the stick.

There was a bit of a whirlwind of calls that evening, me to Mum and Dad, me to Daisy, Daisy to Mum and Dad, Daisy to me trying to get hold of an end of a stick that made sense. You read about dementia setting in or pre-senile dementia or anything that happens when your folks get older. I sometimes worry about this stuff but I didn't think I had to at the moment with Mum and Dad. Dad said they were writing to all and sundry to let them know about this independence thing.

It was funny though what we learned about them in the next few months when things got the way they did. Who would have guessed the things they had got up to before we were born, on holiday and since we left home? Dark horses the pair of them.

Daisy and I went to see them on the next Saturday, to make sure they were okay. Chat to them, make sure they make sense. Take discreet looks at them to check for tremors or shakes, or lop-sidedness on their faces. We saw nothing untoward. They look after the kids while we go shopping and we have a bit of lunch and catch up with each other. I know they like to do that but we had to be sure there was nothing wrong especially when they take them swimming. My Steve thought I was being a bit over the top, a bit too cautious and disrespectful. But I don't think you can be too careful, especially when it comes down to your kids. Can you?

Chapter 7

Sandy

Joe told me he was going to go upstairs to the study to write the letters. He came back down an hour or so later having turned on the laptop up there and tapped away. I don't know what he used to provide any kind of template but it all sounded quite official. This is what he showed me.

Dear Prime Minister

"On the 19th October 2016, a referendum was held in 133 Blossom Avenue, Welwyn Garden City AL7 9AZ and, by an absolute majority, it was decided that Joe and Sandy (Joseph and Alexandra) Quigley, of that address, would secede from the United Kingdom. As residents within the European Union we cherish the ideal of free movement of capital and labour. We will continue to pay our taxes to the government of the United Kingdom. Our new border with the United Kingdom will be that of the aforementioned property recognised by the Land Registry. The new Republic of Hendrix is a secular state and has no establishment links to the Church of England or any other religious affiliation. The new Republic of Hendrix is as the address given above. All correspondence should be sent to either Mr or Mrs Quigley, Joint-Presidents" (he then deleted the titles bit thinking it was over pompous), *"at 133 Blossom Avenue, Welwyn Garden City AL79AZ. Dated 19th October 2016".*

Yours faithfully

Joseph and Alexandra Quigley.

He then wrote a notice for the local newspaper as Charlie, the Solicitor had suggested.

From the 19th October 2016, the address formerly known as 133 Blossom Avenue, AL7 9AZ will now be known as Hendrix. For the purposes of letter delivery, we will retain the post code. Joe and Sandy (Joseph and Alexandra) Quigley of that address would like it to be known that the new country will be free of all religion with no established religious affiliation. We have notified the Prime Minister of our intention to secede from England and have sent letters to the Home Secretary and Her Majesty's Revenue and Customs. She is now your Majesty, not ours as we have declared Hendrix a Republic. As members of the European Union we will respect free movement of labour and capital, the European Court of Human Rights and our obligations to pay all taxes.

He phoned the paper the next day to ask how much it would cost, paid by debit card and emailed the text across. Joe then thought we should perhaps put the notice in the Daily Telegraph or the Times. He phoned them and asked how much it would be for the word count and they told him two hundred and twenty pounds. I thought it a bit much but Joe said it would make sense, that it was what we would spend on a night out in London, theatre and dinner and that it was far more interesting for old codgers like us.

Let me tell you a bit about Hendrix, our new country. We live in what was a four- bedroomed house but is now three with an en-suite, in the grandly titled conservation area. It is a 1920's brick built, double-fronted, neo-Georgian house with a decent sized garden both at the front and at the back. The front has a hedge and a gate, effectively our borders. The front hedge is laurel and about three feet high. The gate is nothing special in fact we should change it. The back garden has a shed where Joe contemplates his lot sitting in a big old armchair he refuses to throw out and keeps his garden tools and the lawnmower. We have a summerhouse that contains the loungers, the swingball set and the croquet There is a greenhouse that Joe tends, a vegetable garden that we both do and a lawn where for years the kids and now the grandchildren play swingball. We have a garage at the side of the house where Joe parks his car. His is the more expensive one. I have to park on a hardstanding and have to clean the bird pooh off every couple of days.

    Across the road there is a green area with a few May trees which look very pretty in Spring and later it would enable what happened to happen. If it had been the ever-present grass verges that are in every street in the town, everything would have been much more tricky. It was all very suburban, very ordinary until the fuss started.

    After placing the ads in the papers and sending off the letters there was a feeling of nothingness. Charlie was right. Nothing happened. Joe and I went to B and Q and had a sign made. We took it home and Joe put it on the front gate. Was the sign going to be a sign?

Chapter 8

Frank, the postman

The Quigleys get their usual post, the circulars stuff, bills and an occasional letter. Their house isn't much different from all the others in the area. I did notice the sign they put on the front gate but thought it was just a tribute. Which it was in some ways. I didn't give much of a toss about it for more than a second. Lots of people name their houses. I thought this was a bit naff, I mean, really. Like calling your house, Elvis, or something.

Chapter 9

Joe

There were no replies from any of the people we sent letters to. (There was a response later on which you'll find out about shortly) We wanted someone to notice, to ask us not to do it, to think of the trouble it would cause but there was nothing. We continued going to work, coming home, having dinner, moaning to each other that nothing had happened, reflecting that that was exactly what Charlie had predicted. It was frustrating. We didn't get any letters addressed to Hendrix. When the girls phoned for their weekly chats or came over with the kids on a Saturday, Sandy told them what we had done and even they thought we were nuts to expect any kind of reaction. Life went on and we still got the religious stuff on the television.

I did make one change to my day. I left for work a little earlier every day so I no longer had to listen the Radio 4's *Thought for the Day*. At work, they thought I was getting in early because I was keen for a promotion to the new job of Group General Manager, Facilities. (I didn't fancy it at all. Too much responsibility and too much day to day travel. We have locations up and down the country. It should go to a younger person)

There were floods in Central Europe and the priests were on. There was an earthquake in the Far East somewhere and the priests came on. The papers were reviewed on the BBC on

Saturdays and Sundays by representatives of faith groups, there were discussion shows with religious leaders spouting on and each time this happened either Sandy or I would shout something at the television. It made us laugh on the surface, but we had set ourselves some ideals about having no religion. Imagine.

I looked all over the internet for something that could block the God stuff. I remembered that there used to be something called a TiVo box that blocked access to certain types of television programmes so kids couldn't see films with adult content but there was nothing I could find that would do what I wanted to do. There are plenty of groups who want to block certain kinds of television but they are invariably at odds with our objectives.

I struggled for a way ahead when Sandy suggested I put an ad in Private Eye. She chose Private Eye because there are a few, shall we say, less establishment advertisers who are there week after week presumably because they get some kind of response. We both read and maintain a healthy cynicism for the world with the help of Private Eye so I emailed them a small ad for the back of the magazine.

"Wanted. Digital Communications and Television expert to help with a privately funded project to block certain imagery from broadcast media. Contact Joe Quigley, Hendrix...etc." or email sandyandjoe@yahoo.co.uk. I waited for a response, hoped for a response and got a sackful of emails and letters from religious pro-censorship organisations saying how they wished me luck. Not the response I wanted. Frank, the postman, even commented on how

much more mail I was getting. Why do the godbotherers believe we are on their side?

Weeks went by and still nothing happened and we were getting frustrated. What's the point of making a point if nobody gets the point? We felt as if the wind had been taken out of our sails and that we might just have been excitable or silly to think anything could be achieved. Had it been fuelled by too much red wine? Had we lost our marbles? What would Daisy and Bec say? Told you so? Neh, neh-ne-neh-neh.

I know Sandy had spoken to a couple of friends about the idea and they had simply thought we were silly. I had met some of the rugby club members when we went to see the game in the pub and they were all more interested in the sport than in any rebellious activities I might want to indulge in. They just teased and drank more beer. They felt the very idea that I could be strongly opposed to anything was at odds with how they saw me. A dull but competent office manager perhaps.

It was back to the daily routine and I began to look for other outlets; other things to do that might make life a little more interesting. I went on EBay and thought about buying and restoring VW Campers. A hobby harking back to the camper we had when the girls were young. It was an orange bay window type 2 with a 1600 cc engine and a Danbury conversion. I always wanted a Westphalia, left hooker, and thought about one now. We could take the grandchildren, take them to the seaside or out in the country. Romantic notions of idyllic, bucolic weekends with grandchildren playing and laughing, cooking barbeque, eating ice cream and going to sleep, snuggling up in the roof of the camper with Sandy and me on the bed below. It would have been a squeeze as it was when we were younger, but you forget the discomfort and concentrate on the good times.

I also toyed with the idea of sailing; getting a dinghy and pootling about on lakes or something with a cabin and sailing in the sea, weekends away, French ports, moules et frites, me and Sandy, romantic, notions of togetherness that were quickly rebutted. "You won't catch me in a life jacket, freezing cold, spray everywhere, wet and miserable while you ready about lee ho."

I also thought we might get a racehorse or two. We could go to the races every couple of weeks, different courses, hotels, romantic notions of winning trophies and having our photos taken in the winner's enclosure. Just a couple of nags, nothing expensive or fancy. I've never been overly interested and Sandy told me it was a silly idea, full of crooks who knew more than us. All that would happen is that we would be mercilessly ripped off and lose all the money we had put in. We hadn't worked to get where we were to throw it all away on a silly scheme that would come to no good.

I just didn't want to wind down into an old age of doing nothing other than existing, drinking tea, eating digestive biscuits and eventually dribbling into a plastic bib in a nursing home that smelt of cabbage and piss. The scale of these ideas was nothing compared to what was going to happen. These all would have been small time hobbies contrasting with the upset that was about to occur.

Something remarkable happened at last. I got an email from buzz@geekmedia.co.uk. He, I presumed it was a he, asked me what I wanted to do. He said he was curious and wanted to see if he could help. I emailed him back and told him that I wanted to block religious imagery from my television.

Chapter 10

Buzz

When I first belled Joe we had a chat about what he wanted to do and what he wanted to achieve. He told me he had been getting wound up at not being able to make any progress with this idea of his and it isn't a surprise. I had to tell him that no one who could do anything was going to see his ad in the back of Private Eye. I found the ad in the online version of the magazine when I was bored one day, snooping around, looking for inspiration. I also told him, or rather, suggested, he needed to do a bit more online because he had no profile. Nothing. Not on Facebook, not on Twitter, not on LinkedIn and, to labour the point, nothing on Instagram. He told me he had all the friends he needed in real life. He wasn't interested in following people and he was happy in his job. Talk about old, not being up with what's going on. You can't say it's a generation thing, even my mum does Facebook and uploads her pictures to Instagram and she is nearly as old as Joe.

I've done a bit of CGI video for YouTube, my degree is in digital media and I work for an outfit, Geekmedia, who specialise in demanding digital solutions to complex imagery problems. That's what the website says. We are a bit specialist but it doesn't mean I have no contact with the real world. I do, I have friends, a family, mates at work, I play in groups over the net on the PlayStation. I am well in touch with the real world. I even go to the pub.

I asked Joe to send over a list of the things he wanted blocked to get a handle on what he wanted to achieve. This is what he sent me.

1. Men and women wearing dog collars whether Catholic, Protestant or whatever flavour of Christian.

2. Men with beards longer than six inches and men with beards but no moustache. The old chinstrap look.

3. Men standing around in crowds wearing little white caps, looking pious and shaking the hands of trembling Congregationalists.

I replied to this one that he couldn't block pious as facial recognition software wasn't sufficiently well developed to recognise emotion in random individuals. Joe decided he thought it would be okay, the man in the white cap always looked pious and as there was only one of him he would have been blocked anyway.

4. Men with unfeasibly long curly sideburns with or without a Kippah.

5. Women dressed from head to foot in black to block nuns and burkha wearing Muslims.

6. Ululating women who apparently don't want to or are not allowed to show hair because it is covered in a veil.

7. Men in purple robes and/or mitres carrying bent sticks either individually or in groups.

8. Men, looking earnest if I, Buzz, can fix it, wearing corduroy jackets, pullovers and carrying leather bound books.

9. Swaying congregations beseeching a well-dressed orator to save them from their sins.

10.   Men nailed to crosses and with their heads bowed as if in pain.

11.   Men in orange flowing robes kneeling in temples or setting fire to themselves.

I reminded him that it was easier to do images than words, and told Joe that pain was a feeling and beseeching was emotional and might not be recognizable and that accents and dialects made the words difficult to decipher. I said I would also try to do headshots, full body shots, people sitting, standing and raising their palms to the sky in supplication. Joe told me he was enjoying himself at last and if it worked, that his wife, Sandy, would be chuffed. The conversation continued and we agreed that would I do images first and look at language software later. I pointed out that "pasta" and pastor" would be difficult as would "profit" and "prophet" and that we would see if we could do context at some time in the future. This was a fuzzy logic thing we were working on in AI at the studio.

Once I had figured out what I was going to do, instead of swapping emails which is how I would normally take a brief, I called Joe and asked him the big question, "what do you want in its place. You might have ten seconds, twenty or thirty or a couple of minutes to fill".

"I've thought about this", replied Joe "I'd like to see the end of the 1999 European Champions league final between Manchester United and Bayern Munich. If we must edit it down, I'll take Sheringham's goal before Solskaer's. If we have a couple of minutes, I'll take as much of the injury time as I can get especially when their goalkeeper, Kahn, was sobbing on his knees at the end of the match. If that doesn't do, add John Terry missing the penalty in the 2008 Champions league final. I can't see that too often. Then, if there's time can I get Sir Alex's retirement when they name the stand after him but before he gets round to talking about Moyes."

He paused. "Hold on, let me ask Sandy, see what she wants". Sandy wanted the time Rafa Nadal changed from one sweaty shirt to another clean shirt in the breaks at Wimbledon. That one from 2009, the semi-final was her favourite. She also said she would like to see some of the British Olympic medal winners when they knew they had won. She said it was always uplifting. Joe said "if you're having that Nadal moment, I'm going to have the time in Trading Places where Jamie-Lee Curtis takes off her pullover ".

"How about you write and email me a list of the clips you want. I'll get them off YouTube and put them in. Give me a couple of weeks and I'll have something for you.

"Um", hesitated Joe, "How much is this going to cost"?

"Nada, my good friend, it's such an excellent idea and it'll stretch me, I'll do it for nothing. I'll be in touch". I knew it would be good for Geekmedia, push the envelope a bit, open up new revenue streams in the future. I had my business head well and truly screwed on. The whole idea might be good for development.

Chapter 11

Joe

And Buzz was good for his word. After two weeks of silent curiosity, we received a small package from a courier. We opened it to find a small piece of plastic looking like a double ended memory stick and a note which read, "Hi Joe and Sandy, have a look at this. Plug one end into the broadband router you have with your TV and internet and then plug the cable into the other end. It's called a dongle. There'll be a five second delay in your getting the pictures because it has to know what to filter and as soon as it goes back to non-religious stuff, you'll be back live. Try it out and come back to me. I've had a go and I'm well made up. Mail me soon".

We couldn't get back into the living room fast enough. Last year we bought a big new television. At forty-six inches, ultra HD, who says we don't have modern stuff. It swamps the room really but the picture is great and the sound is fantastic. David Attenborough's nature programs look incredible. I inserted the dongle into the Sky box and sat back to watch TV. It was eleven o' clock in the morning and all we could find was property shows and nonentities speaking inanities and then I remembered. I tried the BBC news channel. There is always some religion on that whether they're killing each other or finding solace in their faith. We didn't have to wait long. One of the presenters announced that they would be talking to the Archbishop of Canterbury about taking on payday lenders and no sooner had she introduced him than Ole Gunner Solskaer appeared on screen scoring the goal for Manchester United that won the Champions League.

I ran to the phone and called Buzz. "You're a genius Buzz, it's great. Fantastic. Sandy and I couldn't be doing with all that bollocks and now we don't have to".

"Listen, Joe".

"What"?

"I have an idea".

"What"?

"Stop just saying what".

"What"?

"We should develop this idea. I think it could take off".

"I've thought about this too, but I don't know you Buzz, I don't know who you are, where you are, what's in my dongle". Our natural cynicism, born of age, experience and Private Eye was making me defensive. I didn't want to upset Buzz or put the kybosh on a potential relationship but neither Sandy nor I are that naïve.

"No probs, Joe. Let's meet".

"Where are you"?

"Hoxton, East London."

"Come out to Hendrix, Welwyn Garden City, this is going to be great, we can have a beer, get to know each other".

I said to Sandy that the whole thing could work. We've got our country and nobody seems to have objected or raised any concerns whatsoever and now we've got the television sorted out.

The next day, we met up and went for lunch in the Plume of Feathers, a country pub out in the villages north of Welwyn Garden. Sandy just about justified another duvet day and we went out. Bearing in mind the age difference and the fact that we didn't even begin to occupy any part of each other's world, we all hit it off straight away. It was particularly telling when he ordered a pint of Aspell's and so did Sandy and I. We went out to the bottom of the garden where no one could over hear the conversation. "Tell us about yourself Buzz, what do you do"?

"I'm a freelance software developer, some CGI work, some HTML and I muck about with bits and pieces. Haven't you googled me"?

He was talking way over my head and I'm sure Sandy's too, but we didn't let on. "All I have is Buzz and Geekmedia and that doesn't come up with very much at all".

"You're not looking in the right places, mate. We're everywhere but I googled you, Joe, and there you are, a picture of middle-class professionalism. Worked for the same company all your life, it seems, but," He told me again, "you're not on Facebook, you don't tweet and no one can contact you on LinkedIn. And you too. Mrs Quigley, you're invisible on the net."

"Good," she replied.

"That must be why nobody read my ads or wrote back to us. What I'm doing means nothing".

"That's a key question for me, Joe, Mrs Quigley".

"Call me Sandy, please, this Mrs Quigley stuff is ageing me so".

"What does this all mean?"

"It means we got fed up with religion and don't want it in our lives life anymore. We've found a way, with your help, that means I don't have to watch it or listen to it. The whole idea was intended as a bit of fun, something to brighten up our otherwise uninteresting but satisfactory lives."

"What about other people. My point is, I can develop this blocking into an app for Android and iPhone and all the major broadband suppliers and we could charge a couple of quid, maybe make a few bob. We'd have to charge for the dongles, maybe develop it as a download and we could program what people want to see by adding YouTube links."

I loved Buzz's enthusiasm for the project. He said he was a Spurs fan and he would choose Jimmy Greaves' goals, a selection of the best he could find on YouTube. I consoled him about Spurs lack of recent success and he promised that it wouldn't get in the way of the project and that Harry Kane and Pochettino would soon put things right. As far as developing the idea was concerned, while he had put a huge amount of effort into the dongle, I didn't know if I wanted it to go further and to become available generally. I didn't want to encourage this in other people. I didn't want to be responsible but Buzz said we could make some money. I asked him to hold on and to let me think about it. Sandy and I would need to talk about it.

Sandy had got into a bit of a pickle at work. She'd wanted to come out for lunch and meet Buzz but work was reluctant to let her have another day off. She came out anyway. Her work said that duvet days were supposed to be spread over the year and the Chinese were getting anxious about the tests on their polymers. I told Buzz we wanted some time for ourselves to just enjoy the moment and figure out what we wanted to do.

But things didn't go entirely my way.

Chapter 12

Buzz

It turned out to be a bit of a session. We had another couple of pints after we had eaten. The sun was shining and it was my first day out of London for at least a month. The weather was warm, the countryside was beautiful, horses in the field, barns and farming stuff all over the place. Me and Joe and Sandy got on like a house on fire. We talked about the project. Sandy and he described their relationship and it seemed strangely normal for its not being normal. Forty odd years, few arguments, especially when they were younger and money was tighter, no affairs, trusting each other implicitly. We talked about football, they told me about their daughters and what they, the girls, thought about the idea. I said I thought they should loosen up a bit and let their parents do what they want to do. After all, if you've done as much work as Joe and Sandy you deserve to make some decisions of your own. They've had a successful life. For a couple of blokes and his wife, even though we had nothing in common and there was a huge age difference, we had a lot to talk about.

After a couple more pints of Aspall's and a bit of an introductory chat about the app that I had recorded on my phone we decided to get a taxi back to Hendrix. We had a couple more beers while he showed me the app in place, in situ, if you like. I'd developed it and tested it but that was on my kit at home and my television. I wanted to see it in action in a normal house and this was as normal as you might get in the burbs. I got my phone out and filmed the bit where it changed from a religious person talking about the decline of the church on some afternoon property show in an instant to Sheringham's goal.

Awesome. I filmed Joe's look on his face, red and eyes half shut, a bit pissed and shouted, "you're the man Joe". It was truly, and it bears repeating, fucking awesome. I was made up. I made them high five, awkwardly.

The taxi to take me to the station turned up. I nearly fell asleep waiting for the train. The combination of the beers and the warm sunshine and the fact that we had had a good time together had drained me. A large coffee with an extra shot kick started me but I was still a bit pissed.

I fumbled my way through the footage with the editing software on my phone. I could barely focus but managed to put together a reel that I could look back on in time to mark the event. I was pleased with myself, it was a good piece of work. I watched it over a few times, tweaking the footage as I went until I had something I could keep and be proud of. But being still, a bit too pissed, I tapped the share button.

It seems I had forgotten the bit of our conversation where Joe and Sandy had asked me to keep quiet about the dongle. And trains, these days, they have Wi-Fi. I was so used to Facebook and Twitter that I opened two new accounts. On Facebook, it was a page called "Godsblocked" and on Twitter #godsblocked. I've got a couple of thousand friends on Facebook and a few people follow me on twitter. Sorry Joe and Sandy, it's all my fault. The video went viral.

Chapter 13

'Woody' Ashman. Jehovah's Witness Evangelist

I have been an evangelist of the teachings of our lord, the head of our church, Jehovah, in the United Kingdom for three months now. Me and my co-evangelist, my partner, my best friend, Jack and I have been in this country of yours for three months now and we think we know it pretty well. We have met many of your residents in their homes, so close together, so little room you have but with the help of the Lord all things are possible.

We work on behalf of our creator spreading the word of our Lord. Sometimes we do house visits, other times we are in the streets or town centres and shopping malls spreading the word. Hallelujah. Praise be to God. I know that I have been responsible in those three months for converting at least three people to worship Jehovah. One per month isn't bad going for a novice like me. Jack has only done two and one of them changed their mind when they realised we have pecuniary obligations to our Lord. We are taught that if everyone we tell about our Lord tells everyone else it would soon multiply and the membership of our church would grow exponentially and that can only be of the greatest good.

The bible teaches us many things, about love, relationships, family and we have the word to spread. It is a powerful thing and we use the bible to prove the facts and when people listen, when people understand, when people see the truth, they accept the Lord as their God. Praise be to him. I love my job and I look forward to returning home to Sacramento when my work here is done.

The Elders blessed Jack and me with a mission one Friday morning. We were to visit with a Mr and Mrs Quigley and tell them about the word of our Lord. It seemed they had lost their faith and needed our help and our love to find themselves again. So me and Jack put on clean shirts and suits, polished our shoes, combed our hair and went on our bicycles to visit with these poor lost souls.

Back home my mom and pop taught me there was no such thing as coincidence, that everything was God's will. They also taught me about the music and art I should enjoy and music and film and television and magazines that will corrupt a follower. The most mired in sin were rock and rollers and smokers of dangerous drugs such as cannabis. I felt a sense of trepidation when I saw the sign on the gate, Hendrix, remembering how he mocked our beliefs as written in our illustrated magazine, *Watchtower*.

We arrived there at about ten in the morning and I reminded Jack to take off his trouser clips before we knocked on the door. This he did and as we entered we walked up the path and knocked on the door. I always give a loud knock to let the people inside know we are there and pre-dispose them to the strength of our Lord's word. Mr Quigley answered the door wearing jeans and a T-shirt. He hadn't shaved that morning so I thought I was the one with the moral right. I was up, I was clean, I was shaved and my hair was combed. I was prepared.

"Mr Quigley?"

"Yes."

"My name is Woody Ashman and this is my co-worker Jack. We are here to tell you about the work of our church in praise of our Lord and to help you find the truth. God loves you Mr Quigley, praise be to him. May we come in and share the word with you". It isn't often that we get invited in. The many times I have been put off with excuse after excuse why people don't have the time or the inclination to listen to the truth. We are taught that one day, people will believe and if we are not successful the first time there will be a time in the future when people will listen, at the time of the second coming and we are doing important groundwork on that path.

Not only did Mr Quigley invite us in to his comfortable, charming house with its old- fashioned furniture and lamps and cushions, but he sat us down and offered us tea or coffee or something a little stronger. Now I believe abstinence is the best way forward and that stimulants like tea and coffee are not the work of the Lord so I accepted a glass of water, gratefully, as did Jack. It was a warm morning and we had cycled some three miles to be with Mr Quigley.

"Mr Quigley", I said, with sincere hope in my heart. He had proven himself to be a man of gentility. "You do know that God loves you, we all love you and we are here to help you find the truth and the path to enlightenment. You know that Jesus died on the cross for your sins and the word of God is more powerful and sharper than any two- edged sword and that truth comes from the Hebrews 4;12 in the new King James Bible".

Mr Quigley looked quizzically at me, and responded by asking me if I had any children and I said I was too young and had too much important work to do before I could settle down and raise a family. Mr Quigley said he didn't understand how a father could let their son die in agony on a cross and I told him it was because he loved us and Jesus died for our sins. Mr Quigley said that was what he struggled with. He called it something called a non-sequitur which I had to look up when we got back to Kingdom Hall. I said you need to have faith, it is all about faith and Jack agreed. He too said you must have faith, that God is everywhere. Then Jack re-affirmed that Jesus died on the cross to save us because he loves us. Mr Quigley was a bit more stern when he said "I don't see how killing your apparent son to suffer for the apparent sins of the world is justifiable. If that were to happen today he'd be charged with filicide and be banged up, assaulted by the nonces and be made to suffer dreadfully in a way that could be seen by all. 'I killed him because I love you' is no defence".

I struggled with his use of the English language. I didn't know what filicide was or what a nonce was. I asked Mr Quigley for his forbearance and requested he enlighten me. I like to use these biblical terms because they set an atmosphere and can help doubters with their own understanding. Mr Quigley explained the terms and I was shocked to hear of the depth of his doubt. For a moment, I feared Jack might be affected and I considered asking him to attend to our bicycles outside but thought the better of it and so Jack stayed to understand the importance of our work.

I tried to insist that he must have faith, faith in our Lord, faith in our Lord to guide him through the world. Mr Quigley said he was an engineer by education and by training and he had had to have evidence, based on science and maths, in order to make a decision throughout his lifetime. "I can't expect faith to manage the electrical supply to all the IT systems in the building I manage. I need facts, hard facts, tested. Faith won't prove that a new roof won't collapse. It needs to be structurally sound, engineered".

Mr Quigley became a bit more brusque and suggested that we had reached an impasse. He said he would let us get on with our work and that we should talk to some of his neighbours. I said we had been asked by the elders to attend to the needs of Mr Quigley and his wife.

"How did you know about our views on the church?"

"I didn't. I was told that you had lost your way and as one of our more successful young evangelists I was given the God-given opportunity to come to visit with you to help you see the error of your ways". I tried to disagree with him about having reached an impasse and hoped we could continue our discussion with Mr Quigley but we had to respect that fact that we were in his house, albeit in the House of our Lord, but Mr Quigley asked us to leave. He was having a day off work and needed to get some things done. I would have liked it if he bothered to list some of those things but then I remembered that this visit was simply laying the ground work for his eventual seeing of the light, the light that shines. He said something about Onan, we thanked him for his hospitality and reported back to our Elders.

They thanked Jack and I for our strength in the face of adversity and compared it to Jesus being faced with the devil when he spent those forty days and forty nights out in the desert. I did all that was in my power to show the Lord that I was, and still am, a true follower. I had been, as I discovered later, in the house of a drug user and I prayed for salvation with intense fervour.

Chapter 14

Lizzie Bailey, local newspaper reporter.

I thought this might be my chance for a scoop. Nobody reads the public notices in the newspaper. They are put there by local authorities to tell people about closed roads, planning permission to chop down a tree or to dig up a manhole cover. Rarely stuff of any consequence. I look at them every week, it's like panning for gold and I knew I could come up trumps. There might be a planning permission for the removal of protected trees, not that I care about trees per sé but the person wanting to chop down the tree or a developer wanting to build houses or flats maybe pushing at the boundaries of green belt and bunging the Chief Executive or the Mayor to do so. I had found nothing like that yet, but I kept looking.

I had seen the announcement from the Quigleys about what they wanted to do and had hoped to talk to them about it. I had had a few long days in the magistrate's court and too many council meetings to count in the evening and I hadn't got round to it. The weekend had been busy with fetes and a gymkhana and I was out with our young photographer getting snaps of snotty kids and comments from their mothers, all the while they were stuffing themselves with burgers and chips and candy floss. Have these people no idea? Fat parents breeding and feeding fat kids. It's only going to go one way.

I had seen the twitter stuff and the video on YouTube. It seems I follow someone who follows someone who re-tweeted this video of some IT nerd talking about the Quigleys. I talked to my editor and told him I wanted to try to see them and get an interview. He asked me how I knew the Twitter account was them and I reminded him of the notice in the paper and I had recognised the Plume of Feathers from the uploaded video and because we often go there for lunch ourselves, me and Harry, my boyfriend. He wanted to give it to a senior reporter but I insisted it was my idea and I wanted to do it. These senior reporters are a bunch of old alchies. It was after lunch so he was more malleable than he might have been in the morning. He doesn't get the socials and thinks the local newspaper is the be all and end all of the community. So past it. He knows we have an online edition but has no idea how it gets there.

I know, I am ambitious. I think I'm getting a bit of a reputation. My colleagues, the old fellas, those way past It, call me Cold Bailey. I'm pleased about that. Most reporters not stuck on a local in their forties are ambitious. I see a career in the media ahead of me. I see people like the late great Sue Carroll, Suzanne Moore and especially the late and just as great Lynda Lee-Potter expressing their views about all kinds of subjects and I can be just as witty as them. I nearly got fired when I said the lady Mayor was only slightly less effeminate than a trucker and that was one of Lee-Potter's greatest. I have views. I can do bitchy. I have my own blog and no chance the editor will find it. It isn't in my name; I use a pseudonym. It's all about what shit happens in this sleepy suburban dormitory town. Is it any surprise they call it dormitory when everyone is half asleep in these identikit houses?

It doesn't matter if it is Parish Council or District Council, the PCC or local charities. Any group with any self-interest. They all indulge in fighting, the bitching, the back stabbing, the bigging-up, the knocking down. There's so little of any real action they create nonsense and spread it wide. What a bunch of under-achievers.

I wanted the story first. I have to spend my time doing magistrate's courts, council meetings, watching some minor celebrity or talent show runner-up open a local fete. It was time I had a story, time I got a front page, time I got a by-line.

I got to 'Hendrix' (see how I put it in quotation marks. I don't reckon it will last) and knocked on the door. Mr Quigley came to the door looking a bit dishevelled like he had just got up. He was unshaven and wearing a T-shirt and jogging pants. I swear he had no underwear on, but I didn't want to look too much. I introduced myself. "Hi, I'm Lizzie Bailey, from the Times. Can I have a chat with you about your story?"

And he had the gall to answer, "what story?"

I told him I had seen the public notice that he had put in the paper and the video on Facebook and Twitter. "What's going on?" I asked, "are you leading some kind of revolt, some kind of revolution?"

"I'm doing nothing of the sort", he replied. I know he was being cagey, people always are with reporters like me. They always have something to hide and never make their intention clear. You see it at every level from local Parish councillors all the way up to the top. Always have an agenda, always have an ulterior motive and I was determined to get to the bottom of this one.

"Come on Mr Quigley, you can tell your side of the story".

"Show me what you've seen on Facebook and Twitter." I got my phone and showed him. He made it look like the first time he had seen it. "I have to go," he said and darted back into his house.

I opened the letter box and said "I agree with you about the God thing. I think the Flying Spaghetti Monster is just as credible as any other religion. My partner is a Pastafarian." But he didn't come back to me.

I went back to the office, knowing the copy deadline was that afternoon and that I had to fill in some gaps. I needed some background on Joe and his wife, Sandy. Facebook, nothing on its own. The google search gave me the electoral role and his place of work. I phoned them up and they told me he wasn't in. Now there are a few tricks I learned from my mates in different jobs especially in recruitment so I called the Building Maintenance department and found the Office Manager. I asked her what her name was and said she had been recommended as a candidate for a job I had on my books. I questioned her about what she did, her ambition and then asked her about Mr Quigley, what was he like to work for, was he a good employer, was did he do in his spare time and so on? I got a picture of a boring one-time hippie late middle-aged man seeing out his time until retirement. Nothing scoop worthy. Except in the back of my mind I had read that hippies were the original druggies.

So, I downloaded the video and grabbed a still of his face. Now we have a way of doing facial recognition software with our publishing group and I searched Google images to see if there was anything on there. I do like to dig down and deep. And there I found the gold dust. A picture of him and his wife on a naturist website, in the background, on a beach in Spain. Bingo, a story.

Chapter 15

Joe

I had a terrible hangover that day. I don't usually get one but we had had a few in the pub, carried on when we got home and I downed a few Scotches after Buzz had left. You know what it's like when you get a thirst on. I wasn't at my best.

That pushy journalist from the local paper was a pain in the arse. That couple of squeaky clean kids from the Jehovah's witnesses were fun but I did wonder where they got their information from and now I knew. Buzz had put the video of us taken at the pub and then after we got back home up on Facebook and twitter apparently. Now I'm not very au fait with these things but if the local godbotherers had got what they called the story and the newspaper had sent some girl reporter round there was obviously something afoot. The newspaper I can understand. I put the notice in there but you don't think any one reads them.

I was furious with Buzz. We had agreed there would be no effort to attract any wider attention. This was a personal thing for me and Sandy. I called him and he was very sheepish. "Sorry Joe, but I did it yesterday, a bit pissed, I was so excited by the fact that it worked so well, it was kind of a triumph. I was so made up."

"Can we get it removed?" I didn't want to shout at him, rebuke him, because he had done such a decent job, not charged us and if anyone could do something about it, he was the only person I knew.

"We can remove it from our posts but it has gone kind of viral. People are liking it all over and re-tweeting and there's nothing we can do about them. I've got fifteen thousand likes on my Facebook page alone. Sorry, bud".

"Remove it where you can. I don't need the intrusion. I don't want the Jehovah's Witnesses anywhere near my door and I want that reporter long gone."

Buzz said he'd see what he could do. He had persuaded me he was a bit of a whizz with these internet things so I had some faith in him. I told Sandy when she got back from work about what had happened. She talked me round and said that we had at least, got some kind of reaction, an acknowledgement that someone had noticed and she said she thought this was what we wanted. I hoped there wasn't going to be a gap in what the two of us believed we were doing. This wasn't a show off vanity exercise like these minor celebrities try to do to get in the papers to get some exposure to continue a career that starts and ends with nothing. This was supposed to be a moment of rebellion. Sandy pointed out again that I had been pissed off by the lack of reaction and that I couldn't have it both ways. As usual, she was right.

I told her I wanted the acknowledgement, from anybody, from anywhere to come from one of the departments we had written to not from the godbotherers or the local newspaper. She said not to worry. Charlie had convinced her nobody would care; nothing was going to happen and we'd have to wait a couple of days for the paper to come out to see what was what.

That was tough. I didn't know anyone on the newspaper. We had no influence, either Sandy or I or work. At work, we didn't advertise in it anymore. That was all going online. I spent a fretful couple of days worrying about what might happen. The girl didn't phone or try to make contact again. It's hard to exist in a kind of vacuum of knowingnothingness. Sandy and I did what we always did. Go to work, get on with life, cook, eat and enjoy a glass in the evening.

We told the girls about what had happened to prepare them for whatever the newspaper might say. I told them about going to the pub, meeting with Buzz, development of the app and so on. They, probably thinking there was nothing their mum or I could do to interest the local newspaper, just said things like, "uh-huh", "okay" and "yes. Well, if you drink too much."

Then the paper came out online and in print. Do you know what that pushy journalist wrote? On the front page! *Local Nudist Hippie Engineer Declares Secular State in Welwyn Garden"*. One heck of a headline followed by three hundred or so words and a photo of the house and some cribbed photo of me and Sandy on a beach. I was furious. I showed it to Sandy who was apoplectic and she had always been the calmer of the two of us. She demanded I phone the journalist to put her right. I did and she, the Bailey woman reminded me that she had given me the chance to put my side of the story and asked if I would like to give an interview. I should tell you, and I don't swear as much as Sandy, that I told her to fuck off.

She said she come by in the next couple of days to see if I had changed my mind.

Daisy saw it first, phoned Bec and they both said they would be round and asked what all this stuff about nudist beaches was and smoking cannabis. It was like being in front of your parents or a teacher. I smirked at Sandy, who raised her eyebrows. We had decided when the girls were young that we wouldn't take them to the beach. We were both uncomfortable with the idea of them naked in front of other people. You must remember the times, there was too much chatter about fathers abusing their children fuelled by Sunday newspapers and over-zealous pressure groups.

That afternoon I had a visit from the local Imam. I didn't realise that, firstly, there was a local mosque and secondly, that this long–bearded, diminutive man was the leader, until he introduced himself. "Good morning, sir, my name is Mohammed Butt, Imam of the Mid-Herts mosque. I read your notice in the paper and I have had the work of your computer application drawn to my attention. I would very much like to talk to you".

Guessing what was coming, I said "Yes", with a patience I was proud of. "How can I help?"

"It is I who can help you", said Mr Butt.

"How so"?

"You must remember that God is all powerful. The Koran says, and it is not to be doubted…. 'As for the unbelievers, it is the same, whether or not you forewarn them; they will not have faith.

God has set a seal upon their hearts and ears; their sight is dimmed and grievous punishment awaits them".

"I'll take my chance".

"Please restore your faith, read this". He passed me a pamphlet, "and find God, find Allah in your heart. It is the only way you will find heaven".

I flicked through the pamphlet and found a short quotation. "it says here *'There shall be no compulsion in religion'*. This is why Sandy and I didn't want any of this stuff in our lives. And aren't there extreme branches of Islam that wants to behead apostates? We are apostates. Do you want to see me and my wife beheaded?"

"I know what is says Mr Quigley, but context is everything. If you will let me have the time, I will demonstrate to you the relevance of the teachings of Allah and the prophet to your lives and fear not, I do not have any negative intention to either of your heads".

Sandy and I had travelled a bit, Europe, Africa, the Middle-east, before everything kicked off, and some parts of the far-east. I wouldn't say we were worldly wise but neither are we ingénues. We have encountered cultures that are very counter-cultural to our lives and we have been okay. It's a bit like Star Trek where you visit somewhere and don't interfere with the local population. We have never interfered but this Imam was trying to interfere with us, "Salaam Alaikum, Mr Butt. I'm afraid I do not believe in a God, let alone Allah or the Prophet Mohammed and I would appreciate it if you left my house and garden and left me to my own devices".

"I am sorry Mr Quigley, but I am duty bound in my faith to Allah to insist that you reconsider and I must use all the persuasive powers at my command to do so".

"I am sure you are both articulate and persuasive but we are content with our view that our lives will be richer without religion."

"Then you are making decisions without knowing all the facts. Allow me the time to talk to you about Islam, why so many people are converting and how it can and does enrich the lives of millions around the world".

"No" was my brief reply.

"I must insist", he insisted. Plucky little man.

"Then could you please do it from beyond the hedge, over there, the border of Hendrix".

"How can I be expected to reach out to you if I have to do it down by the hedge and you are behind a closed door?"

"Have faith, Imam Butt. Have faith."

The Imam walked down the front garden path and clicked open the cheap fake leather briefcase he was carrying. He took out an A3 piece of white card and a magic marker and wrote "Have faith in Allah. He will guide you." And he stood there holding it up, occasionally turning three hundred and sixty degrees seemingly in the vain hope of finding someone who might agree with him, who might come and hold the card up because his arms were beginning to get achy.

An hour or so later the local priest arrived.

Chapter 16

Father Patrick Corr

I read in the local newspaper about this man who had lost his way with God and how he didn't understand that he was a sinner, what with his nudity, in public, you can be locked up for that. It seemed he had struggled with drugs. I don't know what drugs they were, illegal or legal, prescription drugs but addiction is addiction in my book and the sign of a very weak will.

I had hoped to get to him first, to find out more about him, to try to help him see the error of his ways but as I walked down the street I saw my fellow theologian, Imam Butt outside this newly declared independent state. He was holding up a placard that mentioned Allah. That was wrong in my book.

I acknowledged his presence and said, "good morning Mr Butt."

"Good morning Mr Corr. Have you come to see Mr and Mrs Quigley?"

"That I have, Mr Butt. I have come to show him the error of his ways. He is a sinner who needs to repent for his sins and I emphatically feel the Catholic church is the most suitable church to allow him to establish contact with our Lord. The sins he has committed are best repented with the help of the Catholic church. Of that I am convinced."

"I very much respect your conviction, Father Corr," he said to me, "but you will have to use all your powers of persuasion if you are to get anywhere. I was unable to move him."

"I am sure that as he is a white middle-aged man he will have had some contact with Christianity in his life and my task is to re-open his eyes to the wonderful world of the Lord, our God, our Father, our Holy Ghost." I made the sign of the cross, kissed my vestments, opened the front gate and paced briskly and firmly up to the front door.

I am a bit of an old-fashioned Father. I liked the Latin when we did that. It evoked more solemnity. So, when Mrs Quigley answered the door, I said to her, in a voice that people have said reminds them of that that dead old proddy Paisley, "Behold, I stand at the door, and knock: if any man hear my voice, and open the door, I will come in to him, and will sup with him, and he with me." She looked first at me and then turned to see if anyone else in the house had heard my words. I continued. "I have to tell you Mrs Quigley. I presume you are Mrs Quigley. That you will burn in hell for eternity if you forsake God and eternity is a very long time. Imagine if you will, a ball of steel the size of this planet of ours and once a year a small bird, a sparrow or some such, brushes its wing against that ball and over time it brushes its feathery wing as I said once a year until the ball of steel is brushed away. That's not even how long eternity is, my good lady and that's how long you and your husband will burn in hell, screaming with the other sinners for God's repentance".

Perhaps I was a bit over-emphatic but I have always liked the Sparrow argument. It scares the bejesus out of me. Mrs Quigley said, "good morning, and you are?"

"My name is Father Patrick Corr and I am the priest at Our Lady Queen of Apostles. I am here to sup with you".

"And how can I help you this morning?" Cool as a cucumber she was.

"I have come to tell you that the world has seen what you have become. You are a woman, a couple, who have lost their way and Jesus Christ Our Lord is the Shepherd who will bring you back into the flock."

"Mr Corr," she replied, "we have found our way. We found our way some time ago and where did you get that sparrow nonsense?"

"It isn't nonsense, Mrs Quigley. It is indicative of how long sinners, unrepentant sinners, will spend in hell if they don't see the error of their ways."

"And have you calculated exactly how long it will take this sparrow to brush its wing against this planet sized ball of steel?"

"As I said Mrs Quigley, it represents an eternity. It is indicative. A guide, if you will."

"And what do I need to do Mr Corr?"

"Tell me you have God in your heart and confess your sins."

"And that will get me off the ball of steel punishment?"

"Indeed, Mrs Quigley". I thought I was making good progress. I was heartened by her seeing the light. But it dimmed soon after. "Tell me, Mrs Quigley. If you do not believe in God, what or who do you believe in? You must believe."

"I firmly believe in my, or indeed, our ability to be in control of our own destiny but equally I do not share your view that we must have faith, even a faith, or believe in anything other than stuff happens."

"The Lord God, our Creator, my creator, your creator will ultimately decide. It is His plan that will count."

"And what is his plan?"

"The eternal goodness, the eternal word, the word of God."

"Which is?"

"He loves you, Mrs Quigley."

"I think that is utter nonsense Father Corr and is fatuous. And as we have declared our land to be secular I would appreciate it if you joined the Imam on the other side of the hedge and you can make your protestations from there."

"But, Mrs..."

"No buts Mr Corr. Back to the hedge. I live a good life, as good as anyone else I know. I only covet one thing."

"What's that Mrs Quigley. What do you covet?

"My neighbour's Mercedes sports car. I really want one."

"You do know, Mrs Quigley, don't you, that it was God who gave you the free will to do what you have done."

"No, Mr Corr, it wasn't. Please back to the hedge."

I felt I had given her as good as I have got. I went in hard with the arguments. Perhaps I should have beseeched her, to put it more strongly, to see the error of her ways, been harder with her in my efforts to save her soul. And what's worse is that when I got back to the hedge, that Koran basher said to me, "Christianity is a busted flush, as the Americans like to say."

"Cheeky eejit".

Neither of us wanted to leave. Neither of us was going to be the first to go. Butt held his sign aloft but with weakening arms. I wished I'd had a sign or a chair. What I did have was old faithful, forgive me Lord, my hip flask with a dash of Bushmills. I took a swig, a warmer don't you know, and offered it to Butt. Unsurprisingly he declined. It got dark; neither of us was going to go. I wondered where the Anglican might have got himself, but no sign of him.

I said to Butt, "Imam, we both have a profound set of beliefs, and we both believe we are going to be the ones who want to bring the Quigleys back into the fold, but couldn't we call it a night and get home to our warm beds". And do you know what he said? He said I might not have the perseverance to stay but that he had and he wouldn't be moved. I wished I'd bought my mobile with me, I hadn't expected to be this long. Fortunately I didn't have any family waiting for me at home but I am a little older than he, I am not far off retirement and will spend my years at the Seminary, helping the fathers with new intakes.

When it was dark, Butt let his sign drop and we stood there, largely in silence, all through that blasted night. Dew sodden until the morning dawned on us. What didn't dawn was that the Quigleys had spent a warm and cosy night in a warm and cosy house. We, indeed, suffer for our souls. Perhaps, we could have spent the time more wisely. We could have discussed the finer points of each other's faith. Why there was a Jesus in the Koran, why we both had Adam and Eve at the beginning, but we didn't. We could have discussed joining forces to bring the Quigleys back to a monotheistic faith. But we didn't. The conversation we had was mostly gossip. Looking back, and I would never confess this to another soul, I'm disappointed we didn't do better.

Chapter 17

Sandy

Joe and I went to bed at around ten. We were tired and a couple of glasses helped us off to sleep. We were feeling very doubtful about what the next few days would bring. Charlie had said no one would notice but we had the Imam and that Catholic priest outside the house all night. It was like they were trying to out stay each other; each be more determined than the other to convert us back. It was touching. Their concern, I'm sure was genuine, if misguided. Perhaps they couldn't understand that those of us with no religious faith can have the same level of conviction as the most die-hard of believers. Our minds weren't going to be changed with anything, especially not with a quick chat.

Joe and I talked about how ineffective the arguments were that they put to us and both of us thought that their faiths were built on sand, to borrow from the bible and to push the analogy, they were houses of cards built on sand. One puff of a slight breeze and they'd be down. Perhaps we should have had more respect for their faith in what they believed but we believed that faith itself wasn't a powerful enough concept. Actuality is stronger. Proven science is believable. Myth, fable and parable less so. We are content with our decision. Godbotherers believe they have the answers, we know we do not and we continue to search for them. In science, not concepts.

We didn't like the headline and the innuendo in the paper. Silly girl, so transparent. Yes, we visit naturist beaches on holiday as do thousands of other people. If you have never been naked on a beach, then don't judge. Give it a try. Not on any beach, you get my drift. Nobody judges, big, small, fat, thin, big breasted, little breasted, all sizes of gentlemen's bits and pieces, pert bums, saggy bums. The drug taking hippie thing, well that was all so long ago, I mean forty years plus ago. Everyone experiments at some time and we have had the occasional joint after a pleasant dinner at somebody's house and an occasional, as the youngsters call it, a toot at a party. Never harmed us. Never made us make poor decisions, not that we think so anyway. Others may disagree.

But it was me that took tea out to the priest and the Imam at around seven the next morning. Poor loves they were trying to out stay each other and they both ended up cold, damp and tired. Father Corr, who had looked strong and impressive when he confronted me at the door, looked frail and stooped. The Imam appeared sharper and a little smug with how he had survived the night.

A cry came down the street. "Mohammed, Mohammed, what are you doing, what are you up to?" It was the Imam's wife bustling down the street, headscarf flapping in the breeze as she half ran, half walked looking like a bundle of multi-coloured washing. "Why didn't you call me to let me know what you were doing? We have all been very worried about you. Your mother has been round to watch over the children and help them get ready for school while you have been out here in the cold all night. We have been worried sick.

Worried sick to our stomachs. I only found out you were here because Mrs Abdullah, from one hundred and seventeen, just down the road said you were here. She called me just now saying she thought it was you holding a sign. Foolish old man, you will catch your death of cold".

To which the Imam replied, "hush, woman, I have been very busy."

I asked her if she'd like a cup of tea. She declined. A glass of water? She said yes please. Mr Butt said he was doing Allah's work to try to convert the apostates to Islam and asked his wife to go home and get his phone and a chair for him to sit on. She asked him why he couldn't do it and he just looked at Father Corr and raised his eyebrows.

I came back out with the glass of water for Mrs Butt and we all jumped when we heard what sounded like gunshot but was an old Transit minibus stopping across the road. It was painted with all kinds of symbols, and sign written with Bhaktivedanta Temple. It disgorged robe wearing, shaven headed, white paint daubed youngsters who took to skipping down the street with tambourines and finger cymbals. They seemed to be led by an older, devotee, isn't it, who turned and skipped back to the bus, as if marking out skipping territory.

I went back in to tell Joe to come and look and while I was inside the Anglican Vicar turned up. I called Bec and Daisy to let them know we were fine and not to worry. We were sure it would blow over. I couldn't help hear them tutting. I don't know if it was at Joe and I or the faith leaders' antics.

Chapter 18

Henry Tudor, Anglican Vicar

I got there as soon as I could. I tried to explain to Corr that I'd had to the see the family of a dying parishioner but he seemed skeptical. Doubting Fenian. I do do some pastoral work; it isn't only Mrs Tudor. Corr and I have never really got on, not since I arrived, with my wife, and we took up a more high profile role than my predecessor. I do good works with local charities and community groups, sit on committees and barely have time to write sermons. My wife does a lot of the visiting and supporting, you know, the bereaved, the sick, the elderly, the lonely; she never seems to tire of it and then gets home to look after our two children. We are often in the paper and on local community web sites while Corr sits in his house, grumbling about the demise of the Latin mass, homosexuals and gay marriage.

Me, I'm more switched on, a bit more modern, a bit more inclusive and we have had a couple of LGBMT weddings at the church. The clothes and the flowers were all lovely and you could tell the men genuinely felt love for each other. It was a joyous occasion as are most Sundays. We have a small group of singers with guitars who will sing along with the hymns and often will play something they have written or heard. The Cat Stevens number, Morning Has Broken, a hymn first I'm sure you know, is a favourite and not diminished by the fact that he turned towards the East for his faith.

The scene outside the Quigley house was getting a little intense. Corr and Imam Butt were drinking tea. The Imam's wife was berating him for not having told her where he was and the Hare Krishnas were skipping up and down the road. I asked my two fellow theologians if they had eaten, as I was about to call my wife and ask her to pop to MacDonald's for me. I really rather like those breakfast wrap things. Corr said he'd rather not and Butt said it contained pork and said rather snidely, I thought, that I should have known that it wasn't halal and shouldn't have asked. Mrs Butt scuttled off to do something and I phoned Penny, my wife, to order breakfast. Bless her, she said she'd be as fast as she could.

Corr asked me what I was trying to do. I said that I hoped to talk to the Quigleys to persuade them to re-consider. He and the Imam told me they had both tried and not succeeded. I asked Corr if had done the Sparrow speech and he said he had. I said, no surprise there then. I explained to the pair of them that the Quigleys had both gone to church when they were younger and both had been confirmed as Anglicans. I had spoken to a few parishioners who said they knew the Quigleys. I said it was more likely that they would return to the fold from whence they had come. Corr laughed and said that it must have been the Anglican church that put them off. The Imam simply asked his wife to bring his phone, a chair and some toast would be nice.

As I readied myself to go to the front door, Corr asked, "Can I borrow your phone dear boy?" When I walked up the front path I heard him shout, "there are more bloody Krishnas here than Catholics. Get a group of parishioners together and get them down here pronto. As least twenty," he barked.

I stepped up to the front door and knocked. All seemed quite normal, no pentagrams, no garlic, nothing silly of that sort. I had seen Mr Quigley looking out of the front window so he knew it was me at the door. I waited a little while and knocked again. Almost immediately Mr Quigley opened the front door and said, "good morning, Vicar and how are you today"?

I was taken aback, not thinking the conversion would be easy but thankful that it wasn't difficult, I replied, most courteously "I'm very well thank-you. May I come in"?

"No."

"No? We can't talk here on the doorstep. I do need to talk to you about your video thing, you know the thing you do with your television set."

"Are you on Facebook, Reverend?"

"Indeed I am, and I do think that you are doing the religious community a disservice by having that actress expose her breasts instead of listening to those of us who represent an enormous constituency of right minded individuals".

He had the temerity to say, "if I could be bothered I would argue with you about who is and who isn't right minded, but maybe another day".

"Bothered, bothered. We should all be bothered".

"You seem to be"

"Of course I am; faith is vitally important to us all".

"Nope, not me. And why are you focussing on the breasts and not the football. You didn't see the football clips then?"

"I'm an Arsenal fan myself".

"Do you believe in Arsene Wenger?"

"Of course I do".

"As I believed in Sir Alex before the disastrous Moyes year".

"Do you believe in God, Mr Quigley?"

"No, I don't. I thought I'd made that quite clear".

"But can you tell me why?"

"I really don't feel the need to justify what Sandy and I are doing and I don't want to get into a discussion with you about it. I worry I might upset your belief system and I don't want to be responsible for that. Would you mind making your way back to the hedge, the border, and making your point from there. You have a perfect right to be there. I can't and shan't complain, but please do not try to debate faith with me".

I moved back to the hedge, next to Father Corr and Imam Butt. "That wasn't terribly successful was it Henry", sniped Father Corr. He just had to say something. I called my wife again and said to hurry with that wrap and could she muster some support, about twenty-five or thirty members of the congregation, including a few choir members, would do and we'd need some magic markers, A3 card and some two by one as well as a few screws and a screwdriver. I told her to make sure it was either a crosshead or a Phillip's to match the screws she bought. I told her B and Q would have it all and not to forget the loyalty card. Bless her, she said she would do her best; I know that to be true. We weren't going to be outsigned by the Muslims and the Fenians

Chapter 19

Lizzie Bailey

I was pleased. I had my front page and I had my by-line. This was going to be one stepping stone to a great career. I thought that the nudist thing was a great touch, bound to spark some interest and maybe a backlash which can only be a good thing for me. Keeps the story going. The drugs thing was pure association. All hippies took drugs and there would be one hell of a fight to prove that they didn't so there would be no chance of a libel. I'd had to argue this with the paper's lawyer. Jim, nice but very dim. I set up a Facebook page for the story and posted it on my page so all my friends could see it. I have amassed several thousand friends over the years. I don't know who half of them are but they could be useful contacts down the line. I tweeted like crazy to get the story covered.

The day after publication I hadn't heard from Mr and Mrs Quigley and I wasn't going to let the story drop. I drove over to Blossom Avenue and had to park about two hundred yards away from the house. The road was full of parked cars and outside the Quigleys house there must have been a hundred or so people standing, sitting on picnic chairs many waving placards with a vast range of motifs on them. "Allahu Akbar" was prominent on many of them, being swayed back and forth, left to right by bearded men in robes. Others had written the handy translation "God is great" on theirs. The Christian part of the gathering had placards reading "repent now", "Jesus loves you", "God is love", "Cast the Devil aside" and many more. It takes the breath away to understand how many ways the Quigleys may or may not be persuaded to find religion again. I do kind of agree with them about religion. It does seem to get in the way of a lot of things but I wasn't going to let it get in the way of a good story.

Most of the crowd were older, older than average but then I guess they were either unemployed or retired and didn't have to go to work. They sat there on their chairs, with blankets and tartan rugs over their legs, thermos flasks at the ready and they seemed split into three groups. At the back of the crowd were the Hare Krishna devotees, skipping and chanting and beating their finger cymbals and tambourines providing a musical background to the whole piece that contrasted with the piety of the Christians and Muslims at the front.

This was more pure gold. I took out my phone, rehearsed a few lines in my head and shot a video. My voiceover was, "this is Lizzie Bailey of the Welwyn and Hatfield Times in Blossom Avenue, Welwyn Garden City where a multi-faith demonstration is taking place outside the house of the nudist, hippie, drug taking Quigleys who have decided they don't want to live in the United Kingdom any longer and have decided to declare an independent secular state of Hendrix. Presumably named after the musician Jimi Hendrix, a well-known drug user who died young. These concerned citizens are exercising their right to demonstrate. They are peaceful, mainly elderly with the firm belief that God is one their side". I played it back to myself, was happy with how it looked and how it sounded so uploaded it to the Facebook page, Instagram and to my Twitter stream

I saw Henry Tudor at the front of the crowd near the Quigleys garden gate and walked over to him, holding my phone switched to record. He is usually good for a quote at a time like this. "Mr Tudor, you remember me, from the Welwyn and Hatfield Times. How do you feel about this multi-faith show of unity?"

And then a little man, with a beard, dressed in flowing white robes put his head in front of the microphone and said, "My name is Mohammed Butt and I was here first to try to persuade the Quigleys that Christianity is doomed to extinction and that Islam provides the light he needs out of the darkness of his apostasy." He was then brushed aside by a big Irishman dressed in clerical vestments who insisted he was the most qualified to speak.

"I have been here since yesterday afternoon, overnight, through the wee small hours. I have introduced God into the hearts of more non-believers than either of my two fellow leaders. They, the Quigleys, have rejected the Anglican church. They have decided not to follow Islam and therefore it is only right to conclude that Catholicism is the only way forward for them".

"Hang on Corr," interrupted Henry Tudor, bustling towards the microphone. "I am the representative of the established Church. I will bring them back to God".

I thanked all three of them for their comments and decided I would have another go at Mr and Mrs Quigley.

Chapter 20

Joe

I saw the reporter outside. She hadn't seen me but she was holding her smartphone up in the air and moving slowly round like she was doing a panoramic video. She was speaking to no one in particular, as she was doing this. She walked over to the demonstration. I'll call it a demonstration rather than a gathering because it was all getting a bit noisy and she talked with each of the religious leaders who seemed to be fighting for attention. Silly buggers.

My worst thoughts were confirmed a moment later when Daisy phoned to say she had been pinged by Facebook and that there was a video shot outside the house. She said she was coming over. I tried to convince her that we were okay but liked the idea that she was in tune with the internet and what was going on up there. It might prove to be invaluable.

The reporter knocked on the door and Sandy went to answer. I looked over her shoulder and saw this sheepish looking young girl, certainly less confident than she had been that first time, younger than our daughters, ask if we wanted to comment. Sandy turned to me and I nodded so the girl was invited in.

"Come in and sit down. Would you like a cup of tea?"

"Please, that would be nice."

I said I would put the kettle on and left Sandy with the girl, Lizzie, I recall. I overheard the conversation from the kitchen.

"What would you like to know?" Sandy asked.

"I'd like to know how long you have been taking drugs for".

"Nope, you're not going to get us on that. Next."

"How long have you been going to nudist beaches and are you swingers like nudists are?"

"Firstly, what we do on our holidays is up to us. I'm disappointed that you have written this article in the first place and no, we are not swingers. So, you have two answers to two questions that are irrelevant. Why don't you ask about why we have done what we've done?" I was very proud of Sandy. She was much more controlled than I would ever have been. The kettle boiled, I poured water into the cups, stirred them about a bit and asked the girl if she wanted sugar. No thanks she replied.

"Okay, tell me why you have declared this house to be independent." Sandy gave her chapter and verse. She answered all the questions coolly and fully leaving no apparent room for error. It was a good interview and I hoped our objectives were made clear.

While the interview was going on Buzz phoned. He had seen the video shot by the girl and said there appeared to be three more videos on Facebook, one from someone called Butt, a Muslim, one from a Catholic called Corr and one C of E. I laughed. He told he had something serious to say. "Listen Joe. I've had hundreds of emails and countless posts on Facebook from people wanting the blocker and to do what you have done. All this is today. I can develop it, like I told you for Android and Apple and all the ISPs, put it on a dongle with requested YouTube links for each customer, although many want the same as you and we can sell it for a couple of quid a time. Make some money. Potentially make some serious money. Think about it."

I wasn't up for the idea at all and didn't want the journalist earwigging the conversation so I cut Buzz short and said I'd let him know what we think a little later in the day.

Daisy and Bec arrived and things took a turn for the worse. They questioned Lizzie Bailey about the story she had written and wanted to know why it had been published. They were charmingly naïve but it was positive that they were on our side. Lizzie left the house and walked back down the garden path. Seeing more commotion, I noticed that she once again was filming the scene and pushing her phone into the godbotherers' faces, presumably for quotes.

I called Buzz. Outside, a Welwyn Hatfield Council van arrived with a set of portaloos. The number of people outside had risen to over two hundred and cars were parked on both sides of the road for half a mile in each direction. There was a bunch of Sikhs sitting on the verge across the road. I wondered if they were contemplating the inter-faith fighting over who was going to convert us back. It would hardly have been Sikh like. The toilets were followed by food vendors. There was a kosher food van, Halal meats and kebabs and a Hog Roast. Mr Whippy jangled his jingles and there seemed to be a very positive party atmosphere. The local supermarket had erected a small stand and was doing a roaring trade in soft drinks.

Buzz said, "look mate, I think we might be on to a winner. I have many, many hundreds of people wanting a copy of the blocker and I reckon we can charge them a couple of quid. I've got a PayPal account. Customers can download what they want to see, once the blocker is in place, from YouTube. Lots of people want to know what it was you wrote to the Government and the papers. Can you send me a PDF and I can add it to the app?"

"I don't know, Buzz. How many did you say had asked for a version of the blocker?"

"So far it's over two thousand."

"Shit. Let me talk to Sandy".

"He says he's had over two thousand requests for a copy of the blocker. He reckons he can turn it into an app and charge a few pounds for it. We could make some money".

"Stop and think for a moment. When we set out to do this, did you want to be some kind of leader, an atheist leader taking on organised religion"?

"No, you know I didn't".

"You're on the verge of an all-out multi-faith riot outside your own front door and now you want to cash in on it".

"No, I don't but if there's other people out there who are equally fed up with the diet of religion they are given, shouldn't we help them and if we do, it should be all right for us to make some money. It would be a service".

"Listen, Joe. We could spend the rest of our lives doing what we do, peacefully, quietly, you with Manchester United and that woman with the boobs, me with Rafa, not hurting anyone".

"We're not hurting anyone if we sell the blocker. If we can sell thousands, it means we won't be the focus of all this aggravation going on outside. There will be so many people blocking God that they will dilute the numbers of people demonstrating outside the house."

Buzz said. "We're up to four thousand and I've had them from the United States and Australia now. This could be mahoosive, man".

"I'll call in the morning".

"We need a decision sooner than that", implored Buzz

"Why?" I was settled in my feeling that I shouldn't hurry any actions. I was simply trying to block religion from having any impact on our lives. I didn't want to be seen as anti-religion, it wasn't the point. If people wanted to believe in a God or a prophet, then let them. It's just that it wasn't for me. Equally I didn't want to be seen to take a side, it wasn't a binary decision; religion or no religion. Imagine the consequences of getting involved in that. It could be very difficult to say the least and I had no position on moral superiority or inferiority. Also, I didn't want to spend the rest of my life arguing and justifying.

We had a chat with the girls and they were sure we should go for the money. "Why wouldn't you," said Daisy. "A couple of grand in the bank, have a holiday, but not on a beach, please".

Outside, I watched the collection of the faithful in competition for a conversion and their hardening attitudes were causing more than a commotion. Some of the placard wavers were now threatening other placard holders with their placards. These old people and the Muslim men were getting agitated. It seemed Blossom Avenue was now the fulcrum of a rising tide of religious intolerance. Not against us, but against each other. I called the police.

"Very funny", said the officer. "I've heard about you. In the paper you were. You want to live in an independent country, you sort it out".

"My proposal to the Government was that, as long as I paid my taxes I would be treated like any EU citizen and be entitled to the support of the police". I tried not to sound over pompous but the person who answered the phone was a cocky little shit.

"I do understand sir, but we have enough right now, right in the here and now, so to speak, to do to protect dear old Blighty".

"It is dear old Blighty that is suffering for the noise and commotion occurring on the border between us and your deal old fucking Blighty." You can see I was beginning to lose my temper and that hasn't happened for years. "There's at least one fight going on and the guy with the Hog Roast has had his van turned over and set on fire. In Blighty".

"We'll be right over".

Chapter 21

PC Peter 'George' Cross

When we arrived at Blossom Avenue, the scene was disturbing to say the least. The cars were parked half a mile in each direction and the crowd was blocking the road. Blossom Avenue isn't one of the town's main thoroughfares but it is a through road and the traffic was building up in the vicinity. Car horns were being tooted, people were standing on top of their cars trying to get a view of what was going on. We had to put the sirens on to get anywhere near the Quigley's house.

We parked where we could. I called for back-up, some traffic officers to help disperse the cars. PC Jackson and I walked towards what can only be described as a mob to instil some calm, some order. First, I saw to the Hog Roast vendor. He was in possession of fire-fighting equipment and had extinguished the fire and then it was easy to pick out the ring leaders. I took them aside for a quiet word.

"Gentlemen, please. If you can't stay calm and instruct your various groups to be calm, I shall have to send you all home."

"We have a right to peaceful demonstration."

"And you are?" I always find that if I ask someone their name they back off. He didn't.

"My name is Mohammed Butt. I am Imam of the Mid-Herts mosque and I was here first. Father Corr that Catholic, caused these stirrings when he insisted he had the right to protest nearest the gate to this house." He didn't back off. He was a determined man, I could see.

"Indeed I do. I am the most senior clergyman here and I have every right to take the position I choose."

That was one loud voice. Booming it was. I boomed back. "If you are wanting to be seen to be leading these people and take a position, can I strongly suggest you take a position of peace and calm and ask them to settle down. Now."

Then, you wouldn't believe it. With my car nearby, traffic officers on their way, a van with the BBC logo on it came down the pathway. Tooting its horn, the nearside wheels on the path, the offside wheels on the grass verge, taking great chunks out of the branches of these very trees the avenue is named after. A cameraman jumped out, then a man with one of those fluffy microphones and a woman I had seen on the television. I recognised Jemima Bunn. Coiffed bob, dyed blonde, smart suit, made up like she was one of those Barbie dolls. She and her crew marched right past me and strode up to the front door of the Quigley's house not giving so much as a toss about the damage she had done to the trees.

She was speaking as she strode. "This is Jemima Bunn from the BBC come to investigate the Quigleys and this suburban sect that has been uncovered in leafy, tranquil Welwyn Garden City, just twenty miles north-west of London. Let's see what answers we can get." She knocked on the door, there was no answer. She knocked again. Still no answer.

Then a first-floor window opened and, it must have been one of the daughters who shouted "Leave my mum and dad in peace. This has nothing to do with any of you. Go away."

Then Jemima Bunn asked her, "are you safe up there? Have you been locked upstairs?" She turned to face the camera. "It looks like we might have a hostage situation here. Where are the police? Who's going to stop this?"

Then the girl from the local newspaper, Lizzie Bailey, we often see her in court taking notes said, "this is my story, kindly fuck off and leave it to me. I discovered this".

Ms Bunn then apologised to camera for the language used and said they would be back with a news report for the news at one. Bailey ran at Bunn and started that kind of fight where people can't fight. A bit slappy, but it left them both looking dishevelled. "Help, Police". I had no choice but to run over and break up the fight. Ms Bunn demanded we arrest Ms Bailey as the attacker and we had no choice. The cameras were on us. PC Jackson handcuffed her and led her to the car. She was swearing all the way. "Fucking bitch, that's my story. Let me at her, the fat cow, leave me alone, let me go you stupid pig. Bitch." Colourful language by any standard. We locked her in the car.

Ms Bunn knocked on the door again and Mr Quigley came to the door. "What do you want?" I crept closer so I could hear the answer and to keep the peace, of course. I am an officer of thirty years standing, dedicated to the community.

"I want to see if you want to put your side of this story. We have, seemingly, a nudist, drug-taking family who have no faith in any God who want to set up their own country. Do you see how unbelievable this is? How extraordinary?"

"There wouldn't be a story if it wasn't for that lot over there, hanging around, waving their silly little signs, competing to see who's going to convert us back."

"Is it true that you are nudists?"

Naively, Mr Quigley answered. "On holiday, occasionally, with thousands of others". I presume he hoped the truth would knock the wind out of her sails.

"And do you take drugs?" The wind was still fresh in her sails.

"When we were younger, teenagers, rebellious, like millions of others."

"Officer, shouldn't you be arresting these individuals, or at least searching the house."

"It's not what we are here for Ms Bunn."

"And you have declared independence?" She was really having a go at Mr Quigley. Trying to pin him down. Question after question leaving him no time to expand on his answers. A bit like my detective colleagues in the force.

"Are you swingers, Mr Quigley?"

"Now you're being silly. Emphatically, no!"

"Do you walk around the house in the nude, Mr Quigley?"

"Why, do you want to put a camera in the house to try and catch us out?"

"You can't just answer a question with another question, Mr Quigley. And do you believe in Alex Ferguson as a deity above God?"

"I firmly believe in Sir Alex and have no belief in any God, Sun gods, rain gods, gods the fathers and so on. So yes, I do."

"And are your daughters free to come and go?" She asked. A bit close to the bone, I thought. If they'd had their daughters trapped upstairs, I would have been the first to try to get them out.

"The only thing preventing my daughters leaving is that van of yours blocking the road. Officer, get them to move that van."

"I'm just here to keep the peace, Sir." I tried to explain.

"Well you're not doing a very good job of it, are you?"

"None of this would have happened if you hadn't taken the inflammatory decisions and actions you have."

"None of this would have happened if you hadn't just all minded your own business."

Ms Bunn interrupted. "I do feel it is important to give your side of the story. Come to the studios, this evening and I'll interview you."

"Leave me your card. I don't really know who you are."

Three police cars arrived with the sirens going. Eight officers emerged from the cars, brushed themselves down and gawped at the crowd. This had never happened in leafy Welwyn Garden. A sergeant came over to me and told me I was responsible for the crowd's behaviour, and what was I going to do about it."

Chapter 22

Jemima Bunn

I truly felt that I had given them every opportunity to tell their side of the story. It did seem to be some kind of cult or sect especially when Mr Quigley confirmed that they were nudists and had taken drugs. I should have questioned him deeper but that police officer kept hanging around. When I asked him if he believed in Alex Ferguson more than God and he said yes, I couldn't believe it. For a moment, I thought I should call a doctor. I felt I was taking advantage of someone who maybe had dementia, you know, not all there, but he sounded reasonable. I'm not a medical professional, as you know, but I had seen documentaries about mental incapacity in older people. He was quite animated and I have looked over the footage we shot when we were there and he seemed okay. Not dead-eyed like some of them. Was that offensive? I don't know.

I did ask the first-aider at the studio to take a look, but she was busy. You can't say I didn't try to show I was worried. I'd have liked to have got more out of the daughter's. Imagine finding out that your parents were hippie drug takers and went to the nudist beaches on holiday. I'd be shocked. My parents don't have it in them. I've never met two more normal people than my mum and dad.

After I had asked Mr Quigley to come to the studios, I went to shoot some vox pops with the crowd, get some opinions.

Typically, they all wanted to be on television and they buzzed around me. The little Muslim fellow, who I later learned was called Butt, said he knew Dev, my producer and tried to insist that he should get the interview because he was there first. He said he had been inside the house so I asked him if there were any signs of cults or Satanists. He said he wouldn't know if there were any or not because that wasn't his field of expertise and he kept insisting Islam was a religion of peace and tolerance. A bit over the top I thought, I hadn't said anything about anything to him. Then this big Irish man in a cassock barged over and, sounding like that dead preacher from Northern Ireland, insisted Mr and Mrs Quigley would rot in hell if they didn't refrain from their sinning against God, the creator. He did bang on a bit and we had to edit most of what he said, his droning voice buzzed in my head. Then a chubby, ruddy-cheeked vicar in his black shirt and dog collar, looking every inch the Church of England wanted a few words so I tried to shut the Catholic priest up by interrupting and putting my hand up but he went on and on and on. Mr Tudor finally got his say and told me that he had been in touch with his Archbishop who said he was pleased that the Church of England was at the forefront of a multi-faith effort to convince the Quigleys of the errors of their ways and how pleased he, Mr Tudor, was with the wisdom from on high.

    I thanked the religious leaders and went into the crowd to see what the real people believed. I was surrounded by middle-aged and elderly men and mostly women, it was a weekday after all, who, to a person, all said they we here to support the efforts of their religious leaders. They waved their placards, the Muslims were shouting Allahu Akbar, the Catholics started on the Lord's Prayer while the Christians tried to compete with *Kumbaya.* When I got back to the studio, I looked on Wikipedia and figured out why they had chosen that song. I thought it was just some old hippie nonsense but apparently, it is a spiritual asking for help for those in need. You learn something every day in this job.

The background noise to this hubbub was the Hare Krishna lot who, amazingly, hadn't stopped skipping up and down the street. It did sound quite enchanting with the rhythms and the bells and the cymbals. I tried to get someone to speak to camera but they wouldn't stop. The Sikhs sitting on the grass looked up at me and waved me away. I'm sure I heard them discussing something like the upcoming cricket world cup, but how would I know.

I asked Dev, the producer, to talk to the programme editor for the six thirty news if he could allow time for Mr and Mrs Quigley if they chose to come up. He looked at the footage and said he thought it would be fantastic, but asked if we were sure the couple were all there. I said I'd get a doctor to look at the film.

Chapter 22a.

A fleeting appearance from Mr and Mrs Bunn, Jemima's parents.

It's a bit difficult really. We were children of the sixties too. Of course, we smoked pot and even my husband and I danced naked, stoned completely, with scores of others at the free Windsor rock festival in 1971. Dropped acid, everything, but she's turned out to be such a prude. I don't know where she gets it from.

Chapter 23

Joe

What a day, what a commotion. We didn't expect anything like this. Sandy said we shouldn't complain, that we were moaning that nobody had taken any notice before and I simply said it would have been nicer to have had some kind of response from the people we had written letters to not a bunch of god fearing religionists standing outside the front garden competing for our souls. It did get silly, especially after that TV reporter left.

They had all been quite, moderately if you like, moderate before she arrived, but the prospect of being on television had upped the stakes and they were shouting at each other. Had they been football hooligans it would have been less funny but it wasn't too dissimilar. The Muslim men had their voices raised shouting that God was great and rocking back and forth. It looked like the Imam, Mr Butt, was setting them up for prayers in the afternoon. He took to chanting or singing and then they all lined up, knelt down as one and rocked back and forth. Mr Butt intoned, looking very grave, looking first at his worshippers and then up at the house. I caught his eye and waved at him but there was no physical response. I wouldn't like to guess what he thought. That went on for about twenty minutes.

The Christians were looking on, bemusedly and then their voices got louder and louder. There was a medley of tunes they sung including *Kumbaya, By The Rivers of Babylon, Amazing Grace,* that old Edwin Hawkins number *Oh Happy Day* and a few hymns as well as Psalm 23, the Lord is my Shepherd. Why they thought this would persuade me to join the flock I have no idea. Middle-aged and elderly women, in hats and sensible shoes, with blankets over their knees. I'm sure they meant well. I'm sure they would have been happy to have me come out of the house and say, "yes, yes, I believe, you have made me turn my back on the devil". But it wasn't going to happen. For the followers of their Gods it was a three-way draw. Not even a score draw.

The episodes with the media were also odd, not that I was used to that kind of thing. The girl from the local newspaper we spoke to in depth and gave her a full reasoning for our decision. Unfortunately for her it was very boring, very rational and she had to agree with our motivation in the end. We were not the story I told her. She was creating a story by whipping up a frenzy and that the real story was the godbotherers outside trying to compete for our redemption. I'm surprised at the BBC, though, I didn't expect their girl, the one we were supposed to have seen on the telly, to be so excitable. I always thought the BBC was more measured. But she asked some daft questions.

Sandy and I are perfectly normal, boringly normal. So we take our clothes off on the beach, thousands do. So we smoked a little pot when we were younger and perhaps not so long ago, perhaps we have had a toot in the past but we are not drug fuelled or drug crazed. As I have said we are normal, normal, normal. I suppose that if you add those things together and admit to them it might be seen, by very, very conservative people as being a bit radical. But it really isn't our problem.

I phoned my work and Sandy phoned hers and we took a couple of days off. We didn't want our respective workplaces to become embroiled in all this. It would be inevitable some time, we were sure, but we chose, much to their delight, to say that we wouldn't mention where we worked. Although there was no chance that would remain a secret. Now that we were the focus of so many people's attention, gossip would out.

I did tell Roger, my boss, that I might need to go on the regional news in the next day or two and he laughed out loud. He said it wouldn't be a picnic or a walk in the park, expressions he always used and he said he would make a call to see if he could get us some professional help. I told him I didn't want something expensive. He said they would pay, if necessary. This struck me as unusually generous but then cynicism interrupted and I reckoned he would do it to keep the company's name out of the media.

We heard from Buzz throughout the day. "Whaddup" was his repeated greeting. I'd seen this on *Breaking Bad* and thought it a bit pretentious of him, too cool. I finally gave him permission, not that he needed it from me, to go into production with the blockers and I sent him the letters I had sent to the various Government departments. I did forewarn him that there had been no response from any of them and he said he thought they might think twice if it was going to be on the news. The latest count on the requests for the blocker was twenty-seven thousand and that even if only half of them bought the app at three quid a go it would be nearly forty thousand pounds each.

Buzz told me he had resigned from Geekmedia and was going to go freelance. Was that a problem for me? I said no, but we would need to formalise the relationship. Could he email me?

I went to the bank's website to see about opening a second bank account to put this money into. Sandy had a very large gin and the girls, instead of making more tea and sandwiches, ordered some champagne and picnic food online. It was going to be a picnic after all. For an hour, we sat and chatted, bemused about what had happened and trying to speculate on what might happen. We didn't have a clue, as it turned out.

The next call was from the producer, Dev Choudhury, from BBC local news. "Mr Quigley, I feel it's very important that you come on to our programme to explain what it is you are doing. There are all kinds of rumours about cults, drugs, devil worship and this is your chance to let us all know, in your own words, what it is you are doing."

I was a bit short with him. I am normally quite level headed but I snapped, "These are rumours put about by that reporter of yours who seems intent on whipping up a frenzy for the sake of making a splash. Perhaps we don't give a toss what people think."

"I beg to differ. I believe we are all attentive to what people think about us whether it is your employer, your bank manager or your golf club membership.

"I don't belong to a golf club."

"It doesn't matter. It's just an example of how people might misinterpret your actions. Look, Jemima Bunn wants you to be on her programme tonight. She'll interview you so you can..."

"I know, tell my own side of the story."

"That's right. We'll send a car for you at 4.00pm."

"Don't. It will be a waste of time and effort. I am not prepared to meet your girl today. Perhaps tomorrow." Before he had time to hang up, I said I'd call him in the morning. I didn't want to fan the flames of the religionist's ardour, but in the morning, it might have all quietened down.

Coincidentally, just after that I had a call from a man called Simon Cleve. He said he was involved in Public Relations and Reputation Management. He said he'd had a call from an old colleague in Business to Business Public Relations about a couple, us, who were getting themselves into deep shit, his word, not mine, and needed help. We chatted briefly. We both agreed it was better to see if the fuss died down and that we would talk in the morning.

Chapter 24

Sandy

The girls, who had both taken time off from work to come and see us had to leave to get their kids and go home. They both work very hard, Bec is an Accountant with a firm of Management Consultants up in town and Daisy is a deputy head teacher at a local Primary school. They braved the crowd outside who barked and brayed at them as they walked back to their car.

Joe and I cooked up some supper, a quick carbonara from stuff we had in the fridge. (Joe puts too much garlic in it for my taste, but hey ho) and we settled down in front of the television. There was this local TV reporter questioning Joe suggesting he and I were off our rockers, or cultists or whatnot and our phone rang and rang. We chose not to answer the calls; they could have been from anybody but we did listen to most of the messages from friends who were surprised but supportive. Charlie called on my mobile and apologised for his assertion that no one would care what we did. It seemed they did care and care a great deal.

We sat down for the evening taking an occasional peak outside and, if anything, the crowd had swelled. There were gas rings, torches, some of those half tent things you see when you walk around the lakes, the ones fisherman use when it rains. We convinced each other that it would blow over. How could we be that interesting? We were non-entities, uninteresting non-entities but were drawing the TV cameras, the papers and the crowd outside. Funny lot. Haven't they got anything better to do with their time?

We had a chat about what might happen the next day. Joe was nervous about the possibility of going on television, I was apprehensive about the crowd outside not knowing what was going to make them go away. It certainly wouldn't be reason because it isn't on their radar. (Maybe that was a bit harsh. They will obviously think they have reason but each to their own).

Neither of us slept too well, in fact we were both awake at two-thirty and looked out of the window. Some of the protestors were wrapped up warm, thermos flasks at the ready. Others were asleep in the seats. It must have been so uncomfortable. The weather was holding up for them, not too wet or windy but it was a cloudless sky and must have been chilly.

In the morning, we woke up and went through the normal routine. I was prepared to put kettle after kettle on to help the poor people outside warm up, and we had plenty of bread to make toast but we were beaten to it by an enterprising fellow called Dave and his Diner, teas, coffees, burgers, sandwiches, soft drinks and so on. He did very good business.

Chapter 25

Simon Cleve. Public Relations and Reputation Management

Joe and I spoke in the morning. I gave him some background to the kind of work I do. That's why I insisted on all my professional activities in the title at the beginning of the chapter. I've long stopped doing press releases and seminars for small companies and got myself involved in managing peoples' reputations. Most of my clients are celebrities of one sort or another or business leaders looking after their next career move. I do all the stuff from kiss and tell in the Sunday tabloids to social media. Righting the wrongs that people put on Facebook and Twitter and Instagram. That recent ruling on what google can link to was, if you'll forgive me, a Godsend.

As we were talking he was looking out of his front window and updating me on who was doing what. Many people had apparently dispersed in the evening except for a few dozen diehards. Even the Hare Krishnas had got back in their minibus and gone home to the manor but they arrived shortly after nine. The Catholic and the C of E guy had both returned and parked up outside the house. Joe said he thought they had got there early so they could park nearby. Mr Butt, the Muslim guy walked up with twenty or so fellow Muslims and their placards and the whole thing started again. Joe and I agreed to meet.

We did have a conversation about money. I charge £500 an hour plus travel. He said he didn't know people could earn that much money so I asked him how much his share of the app had been. I had bought a copy so I know it was available, that and the trending on twitter were enough to make him plenty of dough in the short term. I told him I was worth the money and had testimonials. He said not to worry and we agreed to meet at midday.

I called this Dev Choudhury fella and told him I was representing Joe and Sandy and they would be happy to do the six thirty news with Jemima Bunn. Game on.

I have a driver, DeShaun, he's big, and burly and black, drives well under pressure and can take care of himself. He's fifty pounds an hour and worth every penny. If you need to get in anywhere or out of anywhere, he will drive a path thought the most restless of crowds. We arrived in Blossom Avenue at midday in the Mercedes and I surveyed the situation. The crowd was around two hundred strong. There was a satellite truck from each of the BBC, ITN and Sky and they were all focussed on the placard wavers and the religious leaders. The neighbours were out in the front gardens standing, open-mouthed trying to make sense of the situation, wondering how long these demonstrations were going to be going on for

DeShaun and I walked up to the front door and knocked. I waved away the news crews asking who I was. I thought they should have known and if they didn't it was no skin off my nose. I wasn't the story, I was the guy on a monkey an hour plus exes.

Joe answered the door and I saw a man who clearly had looked after himself, no middle-aged spread but he had supermarket jeans and a Manchester United replica shirt on, beige socks and slippers. Sandy was better turned-out; obviously the dresser in the house. It was just the two of them which was fine by me. They were pleased to meet me, after all, I was the guy that was going to get them through this and make sure they got the money. I know this wasn't their primary objective, but if they were at all like me it would become so. I felt like Mr Wolf in that Tarantino movie, Pulp Fiction, the guy that comes to clean up the mess.

First things first. Who was going to do the television? One or both of them? I thought both. If it were just Joe with the accusations of drugs and nudity they might stick harder than if the two of them were together. He looked normal but was balding, wore cheap reading glasses and sandals. Easy to decide on looks alone that he might be a perv. If he was on with his wife, who looked good, there would be none of that. They agreed it was going to be the both of them. I called a hairdresser friend of mine and told him to get his arse out of London and up to Welwyn Garden within the hour. He didn't know where Welwyn Garden was so I said I'd cover the cost of a cab

What about clothes? What did they think they should wear? I gave them half an hour to go and choose clothes and come back down with what they thought might work for them. Sandy came down in a skirt and blouse and a fitted jacket with high-heeled shoes. She looked good. She did know how to dress. Joe came down after ten minutes in a work suit that hadn't seen the inside of a dry cleaner for months. Joe, I said, smart casual, what you might wear to a dinner party? He said he'd wear jeans and a sweatshirt or t-shirt depending on the weather. I called my stylist and asked her to bring down a pair of good chinos, a sky-blue shirt, not 100% cotton as it always shows the sweat, an unstructured jacket and a pair of brown brogues and not to spare the expense. Joe could afford it and he'd need it.

I asked them about their collaborator, this Buzz fella and Joe said he wasn't part of the equation. He was merely the IT guy who had made the dongle that became the app and had put the video on social media and caused the shit storm in the first place. Surely he should be doing his fair share of the flak taking. Joe and Sandy insisted not. It was their call, their idea, and Buzz had simply enabled it. Also, he wasn't the kind of person to wash his clothes, get a haircut and look smart on the television.

Next we did posture. Sandy sat well, upright, legs together, demur looking and she did it naturally. Joe was a funny kinda guy. He sat with his legs apart, on the sofa looking all out like the person he was. We needed to change that. I got him to sit up, cross his legs and look to Sandy, look to see how she was sitting and to do his best to mirror her. He lapsed occasionally during the next bit, the questioning, but by the end both Sandy and I had enough nods and gestures sorted out that he would be okay.

We practised the questions. I asked every question I could think of and I've been doing this for ten years. I had notes from our conversation the previous night and I had prepared a list. The objective was that they would come across as the normal people they were. Professional, well-educated but with a couple of personal habits that had no impact on anyone else and a view that they wanted to celebrate their atheism without religion getting a look in. They weren't attacking religion; they were just not having it.

Joe's clothes arrived as did the barber who cut his hair, flamed his ears and nostrils. They needed it and took the reluctant stubble out of his very sweet dimples. They had made him look a little weird and odd, if you know what I mean and, I must say, we did a decent job. He scrubbed up well, looked a little younger than his years. He was very pleased as he should be. My people know what they're doing and they don't come cheap.

It took four hours and several cups of tea, no booze, and I thought they were ready. I asked them if they wanted DeShaun and I to take them there in the Mercedes and they said no thanks, they'd get the train. It took twenty minutes apparently. I wished them luck, wrote out an invoice, jumped back in the Merc and went back to town.

Chapter 26

Sandy

I was worried about this Simon person that Joe found but he did a good job. He was very flattering and that gave me confidence. Joe was the one who was changed most and I wondered if it made him feel uncomfortable. He said he was pleased and that he would spend a bit more time and money on his appearance. Get a couple of suits made and one day get a pair of shoes like Simon's. Simon had said he bought his shoes from a shoemaker in Florence and that they were one thousand two hundred pounds a pair and worth every penny. You can tell a man by his shoes, he said. I'd never heard anything of the sort.

We were dressed, coached, questioned and went up to the studios on the train. I thought if we turned up in Simon's Mercedes it would look to contrived, too smooth, too prepared and we might get a harder time than if we were seemingly on our own.

A young girl with a clipboard and a pair of headphones ushered us into what they called the green room. I think it must have been a room used by celebrities because it had sandwiches, beer and wine. Joe wanted a glass of wine but I told him no, he could wait until after. There was a television on in this room and we watched the end of the six o' clock news, the weather and then the local news jingles. There was a man in a shabby suit talking about buses with another man in lycra demanding more care from both bus and lorry drivers. Joe and I sat in silence but I knew as well as he did that we were going over questions Simon had given us.

The girl with the clipboard came in and said Ms Bunn would be ready for us shortly and asked if we would like to follow her. She smiled as warmly as she could and I was reminded of the song "*never smile at a crocodile*" as we walked along a corridor. We came to the studio, Jemima nodded at us and invited us to take a seat while there was some footage of the previous day outside our house. Looking back, I can say this felt difficult at the time but we did okay.

She started off hard. "Mr and Mrs Quigley, can you tell me why you are not a danger to society. In favour of drugs, pornography and having less faith in God than you do in Sir Alex Ferguson."

I answered. "I don't agree with Joe about Alex Ferguson, I'm not a football fan, I prefer people like Elizabeth Garret Anderson, the Suffragettes and To Youyou."

"Who?"

"To Youyou, a female Nobel prize winner in Medicine, research into Malaria".

"Okay. It's up to you. But what about the things I mentioned? Porn and no faith in God?"

Joe answered this one. "Miss Bunn, there is no pornography unless you believe it to be pornography, you equate nudity with pornography in your mind and, as for God, we have chosen a route that many have taken before us. That of non-believers. We don't expect to be burnt at the stake. We don't expect to burn in hell. However, we both struggle to understand the logic, the reasoning behind a belief in a God and we think it has no relevance to our lives".

"It's called faith, Mr and Mrs Quigley, if you have no faith in God, and choose not to follow a Christian life, I mean, I heard you said you coveted your neighbour's Mercedes, Mrs Quigley."

"I do, it's lovely. I feel I can justly say I lead a Christian with a small 'c' life, if that's what you like to hear. I don't steal, I don't kill, what else don't I do, Joe?"

"You have no other God; you haven't relinquished the Christian one for a sun god or a rain god or a mountain god."

"Can we be serious, Mr and Mrs Quigley?"

"Miss Bunn, we are serious, this isn't something done on a whim or after a glass of red wine."

"What about those people demonstrating outside your house."

"Yes?"

"What do you have to say to them?"

"We have no responsibility towards them. Their leaders are responsible for what seems to us to be competitive redemption. They are each trying to reclaim us to a religion and they believe they will do it by dint of numbers. It is silly, pointless, wasteful.

"What do you mean by that?"

"We feel that one of the religious leaders believes there is a win to be had from converting us to a faith based belief system and the more people outside the house the more chance of them succeeding."

"I have an idea on how we can make the crowd smaller." Interrupted Joe.

"How's that, Mr Quigley?"

"I'd sooner try it than explain it on television, thank you, Miss Bunn."

"I don't feel as though you have given an adequate explanation of what you have done."

"Miss Bunn. I don't believe we owe you an explanation."

"I thought that was why you wanted to come on and be interviewed, to make your position clear."

"Our position is very clear and has been from the start. You asked us here because you wanted the story and I don't believe we owe you any more."

"You don't believe in very much do you. Thank you, Mr and Mrs Quigley." And with that we were dismissed. Cheeky girl. We were escorted from our chairs, from the studios and out into the streets of London. No "thank-yous". No question of being reimbursed our travel expenses. It was a bit shabby.

I tried calling Bec and Daisy who had gone to the house to see if they had seen the television, but it was all engaged. Home phones and their mobiles. We headed off back to Kings Cross but Joe fancied a pint so we went into one of those city pubs full of men in suits and girls in high heels looking like they all fancied sex with each other but were worried about it seeming inappropriate.

I asked Joe about his idea, he said he would try and negotiate a limited number representation with the faith groups. I said it sounded fancy, he said he thought it might just keep the numbers down and they must be getting tired. It would do us all a favour.

Buzz rang to say he had sold fifty-one thousand three hundred copies of the app. Seventy-five thousand pounds each, we'd made. Not bad. We ordered champagne. Joe told me off for sailing close to the edge when I had said we didn't do this on a whim. It wasn't a whim, but it was not supposed to have had these consequences with more to come.

Bec called back and told us we had looked good and answered the questions well and said she was fully supportive. Simon, the PR consultant phoned and congratulated us both saying if ever we needed any help, just to call. I said at five hundred pounds an hour it was unlikely but thanked him nonetheless.

Chapter 27

Joe

We made our way home that evening arriving just after nine and it was fairly quiet. I thought it was looking good for the next morning and hoped things would quieten down. We had a glass of wine each, watched an edited version of the interview after the ten o' clock news and went to bed.

It was the calm before the storm and what a storm. No four horsemen of the apocalypse but an invasion of religious zealots isn't too strong a word, but they were there at eight in the morning. There must have been three hundred people. Buzz phoned to say he had been up all night sending out the app with dongles to all and sundry and we were approaching seventy thousand sales. He said we needed to chat, that he had spoken to a copyright lawyer and wanted to firm things up. I asked if I needed a lawyer and, and I don't think I'm being naïve here, he sounded genuinely disappointed that I had not trusted him. I told him to come over for lunch. We'd try and go out for a pint.

I went out to the hedge and asked Mr Butt, Mr Corr and Mr Tudor to come into the garden for a chat. They looked at each other, I'm sure they were thinking we had come to a decision about which religion we were going to adopt. There was a very impious look on each of their faces. I told them they were being very insensitive to the wishes of my neighbours, traffic wanting to use Blossom

Avenue, the demands of the police and that we needed to do something about the numbers of people outside the hedge. They agreed. Mr Corr said his congregation was older and getting tired unable to have a midday nap. Mr Butt said the will of his followers was unlimited but many of them had jobs to go to or businesses to run. Mr Tudor said nothing, still hoping I was going to declare his faith the winner.

    I told them the plan but first we had to bring the summerhouse from the back garden to the front garden. They would each need to nominate two members of their congregations to help lift it round. They asked for volunteers and each of them secured the help of a couple of older men. We helped them lift and move it on an old trailer I used to take things to the dump.

    We removed the sun loungers and the swingball set along with the croquet. Mr Tudor said we should play sometime, that he had played for his house at school. I had no inclination to befriend the man so simply ignored him and we all secured the summerhouse in the front garden. I asked the three religious leaders and PC Cross, who had arrived just in time to help, to join me in a meeting. Sandy came in to make sure we were all okay and offered to make teas and coffee. The summerhouse had five chairs and a small table and eventually we agreed the, as we now pompously call it, The Summerhouse Agreement. Each faith group would have a maximum five people at the hedge at any one time, meaning people could go home, get some sleep, do some work and that each religious leader would draw up a rota of members of their respective congregations. PC Cross, as the civil servant, would sign the accord on behalf of all of us.

When we thought we had reached a satisfactory conclusion the door to the summerhouse swung open and standing outside was a Rabbi, a Sikh and the apparent leader of the Hare Krishna devotees. The latter appeared agitated. "We have been here since the beginning and now you leave us out of meetings. Where is the justice. All you people ever do is think we are not worthy of serious consideration."

I was about to answer and the Rabbi made his contribution. "Typical, the Jews are always persecuted. We have a right to be in meetings too. What have you been discussing?"

Then the Sikh has his tuppenyworth. "Our protest has always been peaceful, but we too demand to know what is going on. Don't let our lack of action appear to mean we do not care as much as any other group".

PC Cross tried to explain. "We have decided, for the sake of peace and calm and order that each faith represented here shall have a maximum of five representatives at any one time therefore allowing people to go home, go to work, run their businesses and the free flow of traffic in this street."

I butted in and said, "and it means my wife and I can get some sleep."

The Rabbi, clearly upset said, "so you have two Christian faith groups each allowing five, so a total of ten Christians while we have none. We demand equality. Always, always it is the Jews who are not allowed a voice, who are subjugated."

"Please Rabbi, just stop. You can have a chair."

Mr Corr insisted they were two distinct faith groups and so each should be allowed five. Mr Tudor agreed so for a moment we had that rare thing, peace, until the Hare Krishna devotee said "I will invoke Kali on you unless we can be part of the salvation. We have been here since the start. "You, Sir" he said, pointing at the Rabbi, "are new to this, you are a late comer. You cannot start demanding parity when you haven't put the work in. My boys and girls are worn out."

"You should just stop them then and make them rest, if you had any compassion." Mr Butt interjected.

"Don't you talk to me about compassion, Sir, we do not kill each other, we do not have representatives who murder and maim and rape and enslave."

"But it is well known that you are nothing but a cult."

"We are a recognised faith group with our own set of beliefs and we are recognised by the Inland Revenue."

I stepped in, vociferously. "Can you all please be quiet. Rabbi, you can have five if you can muster them. Is your surname Singh?" I asked the Sikh.

"Yes sir, it is."

"Good, Mr Singh, then you have five and there can also be five members of your organisation, no more. And please tell me your name."

"I am named for Paurnamasi, but you can call me Dave."

And then Sandy bought the teas and coffees in and it all kicked off again. Accusations of discrimination from the Sikh, persecution from the Rabbi and indifference from Dave. Butt, Corr and Tudor looked smug with their drinks. Sandy made more and five minutes later the summerhouse was emptying.

Ten minutes later the road was much quieter. PC Cross was happier. "You did a good job there, Sir. I appreciate all your help".

"It's now up to you to keep everyone to the word of the agreement."

The television news vans all buzzed and whirred as the faith group leaders left the summerhouse and the reporters were on them like, I don't know, forgive me, flies on shit or should I say bees around a honeypot if I am trying to protect my reputation. Why they couldn't all just bugger off and leave us alone, I don't know.

Sandy came out and said she had an idea.

Chapter 28

Buzz

I had a call from Mrs Quigley. I'm reluctant to call her Sandy, she is a bit older but I'll give it a go. She said she would prefer it if she and Joe could come to me that evening so we could have a chat instead of me going to them the next day for a pint or two. I said I had no problem with it, nearly called her 'love' and she said they would be at mine, if I gave them my address, within the hour. And would I order a Chinese and did I have any wine at home.

I'm the first to admit that house pride isn't my thing. I haven't had a girlfriend for about six months and the flat was looking pretty skanky; socks around the place, unwashed dishes, overflowing bin, Rizlas and baccy back in the drawer like I hadn't moved on since I was a student. I tidied up the place as best I could, opened the windows to let in some fresh air, ordered the Chinese and popped to the offy to get a couple of bottles of white.

Mrs Quigley had explained that they had managed to reduce the numbers but wanted to get away from the noise and the TV Cameras. An hour and ten minutes after they called, they arrived, looking a bit wired, stressed. Joe asked about the wine situation and I poured glasses. The Chinese arrived and they both settled down. I didn't know what the next part of the plan was. I only have one bedroom and the sofa is no place to kip. I said we should look at the agreement I had drawn up and I gave Joe and Sandy both a copy.

Essentially it said we would share the copyright on the software, any patents that we might get on the app and the dongle and share the revenue 50/50. They agreed in principle but said they'd like more time to read it.

(A little later, we started a business in which Joe and Sandy had fifty percent and I had the other fifty percent. I didn't need access to the money and neither did they and we opened a bank account requiring at least two signatories, mine and one other. The business would cover costs but take the money and then pay a dividend. It was all worked out by one of their daughters and I didn't have a problem. We all had the same point of view that we wanted fairness and nobody expected us to make any real money out of this).

Back to what happened. I saw Joe looking around a bit, being a bit nosy and I asked him if he was alright. He said, "I don't want to be rude or judgemental, but this is very student, this flat and there's one thing you can usually find in a student flat that wasn't obvious here."

I was curious and asked, "what do you mean?"

"Do I have to spell it out?" he asked.

"Yes," I said.

"I could really fancy a smoke," he hinted

I skinned up and we had a smoke. Mrs Quigley said she wouldn't, that somebody had to keep a clear head. The next thing, Joe asked if I had a credit card and I said yes. I thought he wanted to do a line or two but he said they wanted to get away for a day or two, where no one would recognise them and no one would see them. "Can I borrow your card to book a hotel and use your laptop to find one?" he asked.

We had a look on the internet for a hotel and found one in the Cotswolds. Funnily enough I had stayed there a couple of years ago with this very fit girl I was dating. I had won some money on one of the poker sites and wanted to be flash. Those were the days, when I could date a good-looking girl. This place still looked pretty good so I said they should go there. I gave them card details to book, luckily it was a different card from a couple of years ago. Joe was very sensitive and asked if I had any cash. He didn't want to use a cashpoint in Hoxton or in the Cotswolds and they would need a cab. I think he had watched too much '*24*' but he was either serious or a bit paranoid from the excellent grass we had smoked. I went to the cash point and got him a couple of hundred quid, after all, we were fairly minted.

They stayed an hour or so and then they were gone, in a cab, to Broadway, in the heart of the Cotswolds where me and my then girlfriend had had a very good time. I was jealous and thought it would be nice to get away, nicer still if I had a girl to go with. I washed the dishes, skinned up again, finished the wine and went to bed.

Chapter 29

Sandy

I was very stressed out. Normally I can cope with stress but Joe's summerhouse thing and then the other people turning up demanding chairs around the table and tea and the TV people, I needed to get away. We packed overnight bags, called a taxi to meet us around the corner from where we live so we wouldn't be seen and then we snuck out over the back fence, into the neighbour's at the rear of us, through their garden and out by their garage. I felt like a naughty teenager holding Joe's hand as we waited for the taxi.

We did this thing with Buzz that I'm sure he has told you about and by half ten we were in another taxi taking us to a very romantic looking fancy hotel in Broadway. I called Bec and asked her to call Daisy to let them know we were going to be okay and not to worry. She said she thought we were being over the top but I know we weren't. Now I felt more like a grown up, it was exciting, romantic, fun, like we hadn't had for years. I snuggled up to Joe in the back of the taxi and gave him a big kiss. He was a bit startled and a bit stoned, but it was making my heart beat a little faster. I was quite relaxed, relatively relaxed. We were going to get away for a couple of days. No TV, no crowds, no religious leaders. No one would know who we were because all the telly stuff had happened in our area, it was all local news.

We got to the hotel at about one in the morning. Joe had nodded off so I nudged him awake and reminded him that his name was Buzz. I don't know how Buzz had got a card with that name on it but he had said he was now, officially, Buzz, by deed poll and his passport, bank account and so on was all as Buzz. It didn't quite ring with his surname, Fotheringay, although luckily enough, not Lightyear. Apparently, his parents had named him after the buzzing feeling she had got when newly pregnant, the feeling she had before the tests confirmed she was. His real name was Nigel, after his dad, but he hated that and from the age of eighteen had been Buzz. His parents had complained but he said it was his life and he wanted the name. It's funny what you find out about a person over a Chinese, a glass of wine and the joint he shared with Joe.

We checked in to the hotel with the night porter, were shown to a lovely room with a four poster and promptly fell asleep, even without brushing our teeth. Neither of us had had an adventure like this before and we slept the sleep of babies.

We didn't wake up until nine thirty. That's not like us. Normally we get up at around six. It was too late to hurry for breakfast downstairs so we took our time and ordered room service. It still seemed very indulgent, very naughty like we were in a film script or something. The breakfast was great, meaty sausages, buttery mushrooms, soft poached eggs and granary toast with marmalade. The room was quite luxurious as well. Joe had to remind me that we had nearly eighty thousand pounds in the bank account now and we might as well enjoy it. We had beamed ceilings, comfy leather chairs, his and hers robes, slippers and one of those roll top baths that we could both get in. And we did. It was fun. It was naughty.

We finally decided to go out at about midday. The village is quintessentially pretty, like it has been preserved for tourists and there were coachloads of Japanese taking photos, Americans braying to each other saying how quaint it was. Hanging baskets were everywhere along with antique shops designed to catch people out with their supposed authenticity, tourist tat shops and up market country clothing shops. I'd always fancied a pair of proper stout walking boots and a couple of those walking stick things that make you look like a crab so we bought a pair of boots each for over one hundred pounds, each. One hundred pounds for boots, I was shocked, but Joe said we had the windfall and we might as well treat ourselves.

The next stop was the newsagent/tobacconist. Joe said he'd like a cigar to go with a pint at lunchtime in one of the village pub gardens. He then said he felt like he had been, metaphorically, punched in the head and kicked in the balls reading a newspaper headline (later he couldn't remember which newspaper it was) asking, in bold type ***"Is this the most dangerous couple in Britain?"*** followed by a paragraph reading

"Mr and Mrs Joe Quigley, the cultists who want us all to abandon the morality of religion have gone on the run to infect others with their crazy idea that there is no spiritual life, there is no God, the Church of England has no place in society and their obvious disregard for the Queen. They believe we are all free to do and think what we want irrespective of the wishes of others. If you

see this couple, don't approach them. They have no convictions for any violent crime, but this newspaper believes they are capable of anything. They have disappeared and are believed to be on the run. They are avoiding providing us with the information we need so if you see them, please call this newspaper and we will pass on your information to the authorities so they can be stopped".

There were more photos apparently downloaded from other people's uploads to Flickr and Instagram and they all made Joe look like a crazed maniac intent on destroying the world as we know it.

"Call Simon," I said. "Call him now, pay him his ludicrous amount of money and get this silliness stopped."

Joe turned on his mobile to a barrage of pings and called the PR man. "I need some help."

"I've called you half a dozen times and your phone's been switched off. Where are you?"

"In the Cotswolds."

"What on earth are you doing there?"

"Trying to get away from the noise but I've just seen this headline. Am I the most dangerous man in Britain?"

"Of course not, it's just some right-wing rag edited by a reactionary old Christian. However, we do need you to come out and defend yourself."

"Every time I do something the situation just gets worse".

"We'll have to knock it on the head. I'll call you in an hour. I think I have a plan".

Joe didn't buy the newspaper and fortunately he wasn't recognised. He fancied an early pint and a smoke but thought he'd better keep his head for whatever might happen. Self-aware, he knew one pint would become two, would become three, he'd get a thirst and be in the pub for the afternoon. Me, equally self- and Joe-aware, I knew not to suggest a pint. Instead I suggested a return to the hotel, order lunch from room-service and try to rest. "I'll have to keep my new boots for another time".

An hour later, Simon rang back. "Listen, Joe. I've got you a ten past seven on Sky News tomorrow, Suzanna Reid on *Good Morning Britain*' just after eight and a studio visit to BBC *Breakfast* for eight forty-five. There's a car organised to collect you at four thirty tomorrow morning, so catch some sleep, don't drink, shave, dress normally, eat safely, we don't want you sitting on the toilet all night because you had a dodgy curry. I'll meet the car just before the Sky interview and I'll be with you all morning."

"Sounds like a plan, Simon."

"It is a plan. Both of you practice like you did before. Answer the questions you believe they'll ask, the ones we went through. Breathe in through your nose and out through your mouth. You did well the day before yesterday, shame about the outcome. All you can do is remain calm, follow your own thoughts. Steadfast is the old-fashioned word I'm looking for".

As Joe was being coached, I was taking calls from Bec and Daisy, concerned friends and work colleagues. I hadn't had a day off work without phoning in for ten years and hadn't phoned in to say I wasn't coming to work. In the hubbub, I'd quite forgotten the real world and the real job and the real people. We were like a couple of runaways. This was bringing us back to reality and I didn't really like it. My colleagues were calling the girls and they needed information to be assured that while Joe and I had got ourselves mixed up with religious leaders and the television, we were quite safe. After four hours of phone calls I finally put the phone down and climbed onto the bed next to Joe for a cuddle.

"Did you have any idea this might happen?"

"None at all."

"That we'd be running away, holed up here to escape the faithful."

"Nope."

"And that we'd end up as the 'most dangerous couple in Britain'?"

"I have to say, it's laughable. It's nobody's business but ours and nobody would have been any the wiser if Buzz hadn't uploaded…is that the right word? stuff to the internet."

"I don't think we can blame Buzz. And it is because of him that you'll have more money in the bank than you've had for years."

"The eternal question then. How much money makes all this worthwhile?"

"If we were doing it for the money".

"Which we weren't of course. It was all just a thing, not a joke, not a serious statement of any intent, not meant to upset, not meant to provoke such anger, maybe fury. Are they all so extreme?

"I've no idea, love. But some of them are and I guess those are the ones we need to look out for".

"I'm not sure any amount of money would make up for this, running away. I don't know if we are going to have to be in hiding for days, weeks, months until it all dies down. If it does all die down".

"What do they think they're going to achieve?"

"An apology, repentance, the both of us going to church? I've no idea really."

Chapter 30

Joe

We lay in each other's arms until six o'clock when we thought we had better watch the early evening news. Pleasure to see that we weren't the leading story became anxiety when the photo from the morning's paper appeared on the screen. The newsreader seemed to follow the tone of that morning's newspaper but then said "The Home Office have confirmed that they have received two thousand three hundred and twenty applications to secede from the United Kingdom, using the form of words first used by Mr and Mrs Quigley. Local newspapers have reported a number of advertisements placed in their Public Notices sections by nearly two thousand people. Tomorrow night at eight o'clock on BBC one, we will be airing a discussion on the subject. Please visit our website, follow us on Facebook or Twitter to join in the discussion."

I was, as they say, gobsmacked. We sat back on the bed, looked at each other and laughed. Perhaps the tide was turning; perhaps there wouldn't be so many agitated believers outside our house as they would be too thinly spread across the country. Our telephones pinged and rang until we turned them off. Satisfied that Daisy and Bec knew we were okay and that close friends had also been reassured we ordered an early dinner from room service; each choosing steak and chips, with the steak medium to avoid all chance of an upset stomach. Ice-cream for dessert and a glass of port for me to drink while I smoked a big fat cigar, puffing smoke through the open window, relishing the idea that I still had a more than a trace of rebelliousness left in me.

The following morning at four thirty our room phone rang; reception telling us that our car had arrived. We, dressed and looking as relaxed as possible, walked out of the room, down the corridor, down the stairs. I paid with Buzz's card and the more alert-this-time receptionist said, "they asked for Mr Quigley. This card is for Buzz Fotheringay. Are you Mr Quigley or Mr Fotheringay?"

"Fotheringay", I lied, aware of the consequences of being caught out. "Quigley is my stage name, isn't that right, dear".

Sandy, quick on the uptake, couldn't restrain the laughter. "Have they done it to you again darling. I wish they'd just get it right". She took a handkerchief from her handbag and wiped her eyes. Luckily the receptionist felt she might be in on the same joke with someone famous enough to have a Mercedes arrive for them with a uniformed driver. She took the credit card, I entered the pin and the danger was averted.

The drive down the M40 was pleasant as the sun rose. We practised question and answer sessions, Sandy occasionally trying to catch me out. "If they were to make a movie of your experience, who would you like to be you?"

"I don't know. Clooney, Pitt, Bradley Cooper, you?"

"Cameron Diaz."

"So, if you were Cameron Diaz who would you prefer for a screen partner or husband?"

"Brad Pitt", was the very quick answer. "What do you say to the people who are outside your house, waving placards, accusing you of being the devil incarnate?"

"Go home, go back to work. Get back to the hedge. Just leave us to get on with our lives".

We picked up Simon from his home in Beaconsfield and drove to the Sky studios in Isleworth. We were a little more confident this time, having been through the same scenario on the regional BBC programme and knowing we had each other. The game had changed but not in the way we had hoped. We worked out a strategy. I knew the Irish presenter was a Manchester United fan and we thought we'd get on better as a pair of blokes, men, fellas if you like and we would try it with just me. I was happy with that outcome. I know Sandy is strong but I also knew the day was going to be difficult.

Interviewed by the Irish male presenter with his Irish brogue he asked me, "what does it feel like to be a leader? To have followers, people who believe in you?"

I was really taken aback. No one had said anything about being a leader and I didn't want to be a leader. It wasn't me. "I'm not entirely sure I know what you mean, I'm not a leader."

"Sure you are, you have a Twitterstorm in your name, countless tens of thousands of followers on Facebook and you say you're not a leader. Come along now Mr Quigley."

"I haven't put anything on Facebook or written anything on Twitter, I wouldn't know how."

"But you, maybe not you yourself but this accomplice of yours uploaded video to Facebook showing your gizmo in action and I have to say, as a fellow United fan, I really enjoyed the clip. Nonetheless, you started this whole shebang".

"Shebang?"

"All these people demonstrating outside your house, the noise, the threats of violence against you and your family, all over twitter. You brought them on."

"Are you telling me, that my not wanting to have religion as a part of my life, brought on those threats of violence from religious, God fearing, peace loving individuals and groups?"

"I'm not sure I want to go there, I'm not sure I want demonstrators outside my house. Anyway, you are the leader of this development in faithlessness."

"How many times? I'm not a leader. I'm not leading. I am a Maintenance Manager. I am the husband of Sandy, the father of Bec and Daisy and that is all."

"I think you're being modest Mr Quigley. You have hundreds of thousands of followers whether you like it or not. And where there are followers, surely there are leaders."

"There are people who have downloaded the app and for reasons of their own have chosen to do what I did."

"But my point is, if you hadn't done what you did, there wouldn't be people copying you."

"I'm not going to get into a philosophical discussion with you about the nature of leaders and followers. I'm not an ogre, nobody who knows me would call me a bad person, I'm not necessarily anti or against or whatever, religion, I just don't want it in my life. Other people can choose their paths, their beliefs, their vocations. I simply choose God-free existence for me. Thank-you."

"Thank-you for coming in Mr Quigley."

And it was over. I managed to keep my temper although there were times when I felt it might have boiled over. I wasn't used to this kind of pressure. At work, I worked alongside colleagues. There had been a few career motivated machinations at times from more ambitious colleagues but I tended to steer clear and enjoy the satisfaction of getting work done well. Making sure the building and the work environment was good, was right, not too difficult, not too demanding, but enough to keep me switched on. But to be under the spotlight, physically as well as metaphorically was different. It was tough. Presenters with agendas. Tricky buggers trying to force words into my mouth.

We sat in the car to the ITV studios with Simon preparing for the next round. "You did well," offered Simon.

"Yes, you were very good," added Sandy. "You didn't rise to his bait. That bit about faithlessness. What a contrived load of old bullshit." She always said it as she meant it.

"Or the followers and leaders gambit he played," added Simon. "As I said, remember what the politicians do, have your own agenda and don't feel as though you have to answer their questions directly. If they give you a choice of answers, like are you a believer or are you faithless, you have more options that the answers they gave you to give. Tell them you are simply a human being."

"I feel like an amateur boxer fighting professionals and you sponge me down between rounds with gobbets of advice and words".

"Just here to help," said Simon.

"Don't be miserable, Joe, love. Treat it like the adventure we said it was. Nobody's going to best us about the idea and what we want. For us, Joe." After forty odd years she's still very much on my side. Love her.

I'm not sure why I was getting the brunt of the attacks but I didn't want Sandy to get stressed out again. I said I would do the interviews alone. Simon thought it would be better if we both did them and Sandy thought I was going to be thrown to the lions, she wanted to be there to support me, but I felt good that I was going to be okay. And I was.

More accustomed to the process now, we were led to a green room at ITV where coffee, orange juice, Danish pastries and croissants were laid out. I sat with Simon and Sandy, we were all three in quiet contemplation. Simon contemplating his job and potential income, me contemplating another round or two of word play and Sandy told me not to get all stressed out, try to keep calm.

The exchange with Suzanna Reid was less confrontational. Perhaps she was less concerned about viewers wanting her to topple me from my apparent self-imposed importance. Perhaps she was more curious. Perhaps because she was a woman.

"What gave you the idea for, what do you call it?"

"It doesn't have a name. It was just an idea. Sandy should take the credit. It was her action that turned the idea into something we actually did."

"So, what started the idea?"

And, to summarise because you've heard this all before, I told her about the Muslims shooting, raping, beheading other Muslims in the name of a God. Israelis, bombing Palestine, killing women and children to defend their state, their land of milk and honey turned somewhat sour and bitter. I told her about Church of England Vicars urging God to be on their side in warfare, Catholic nuns and priests abusing children and covering it up and I said that we felt we had no wish to be a part of that. We didn't want it in our lives.

"Sorry, was that a bit of a rant?"

"No, no, no. But how can you ignore the suffering, do you have no compassion?"

"I am a compassionate man. I care very much for my family and friends. I donate to charity. Comic relief always gets money out of my wallet. A religion does not equate to empathy, understanding and compassion."

"But don't you have any compassion for the victims of war?"

"We could have a chat here about Holy wars over the centuries and you could ask me if I feel compassion. We could continue with the Sunnis and Shias shooting the (I was going to say shit here but managed not to) others to death in what they might describe as a Holy war."

"But what about the kids, in Aleppo, for example?"

"Yes, of course I do, for victims, but, like everybody else I am limited to what I can do. I can't dictate Britain's foreign policy or defence. I can express an opinion in a poll, if ever I was asked but I never have been."

"And tell me about Hendrix. What made you do this?"

"I guess that the Scots were being offered independence on a single simple question. That would have set some kind of precedent and I thought, we thought, me and Sandy thought it would be fun, something interesting to do; something that would really mean nothing to anyone but us."

"Mr Quigley. I wish both you and your wife good luck. Thank you for coming on the show."

The session on BBC Breakfast was easier. Timed later in the show when they usually have celebrities on, I quietly but, I think, assertively repeated that I wasn't the devil incarnate in chinos and a sweater determined to ban religion. I continually repeated our mantra that it was mine and Sandy's decision about what we wanted to do with our lives and Charlie and Naga didn't push the point.

We dropped Simon off back at his office and decided to venture home. Surely those of faith can't still be demonstrating when there is no one there to hear their objections or rise to their bait. With their numbers rationed to five per faith, assuming they had stuck to the Summerhouse Agreement as it had become known, there wouldn't be any fuss.

Chapter 31

PC Cross

I saw their car turn into the road and the looks on their faces. It had all kicked off a bit. What they will have seen is a mass of placards and two groups of people baying at each other. On one side were the anti-Quigley placards held aloft by Mr Butt, Mr Corr and, not to be outdone, Mr Tudor and their followers. A brief selection, if you will, said things such as *'down with the infidels'* *'God have mercy on your souls'*, and *'have faith in the lord our God, Jesus Christ'*. They were still joined by the Hare Krishna lot, the Sikhs, generally sitting on the verge miming cricket swings, bowling and batting, a group of orthodox Jews and recently arrived some Methodists with their arms aloft in supplication, fingers pointing to where they thought heaven was. "Praise the Lord", they chanted. There was also a small group of what appeared to be Africans, in grey suits, white shirts and the shiniest shoes you ever saw outside of the Force.

On the other side of the demonstration, which several officers and I were doing our utmost to keep calm were a large group of individuals. The car stopped and Mr and Mrs Quigley exited the vehicle and came towards me looking a little bewildered by the turn of events. "Who are those other people?" asked Mr Quigley of the demonstrators whose placards and bedsheets said, *'in myself I trust'*, *'the faithless shall inherit the earth'* and *'The Godbotherers are a bunch of arse souls'*

"They appear to be in support of you Mr and Mrs Quigley". I had been assigned to the demonstration as an experienced officer with a barely adequate number of young officers trying to keep control and keep the two sides from killing each other, to marshal the demonstrators, to keep the peace. I must tell you that under my helmet I was sweating profusely, sweat patches grew around the armpits of my shirtsleeves and if I had had a mirror I am sure I would have seen myself very red in the face. "Look what you've started now, Mr Quigley. There are at least four hundred people here shouting and hollering, shoving and heaving. We don't have the resources to control it".

The demonstrators in support of Mr Quigley and his wife seemed to recognise them from their television appearances and the photographs in the newspapers. They held their arms up, swayed their placards and from a whisper to song to a chant one could hear them saying "leader, leader." As more people joined in the cries became louder "LEADER, LEADER, LEADER"

"Oh for fuck's sake," said Mr Quigley using an expression I could have had him arrested for breaching the peace. "This I do not need."

I had to ask Mr Quigley for some help. "Can you give me a hand trying to keep these people apart and help me disperse them. Please?"

"I am not their leader."

"But they believe you are. Speak to them."

"If I speak to them it will only compound their misguided, flawed view that I want anything to do with leadership."

The cries grew louder. "LEADER, LEADER, LEADER". Some fell to their knees. One shouted "I waited years for this to happen. For someone to do something about the stupidity that is religion and you have come along."

Another, brandishing a Tannoy shouted "Let's hear it for the atheists, let's hear it for Joe. LEADER. LEADER. LEADER."

The cacophony grew as those of faith on the other side of our hard-pressed police line shouted back to drown out the noise of those who felt they had a new messiah, not their messiah. "There is only one God", shouted the monotheists. (A word I had learned the day before from my mate Bill, a bit of a religious nut).

"Unless you're Hindu", responded one of the faithless.

"Can't you do something?" I pleaded again with Mr Quigley. I had to shout into his ear to make sure I was heard over the din.

"I'm not a leader. Get me that Tannoy!" A couple of officers and I strode into the atheist's group and grabbed the man with the Tannoy. Mr Quigley grabbed the Tannoy itself and spoke into the microphone. "I am not your leader. I do not want to be your leader".

However, the only words the crowd chose to hear were "leader" and "leader" so they responded with "LEADER. LEADER. LEADER".

In a vicious spiral of two syllable noise, Mr Quigley and the crowd wound each other up to the point where he flung the Tannoy to the ground, grabbed the owner of the Tannoy, summoned me with a hand pointing towards his summerhouse and went looking for Messrs Butt, Corr and Tudor. He gathered them up and took them inside. Mrs Quigley gestured cup of tea to Mr Quigley and, I must tell you, I was parched.

The Tannoy owner was called Julian. He had no idea of what was going on but saw that Mr Quigley had three religious leaders and only him. "You'll be fine," said Mr Quigley, in the most re-assuring voice. "Our agreement was there would only be a maximum of five people from any faith group here at any time and you lot have broken the agreement".

"They", said Mr Corr, "all came down here in their cars and minibuses. They outnumbered us and we had to do something. We had to call for reinforcements."

"And it didn't occur to you to turn the other cheek?" I learned later that Mr Quigley disliked using biblical exhortations but felt they would be understood.

"It never does with those Christians", accused Mr Butt. "They say one thing and then do another."

"That's not fair," shouted Father Corr. "There are at least fifty of your lot out there. Ululating, praying in supplication to your Prophet."

"Do not take the name of the Prophet in vain, Mr Corr."

There was a knock at the door. The Methodist preacher, a Rabbi and Dave the Hare Krishna leader stood outside. Mr Quigley opened the door to be told by the Rabbi that it was only fair that they should all part of the council.

"This isn't a fucking council gentlemen."

"Allah have mercy on you".

"God have mercy on you"

"Praise be to the Lord."

"You have succeeded in offending all our sensibilities, Mr Quigley," said Mr Butt

"You have succeeded in offending me and offending the agreement we had."

"Can you offend an agreement, Mr Quigley, Leader?" asked Julian.

"Don't you fucking start. I've been up since half past four putting up with intrusions on my sensibilities and I'm not your fucking Leader."

Sandy came in with tea and biscuits for six. Myself, Mr Quigley, the new man Julian, Mr Butt, Mr Corr and Mr Tudor. " Is this not discrimination against us Jews, there is no tea for me. We have put up with discrimination, being treated as second class citizens for thousands of years. I told you this the last time we were here."

"I didn't know you were in here, Rabbi. Would you like a cup of tea and I can always get more biscuits?"

"Yes please. Do you have chamomile?"

"I believe we do. And you, gentlemen, would you like a hot drink. I wouldn't like to be seen as discriminatory, is that how you say it?"

Tea issue settled, Mr Quigley continued. "You", he said looking at the believers, "If you have to be here have a maximum of five people and you, Julian, get them, your lot, gone. I am not your leader. I do not lead anything. If they need a leader, you do it. You came with the Tannoy, you were prepared to lead the shouting and the chanting. As I said, if they need a leader, lead them. Otherwise send them home."

Chapter 32

Julian

I couldn't believe it. I've tried to do something, to be seen, to justify for years. I've wanted social change, I've been at the front of demonstrations and marches for most of my adult life, certainly since I was about fifteen years old and never have I been noticed. This Tannoy, I got it on eBay for fifteen pounds thirty-seven pence, has been a godsend, well not a godsend if you know what I mean but it has made me into a person who can be and will be noticed. I will be recognised for my beliefs and convictions. Not the convictions for dope smoking and affray, but for the convictions I have held for around twenty years that we should believe in ourselves not some figure head crutch man in the sky with a beard and bony fingers if you believe that painter, Leonardo di Caprio or something painted the chapel in Rome and was paid a load of money to make God look like the everyman's grandad he isn't.

I drank my tea with the other people in the summerhouse not waiting for it to cool and went outside. I made sure I was in Hendrix when I made my announcement, through the Tannoy, to the crowd who were waiting for news. "Joe Quigley has anointed me leader, not anointed, that's that lot, isn't it? Has appointed me leader and asked me to ask you to disperse. Working with Joe, as I can call him, I want to suggest we meet in one hour, on the Campus in Welwyn Garden town centre. We need to give Mr and Mrs Quigley some peace and quiet and to let these religionists know that we are not going to have a shouting match here in Blossom Avenue." The crowd who were in support of Joe and Sandy murmured and shuffled, collected their coats and bags and headed off towards the town centre.

I was blown away, gobsmacked. People had never paid me any attention and now I had all these people doing what I was telling them. This little bit of authority, this little bit of power made me feel I had arrived. My mum would have been so proud. Up until then I had done a bit of selling Socialist Worker at conferences, odd jobs, a bit of community service but I had never had a focus. That's what my therapist calls it, a point to my life and now I had one. Man, it was awesome. What a man with a Tannoy can do. And now I was a leader. Joe told me so.

I didn't have a plan. Life had taught me that there was no point in having a plan because they never work out but I must have sounded like I did because when I suggested people go to the Campus they all went. They all went!

I thought, what am I going to do when they all get to the campus, what am I going to say, how will they react, will they accept me as a leader, a spokesman, a representative, a delegate, I had no idea? Would a pint help me prepare? Better not. A spliff? Nah. Stay in control. My legs were shaking, I needed a piss. I got my bike and cycled home. Another cup of tea and a sandwich, I only had a tin of tuna in the cupboard. Never mind, focus, focus, focus. I had the Tannoy. I had been told by Joe to disperse the people.

I brushed my hair and made sure there was no food in my beard and cycled to town, to the Campus. If you don't know it, it's by the F. E. College, at the front of John Lewis and next to the library. There is a kind of concrete arena with benches surrounded by lawns and trees and in the Spring there are daffs and crocuses. It's very pretty. The police station used to be there but they moved that and now they've got housing for the olds in its place. I made sure I got there early and positioned myself at the apex of the arena. There must have been a hundred people there when I arrived and more turned up. After about ten minutes there it must have been five hundred or so people, after twenty minutes we must have had a thousand. My balls shrank right into my scrotum.

I was doing his best to fire up this growing crowd. "Joe has asked me to lead this organisation, us revolutionaries against the political status quo, against religious intervention in our daily lives. We need to define our objectives, organise, set up committees, train spokespeople. The first thing we need to do is organise a ballot to confirm leadership on me, or are there any other volunteers?" I thought it all came together well. I surprised even myself.

A middle-aged woman got up from the crowd and took my Tannoy. "My understanding, having seen Joe on the television a couple of times this morning, is that he and Mrs Quigley simply want to lead a life without religion getting involved, He doesn't want to change things. He doesn't want revolution, Julian, he doesn't want to organise, he doesn't want committees, he just wants to be left alone." There was muted applause and a couple of whistles from the crowd. It wasn't an inspired bit of oratory.

I wasn't having that. I snatched the Tannoy back and, fearing the loss of this quickly won authority declaimed, "if there are two schools of thought, one radical and one passive, can I say, then I would like to lead the radicals. It's time we did something; we can use our numbers, our will, our collective energy, our anger to change this country for the better. All those with me, let's meet again here, at three this afternoon." There was cheering from pockets of the crowd as my words hit home amongst the radicals. "Tweet your friends, update your Facebook, put pictures of this on Instagram and Flickr. We will lead and others will follow". The radicals all took out their smartphones and did as they were told, taking photos of each other, fists clenched, arms aloft, sneering snarls on their faces as they took selfies and uploaded them. Here was a cause they could grab on to. I had a fucking erection.

Those who preferred this older woman's idea of what Joe wanted, described as passive, drifted off, back home. They weren't going to be part of my movement. Or mine and Joe's movement.

Chapter 33

Daisy

Hello, you haven't heard from me yet. Probably because I am the younger daughter and Bec tends to take over. I was dead proud of Mum and Dad. I know it was all a bit silly and probably started off after a couple of glasses of wine with Mum and Dad winding each other up and doing this independence thing. But I tell you what was weird, the day they did it was Seffan's birthday. Have they told you about Steffan? No? He was mine and Bec's little brother and died of leukaemia when he was eight, about ten years ago. It might have been coincidence but that would be one hell of a thing, wouldn't it?

It broke Mum's heart and I was worried about Dad because he seemed to bottle it all up. Don't get me wrong, he was brilliant with Mum, supportive, understanding, helped with the housework and the cooking and being in touch with everyone. I heard him crying a few times, in the middle of the night, but never in front of me and Bec. We didn't have the kind of relationship that I could talk to him about it. He would have been embarrassed if he'd known I'd heard him. Anyway, he made sure we all ticked along, me and Bec at Uni and got us new phones so we could all be in touch, he was great really, sound, solid, it was like he was trying to be our rock. But I think I know what might have kicked all this off.

Nana and Gramps, Dad's mum and dad were still alive then. They were regular church goers and they insisted that Steffan should have a Christian funeral. They didn't like, inflict us with their beliefs but they were devastated when Steffan died and I think they thought he might have gone to what they called a better place. He was a fantastic little brother. Naughty, fun, a mop of hair and two older sisters who loved him and parents who spoiled him rotten especially after his diagnosis and he was a boy who deserved better than he'd got. A Christian funeral, they thought, was what he needed and Mum and Dad agreed to it.

It was an awful day, the black, the cars, the clothes, the vicar and, to put it bluntly, he fucked up. Called Steffan Steven, went on about God and his mysterious ways, ashes to ashes, called to heaven and the coffin was so small. Me and Mum and Bec were all in bits, Dad, tried to stay together but couldn't. It wasn't grief, it was anger and he said after that he couldn't say anything because he was worried he would upset Nana and Gramps and Steffan's teachers, school friends and the doctors and nurses that came. That was sweet that they came. He'd been being treated for a couple of years and everyone had fallen in love with him. It cuts me up just remembering now.

Anyway, back to today. Dad was trying to organise the religious rabble that had collected outside the house and a bunch of people who had seen them on the telly that morning who looked like they wanted to support Mum and Dad. I know he was on the edge because he doesn't usually swear that much but he was getting angry and normally he keeps a lid on that. They went into the summerhouse, had some kind of discussion and first of all this guy with a Tannoy came out, full of himself and made an announcement. Then the religious lot went to their groups and most of them left. I don't know what Dad said to them but it got a bit quieter from then on.

I checked my Facebook page and I can't believe how many friend requests I had. I didn't want to get that involved, this was Mum and Dad's thing so I ignored most of them. Then I searched the groups and there were hundreds, both in favour and against what they were doing. Some of the comments were vile and the threats from the religious fruitcakes were odd. How is it that people who say they believe in peace and love and God can be so nasty and so full of hate?

I didn't want to but I went on twitter and tweeted about the comments. I shouldn't have done because the response was quick and very nasty. Why can't people be interested in the important things, not what my parents are doing.

Chapter 34

Julian

I know I shouldn't tell you this but I went home and had a wank. I felt like I had found my purpose but needed to suss out a plan for that afternoon. What's the point of being a leader if you haven't got anything to lead with, no ideas, like?

I haven't got a pot to piss in, no credit card, no bank card, no bank account, they don't let you have one when you're claiming but I phoned my mate Jezza and asked him to set up a website for me, see if he could get something like jj.com, like, for me Julian and Joe, you see. I needed to have something to say when I went back to the campus at three. I needed more than to have them post on Facebook and twitter and Instagram. I wanted a movement.

I couldn't get what I needed, bit shit, really. I went back to the campus and there were hundreds of people watching, waiting but I had nothing to say. I tried to wind the people up getting a cheer for Joe and Sandy but things only kicked off when the telly van turned up. It was only Sky but the crowd started cheering and waving their signs supporting Joe and Sandy and I thought we should perhaps have a march like we had when they wanted to get fees for university tuition. I shouted into my Tannoy. "Supporters, let us make our way to St Albans, to the Abbey, to show the Bishop what we mean".

I hustled and bustled through the crowd to the bit outside John Lewis and led my people down Parkway. This is a posh part of the town centre with cherry blossom in the Spring, a fountain and nice lawns. I looked behind me and some people were following me but most weren't. I shouted again "Let us show our support, follow me."

A bloke came up to me and said he didn't have time to go all the way to St Albans, his wife was going to be home soon and he had to make tea. Someone else said they didn't have the right walking shoes on and another said it would be late and dark by the time we got there and if he left his car in the car park, how was he going to get back. It's not as if I ever said I had all the answers.

It was a bit embarrassing. Out of all the people that had been there at three only about twenty followed me down Parkway and then seeing as how it all looked a bit sad, one by one, they stopped, or went into John Lewis. By the time I got to the Parkway Tavern, a place I know well, it was just me and the Sky people. Dis-fucking-aster.

Chapter 35

Joe

The next morning, things had settled down outside the house but on the internet things had taken off. Bec and Daisy showed us the comments being made. Like the girls, I couldn't believe people could have such intense feelings about things other people did. I guess it was the anonymity but I would never sink so low. Sandy was visibly shaken and I told her I thought it would all blow over soon.

She phoned Charlie, the solicitor to see if there was anything we could do and he explained that even though people were saying such dreadful things it would be impractical to sue. Bec said it was the internet and that people just ranted because it was easy from their laptops and tablets because no one would know it was them.

The first visitor of the day was the postman. A red post office van parked outside and the postman dropped of three sackfuls of post. We looked at a dozen or so letters, half or so in support and the other may just as well have been in green ink they were telling us how wrong we were and the same old nonsense the religious lot out front had been giving us. Bec went through the envelopes looking for interesting stamps and found a couple. There was nothing official looking, as we had hoped in response to the letters we had written. The rest we put in the shed to take to the dump later. I made a note to buy a shredder.

I phoned Buzz to see what was going on. We hadn't spoken in thirty-six hours. "Joe, man, where are you?"

"I'm at home. We've just had three bags of hate mail delivered."

"That's nothing, Check out twitter. You've got tens of thousands of people having a go at you."

"It doesn't seem so bad when it's not physical."

"There's some pretty strong stuff on here but you can tell where it's coming from by the hashtags. We've got Mohammeds, Begums, Singhs, O'Reillys, Smiths and Jones's, Mkwezi, Ng, Li; all kinds of shit from all over the world. Which reminds me. I hope you don't mind but I've done a couple of things. I put the price of the app up to £9.99 and it doesn't seem to have harmed sales and I have instructed a translation company to re-write the notices and the app instructions in French, German, Spanish. We've got orders for nearly two thousand from France, eight thousand from Germany and fourteen thousand from Spanish speakers. There must be nigh on a million quid in your bank account if mine is anything to go by. Not bad for a less than a week, eh?"

"No, not bad". I was tired by all the rushing around; made weary by the constant misinterpretation of what I was trying to do. Both politicians and the media seemed to be lusting after a new story or a story to attach themselves to. "I'll call tomorrow for an update, and we should meet again soon for a pint."

"We should. And I have a great idea I need to talk to you about, partner".

The weirdest thing that day was the arrival of a Rolls Royce limousine. A liveried driver opened the passenger door and out stepped an extravagantly dressed African man who promptly knelt to the floor and held his arms up in supplication to his Lord. He was helped to his feet by the driver who was then shaken off and the man strode to the front door and knocked. I answered, "Good afternoon".

"Brother, I have come all the way from Nigeria to speak to you, to help you".

"I don't need your help."

"You may not think you do, but I can help. There are ways of the Lord that can be used to your advantage. Look at me. Can I come in?"

"No".

"But I have come a long way".

"Still no".

"But isn't it your common British decency to invite a weary traveller in. To offer them a cup of tea and a biscuit, that is your traditional afternoon repast is it not?"

Sandy stood behind me. "Invite him in. I want to see what he can possibly think he has to say."

"Thank-you, gracious lady. You will not be disappointed." He stepped in and looked around at the quintessentially English furniture in the very English house. "May I sit down?"

"Of course."

"Let me introduce myself. My name is Pastor Adejoba. I run the God's Salvation churches in Nigeria. I have over twenty-five thousand followers. You too have followers and how I can help you is this. Take this chance to make some money from them. Use the money you have made from your app to make more money. This will all be over in a moment and you need to establish financial independence. Establish a foundation; get them to offer ten pounds per month of their income to your foundation. Build a school and charge for their education. Sell them branded products. You will know of course that Kabbalah makes its money from bottling tap water. We do the same and we make a fortune."

"It was never my intention to make money from what I'm doing. I did not set out for commercial gain. I wanted to banish the hypocrisy of the church from my life and you come here ramming the same hypocrisy down my throat."

"But it is all for your own good. Look, I came here today in my own private 747. I drive a Rolls Royce and have three Ferraris at home. This on my arm is a fifty thousand-pound Patek Phillipe watch and I have three more at home. These teeth, twenty-four carat gold."

"How many pairs of those do you have at home?" asked Sandy

"This is my only pair and I fear you are pulling my leg. But I mean this from the bottom of my heart. Make money where you can".

"What about overturning the tables of the moneylenders; the separation of God and Mammon. I remember Thatcher saying she believed Conservatism was in line with Christianity. It is rubbish. People like you are nakedly self-interested. This is your job and you do it to extract money from unsuspecting, gullible people who seem happy to believe you, you're no better than a Hedge Fund Manager."

"But you do not understand. This is God's way of rewarding me for spreading the word of his love, his power, his glory. It is a mutually beneficial arrangement we have. After all, I do not take the money from these peoples' hands. They give it to me willingly."

"I think it's time you left, Mr…, I can't remember your name".

"Do not worry. I will remember yours Mr Joe and Mrs Sandy Quigley. Oh yes, I will remember them well. Goodbye, Sir." And he left the room, left the house, left Hendrix, strode past all the other assembled faithful, waving his fingers in a fashion that suggested he was blessing them and swooped off in his Rolls Royce, teeth glinting from his broad smile.

Chapter 36

Buzz

I couldn't handle all the work. I know Joe and Sandy were having to fend off all the religious nutters so I couldn't get them in to help and I'm not sure they would have known what to do. I had a couple of mates help with the app and paid them well but I was being swamped.

The idea I had for Joe was to extend the app so we had some choices available for different people and if I didn't do it first someone else would get in. The app wasn't that complicated. Some were asking if they could have letters that were not in favour of the EU thing that Joe and Sandy had in theirs but then the great idea came about when people were emailing and asking if they could block politicians and footballers and was there a way to turn the blocker off and on. One person had been watching The Godfather and every time there was a Priest, the film was blocked. It really pissed him off. I should have thought that one through at the beginning but we were so up about the whole idea that it didn't occur to any of us.

I sent out an update on the on/off thing so customers could have a choice and I started work with a couple of mates on a website. It didn't take long because we all know what we're doing. We got all the .com, .co.uk, .net and so on and set up a number of email addresses. We knew there would be plenty of shit flying around so we built in software tools that could read comments people were sending and trash the stuff we didn't want to read. The ordering process was simple. Customers could select from various groups who or what they wanted to block. We started off with the religious stuff Joe and Sandy wanted, then, and this is the killer I told Joe about, we had politicians, so we put images of senior British, European, Indian and American politicians and they all went on and eventually many, many more. The footballer stuff was difficult. We didn't want actual individual footballers so we went for team kits. England and English teams first, then Scotland then the European teams.

    We had a pretty good site going and when we uploaded it within minutes we had a deluge of orders, emails objecting to any or all of it and, you won't mind this I'm sure, money in the bank. We were a real part of the democratising of the internet. I was chuffed. We all know the internet and the web was all about personal expression and then the corporates took over, Amazon, Google and all those behemoths and now we were giving people a chance to choose what they were exposed to. I felt I understood what Joe and Sandy were up to and it was like, the people could be their own editors of what they saw on the telly or heard on the radio.

    We thought about developing the app for the internet but that was too big, too much and would have slowed everything down. I know more and more people are getting their news on their phones and laptops but I couldn't see how it would work. The fault in the system. What we did do was put it on a USB that people could put into their car stereos. We had a lot of people asking if we could get rid of Radio 4's *'Thought for the Day'*. We came up with a deal with one of the music download organisations and allowed our customers to download fifty tunes to a USB and have them shuffle when that bit of religious stuff came on. Money in the bank. Loving it.

Joe rang and said the money was fantastic, but he felt awkward that we had all made so much in so little time. I knew his politics was a bit left of centre, we'd had that chat in the pub garden and he was finding his new-found riches a problem. I suggested he shouldn't be hasty and that he should chat with Sandy about what they might want to do. It was bit of kind of role reversal, me advising someone the age my mum and dad are about what they should do.

I was stuck with something of a head fuck as well. I had never learned to drive so couldn't spend money on a car. I rented my flat but had never thought about where I would live if I ever had the money to buy a gaff. I didn't want to get furniture or a watch or anything flash but I did order the biggest, most powerful, most expensive Mac I could find. Fuck them all, spend it while you've got it. I booked driving lessons and ordered a provisional driving licence.

Chapter 37

The Prime Minister

With Mr and Mrs Quigley and the media unaware, I called a meeting of COBRA, the Government's security specialists and some senior Ministers. The Home Office has received a few hundred thousand letters from all over the country wanting to leave Great Britain.

"Look. What's happening here seems to have been started by those bloody Scots wanting self-government. We can't have three hundred thousand separate states in the UK, it's ridiculous. The map of the United Kingdom looks like it has measles with all those red dots. I need to know what's going on. Home Secretary, this is your field. What do you know?

"They're mostly split evenly across the country, there appears not to be a centre but quite a few in Welwyn Garden City itself." Her head bobbed up and with emphasis when she said Welwyn Garden City. As she bobbed her neck fat rose over the collar of her blouse and I thought she'd better go on a diet again. She was fed up looking like a nodding dog in the back of an old car.

"Wasn't that the place described by George Orwell as a magnet for 'every fruit-juice drinker, nudist, sandal-wearer, sex-maniac, Quaker, nature-cure quack, pacifist and feminist in England'?" asked one of the better-read ministers.

"No, that was Letchworth, but they're all the same," answered a much better-read Oxford educated Military man. "De Soissons, Bessemer, Howard, idealists the lot of them."

"Can we describe these people as nutters or something, living on the fringe of our British societal values, not really a part of the country we know and love? I'm sure we'll get the newspapers on our side. I'll speak to some of the proprietors and get them to put in a shift with their editors."

"Yesterday's headline about the 'most dangerous man in Britain' was a bit extreme, I thought," said another minister. "Perhaps we should tone it down a bit; not let them see that we are concerned about what we should regard as simple childishness."

"What about revenues Chancellor?" I asked.

"The letters they send in say they'll continue to pay tax and we can't afford to go after these small fry at the same time as not go for Google and Starbucks and the others. We don't have the resources."

"What about their passports, Home Secretary. Can we de-recognise them or something. Keep the buggers in their new 'lands'?" I gestured 'bunnies ears' with two fingers of each hand together raised above my shoulders.

"I feel we still have a strong position on the free movement of capital and labour within the EU, Prime Minister. If we take away their passports they can't travel which means they can't get to work which means, as I'm sure you are aware, reduced tax revenues".

"I want to go back to the idea that they are unpatriotic and somehow out to destroy a British way of life," I tried to impose my will. As Prime Minister, I had to lead. "We can't possibly have three hundred thousand individual states within the United Kingdom."

"I think they might contend two things there, Prime Minister. One. What is a British way of life and that they remain a part of the European Union?"

"Well we must press the media into defining a British way of life. Values such as hard work, loyalty, respect, after all they no longer recognise the Queen as Head of State or the established church. How unpatriotic is that? How about supporting the right football team; they won't have their own teams."

"I'm not sure that is a priority Prime Minister. People tend to be more loyal to their football team than to their family and certainly to any allegiance with any political party. There is no ground to win on that one."

"But what will the French President and the German Chancellor think when I go to the next summit as leader of a country that is falling apart from the inside?"

"I believe, Prime Minister", said the well-read military man, "There are two things. One. The Krauts and the Frogs have the same problem and two, you can point to a libertarian view of Britishness, allowing freedom of choice, freedom of speech and freedom of action. It is a testament to your understanding of these essential parts of British democracy that will see you though. Either that or we could round them all up, put them on the Isle of Man like we did with the krauts in World War two or maybe the Isle of Wight if they demand better weather."

"Please don't start on rounding people up again, General, it doesn't poll well. However, I like your idea about the British freedoms. However, again, we can't deal with three hundred thousand individuals. There must be a leader of some sort we can talk to.

Chapter 38

Joe

I took a call from Simon Cleve, you remember, the PR man, who said he had had a call from a producer at the BBC asking if we wanted to be on a discussion special with Julian about the way ahead. It seems Julian had been kicking up a storm with talk about organising and representation. This wasn't on my agenda and, I have often said, I didn't want to be part of a movement let alone be a leader. I probably made a mistake when I told Julian, that because he had the Tannoy, he could lead the people who were supporting me but I had just come back from a round of television studios to be confronted by baying demonstrators outside the house. I was a bit short tempered because we hadn't slept that well in the hotel in the Cotswolds and I didn't think it through. I didn't even know where this Julian lived.

The TV programme was going to be pre-recorded that evening, the idea being it would avoid people gathering outside the BBC to make their voices heard in either support or protest. I told Simon I would do it.

While the demonstrations outside the house had quietened down a little, I did notice that the age of the people had gone down and there were more young men. I didn't point this out to Sandy because I didn't want her to worry. There were more scuffles amongst the diehards out there who had pitched tents and made campfires on Welwyn Gardens' grass verges up and down Blossom Avenue and on the greensward across the road. I asked Simon if he knew anything about security and he said he would get back to me within the hour. We had a brief discussion about putting him on a retainer. He knew we were making a whole load of money and he wanted a share. I agreed to £1000 a day plus expenses for the next couple of weeks.

He duly called with a proposal. He thought we should have a uniformed guard by the gate and a couple of people in the crowd acting as eyes and ears. His view was that there didn't appear to be any fundamentalism but you couldn't be sure and better safe than sorry. Fifteen hundred pounds a day was, to my old self, a lot of money, but I was making it every five minutes with what Buzz was up to. And I thought, was I turning into a prick?

I said to Sandy I was going to have a kip and could she wake me around four. I went up to bed and slept the sleep of the peaceful contented. The worst was over, the crowds diminished, one last television thing to do and back to some kind of life.

I was due at the BBC at six o'clock for the recording and they sent a car at four-thirty. I had the same clobber on as I had that first time, had shaved and felt pretty good. I was becoming more confident about these telly things. The car was a Mercedes, it was incredible, an S Class apparently, according to the driver. I told him I would quite like one and he said I should use my imagination and not get a car that made me look like a chauffeur.

We arrived at the studio in good time and, as per usual, I was shown to the green room and there was Julian, with his

Tannoy. "Joe, man, you're here. Fantastic, man, great to see you again."

"What on earth have you been up to, Julian?" I asked.

"What do you mean?"

"Why are we here?"

"To spread the word. You don't have to say much, leave it up to me, I will do what needs to be done to get this country put right, get religion put in its place. I've launched a website, it's called www.doublej.org.uk. Double j, that's you and me. I've had hundreds of hits."

A young man, with another clipboard came and took us to the studio. We were seated with a man I recognised, but I couldn't tell you his name. He explained what was going to happen and we started.

The interviewer asked me, "do you have any regrets appointing Julian here as your representative?"

"He's not my representative. He's just someone who had a Tannoy, someone who could shift all the people away from my house and leave me and my family in peace."

"Man, you asked me to be a leader."

"I know, to lead people away from my house."

"Is it true, Julian, that you have organised a movement, the proJoes is it to politicise this movement?"

"Yeah, sure, it's sick, man, we're gonna have committees and chairs and everything."

"And what is your plan, Julian?"

"We want this government to let people have independence, to make their own lives free from religion. We need to teach people that there is no God, no old man with a white beard sitting in a cloud listening to and answering peoples' prayers and being in charge of everything and being some kind of control system so people behave as those elites want them to, being all goody two shoes and kowtowing to men who believe in imaginary friends and wear silly outfits and make women wear burkhas or feel dirty if they are menstruating."

"And this is all your doing Mr Quigley?" This presenter was enjoying himself wanting me as the target knowing that Julian was all the ammunition he needed.

"Not a bit of it. Julian here has assumed a role that I did not give him and he doesn't speak on my behalf. Tannoy or no Tannoy".

"Joe, man, you told me to lead the people, I felt like I was a kind of Moses figure doing your work for you, doing what you wanted. It was kind of unsaid but I thought you wanted religion to be exposed for the sham it is."

"Julian, I wanted you to take the demonstrators away from my house, away from my family, away from my neighbours, to give me some peace and quiet."

"Did you know, Mr Quigley that when you appointed Julian, and he only wants to be known by his first name, that he had convictions for affray, drug possession and had been under psychiatric care for many years when he was younger?"

I got in first, "you must know I don't care about the drugs bit and if he was mentally ill and was convicted of affray, then he should be getting help, not being exposed and being open to ridicule on your television programme."

"Joe, man, I can speak for myself. Yeah, I was bit fucked up when I was younger."

"Please be careful with your language."

"A bit fucked up but I had pressure, man, my dad left when I was twelve, my mum started on the sauce and I had no one. I started on glue, went on to skunk and it did my head in. I can't hold down a job, I do or did Big Issue and I try my best to get by. This is my big opportunity. This is what I can do to make a difference. My heads in the right place, I don't have voices any more, I take my pills."

"Julian," I tried to get him to stop before it got worse. "We'll have a chat after this and sort something out, but we need to do it away from this studio, away from prying eyes."

"You're right, man, we don't need this puppet here to take the piss anymore."

"Julian", I said, "take off your microphone, I'll see you in the green room in five minutes."

I turned to the interviewer. "You are a disgrace, you can show this whenever, it might make one of those clip shows you do when you laugh at people but you are a disgrace for taking advantage of this young man who obviously has issues. I'm going to apologise to him for having given him the wrong idea. I think you should apologise for setting him up like you have only to see him fall."

Chapter 39

Sandy

Joe got home from the television thing at about eight and went straight to the fridge and helped himself to a large glass of white. I asked if he had eaten. He hadn't and neither had I so I suggested we pop out for a curry. There are times when I can see Joe is stressed. There was the time at work when there was subsidence in the offices and another when the IT went down. He gets a bit of a tic and his left eyelid droops. It was funny when I first saw it donkey's years ago but now it is a warning sign.

I had watched him on the television and I thought he had been fantastic. All this stuff is way outside both his and my comfort zones, way, way outside but he has taken the brunt of the shit, forgive me, stress. I needed to think how I could help. Not telling him about his eyelid was one way, he would only have stressed more about it. We're both getting on and I firmly believe that a little bit of stress, usually at work, is a good thing. It helps you cope with spikes in stress levels. I didn't want him having a stroke or something. It wasn't the purpose of what we had dome. What we had intended was to have a little fun. Cock a snook at religion.

At the Indian, we ordered a bottle of wine and our food. When the poppadums came, I asked Joe "Do you regret what we've done. It's a lot of hassle for you especially." He spooned chutney on his poppadum and shook his head. I knew he was tired. "I'm more worried about you. I've agreed with Simon, you know the PR guy, that we are going to have a security guard at the front gate and we're going to have a couple of, I don't know, ringers, stooges, eyes and ears in the crowd. I'm worried something might kick off."

Then one of the other diners came over to our table. I feared the worst, a screaming match, accusing Joe and I of demeaning his God, his religion, his faith, his beliefs but it turned out the other way. He said, "you're Joe Quigley aren't you, I've seen you on the television. I've done what you've done, bought the app, wrote all the letters." He reached out his hand and Joe tentatively shook it. He was wary. "You must be Mrs Quigley. I love this whole idea. I've got Micky Thomas's goal for Arsenal against Liverpool in the 1989 football league decider when he scored in added time, it's so easy when you can put in a YouTube address. How did you do it?"

"Nothing to do with me. An IT geek called Buzz is the brains behind the tech. I'm just the person who started it all off, well, Sandy initially and me".

Joe's face visibly lightened and his eyelid stopped drooping. The man introduced himself as Peter Bartlett and said he lived just around the corner from us. "I'm here with my wife, Judy. Judy, come over here and meet Mr and Mrs Quigley." His wife, a pretty woman in her forties came over.

"You did the telly thing didn't you. Pete's got all this old football stuff he gets when the religious stuff happens. I've got Richard Gere in Pretty Woman. He makes me go weak at the knees. I've fancied him ever since American Gigolo. What a man he is."

"Yes dear, now come back and sit down, we mustn't disturb Mr and Mrs Quigley, although, can I buy you a drink, you know, to say thank you."

I said to him that we were okay and asked if he would mind if we got on with our meal. My Jalfrezi and Joe's Madras had both arrived and neither of us like eating too late. We get indigestion. I didn't want to be rude, you feel as though you are treading on tiptoes not knowing how anyone will react to what you say or do, whether they will take umbrage and call the newspapers or put something on Facebook. The man's wife took out her phone and took a photo of us saying she wanted to post it on her page. I didn't want to make a fuss and neither did Joe. We thanked them for their encouragement and ate.

We finished the meal and walked back home. Arm in arm. Joe was smiling broadly. Not because of the wine but he was chuffed to bits that he'd actually met someone who agreed with what we were doing, who didn't judge us, who didn't heckle.

"To answer your question from earlier, about is it worth it. I think it is. That one little thing. It's nearly as good as the money in the bank and it's nice to know that he's local. I'm going to search the paper's website for his announcement, get his address, send him a bottle."

"You can see if he's got anyone outside his house waving placards and chanting at him. We might get to the stage soon when there are more people with the app than protesters and they get thinned out across the country,"

"Wouldn't that be nice. Night cap?"

It's funny. We had both got so used to having people outside the house that we didn't notice them as we arrived home. They were just there. You must admit their staying power is very good. I looked through the curtains just to satisfy my curiosity. There were about twenty people there, sitting on chairs, wrapped up in blankets, chatting amiably, seemingly, with each other.

Chapter 40

Joe

I didn't sleep well that night. The curry sat heavy in my stomach. I think Sandy told you that we don't like to eat too late and we ate too late. I was so tired after the telly thing and travelling up to London and back that I conked out on the sofa.

There was another sackful of mail from the postman. I binned it. I checked my email and there were some from Buzz. We had sold nearly a million copies of the app and our bank balance was looking quite unlike it ever had before, by a distance. We'd never been broke, a little short sometimes, when the kids were young but this was unheard of. We would have to ask ourselves some big questions. Could we retire? Could we move? Could we do both? I didn't know what we'd do if we did retire. I just thought we'd see the grandkids, travel a bit, garden, see friends, pensioners' lunches, three courses for £9.95 at the village pub. But now we had more money that we ever imagined. A then a bolt out of the blue. A call.

"This is the Prime Minister's private secretary. The Prime Minister would like to meet you."

"What for? Eh? Who? Are you joking with me?"

"Mr Quigley. The Prime Minister would like to invite you to Downing Street for a meeting. We'll send a car for ten-thirty." And then the voice hung up.

"Sandy. I've just had a call from the bloody Prime Minister's private secretary asking if we want to go to Downing Street for a meeting. They're sending a car." The only word I caught in response was "shit".

I showered, shaved and pulled my least shabby suit out of the wardrobe. Sandy was in a bit of a panic, couldn't decide on clothes, shoes, earrings but we managed it and then, at bang on ten thirty a Jaguar XJ, the new fancy one, stopped outside and a driver came up the path to the door. The people outside stood up and started their placard waving, but the driver, a man in a dark suit, about our age, walked up and knocked on the door. "Good morning Mr and Mrs Quigley. I'm here to take you to Downing Street."

"I guessed. What's it all for?"

"I'm afraid I'm not privy to that sort of thing. I'm here to drive". We walked to the car, he opened the rear doors for Sandy and me, the smell was incredible, the leather so soft, he got in the driver's seat and the Jaguar purred its way to Downing Street. It was unreal. Fancy cars, liveried chauffeurs, invitations to see the Prime Minister. We drove past the gates at the entrance to Downing Street from Whitehall and pulled up outside number ten. It was, unsurprisingly, I guess, exactly like it looked on the television. I looked at Sandy, who smiled at me, touched my arm and got out of the opened door. That driver was good.

Photographers, perched on ladders, did their stuff. I don't know if they recognised us or whether they just took pictures of any and everybody that turned up. The Police Officer opened the black door of number ten and we were shown into a room with a couple of sofas, pictures on the walls, rugs, comfy chairs and those lamps you see on the television that people have on over their shoulders when they are being interviewed by Andrew Marr. A woman in her fifties breezed in and asked if we would like tea or coffee. She sounded brisk and efficient. We both asked for a coffee.

Then the Prime Minister came in. She walked over to us, with a big beaming smile and her hand held out. She looked tired, like this was a façade and a bit of a struggle for her. "Good morning Mr Quigley, Mrs Quigley, how the devil are you?" I let that one slide, perhaps she was just trying to be jolly.

"Very well thank you".

"Have you been offered tea and coffee?" She was making every effort to be friendly. "We'll just wait for my secretary to come in. You appreciate, we have to have notes made, records if you like, of the meetings we have." The brisk woman came back in carrying a tray of tea and coffee. I expected a maid or an intern but no, this powerful woman, working for the Prime Minister, was pouring our drinks. Tea and coffee sorted, the Prime Minister cut to the quick.

"Tell me, what inspired you to declare independence and to do this anti-religion thing?"

I explained why we had done what we had done. It doesn't bear repeating again, you'll get bored, but I did have to ask her why she thought I was anti-religion.

"You have this app thing, that block religious symbols and religious leaders from your television and you are marketing it across the world, for all I know, on the Internet".

I had recently read that her father was a clergyman in the Church of England and my natural proclivity was not to offend or personalise this. "I simply didn't want to have religion in my life, the same way other people choose to have it. It was a simple binary decision, if you like. Religion or no religion. The outcome was unexpected."

"We didn't expect to have hundreds of people outside our house, temporary toilet facilities, a hog roast and other food stalls," said Sandy. "We have had greater religious intrusion than if we had done nothing."

"But you have thousands, hundreds of thousands of people who have followed your lead. Local newspapers are crammed full of announcements that people are declaring their homes and gardens to be independent. It is very disturbing for the integrity of the country."

"I think the parallels are with all those people in that census who described their religion as Jedi. It's a game, a fun thing."

"It may be for you, Mr Quigley, but it is a very serious matter for us. There are issues of borders, constitutions, policing, tax revenues, healthcare."

"Did you read our letter?"

"What letter?"

"The letter we sent when we declared independence, the same letter that set the template for all the other letters you must have received. It said we would continue to pay our taxes and national insurance and in return expect free movement."

"But things have changed. Now we are leaving the EU, the freedom of movement question comes up. Why should we give it to you when we are negotiating to clamp down on it for other Europeans?"

"Because you don't want to isolate however many there are of us in our houses and gardens. The implications are far too wide ranging."

"But we may have to."

"I'm sorry", said Sandy, who was quicker on the uptake than me. "Are you threatening us with house arrest for our declaration of independence. Are you suggesting we are not allowed into the United Kingdom?"

"Well you really are rather disuniting it, aren't you? I think you should think through the implications of what you are doing and would strongly suggest you stop playing silly buggers, and go back to work." She sounded like that headmistress in St Trinian's.

Sandy was quicker than me again. "Prime Minister, we are of similar ages and similar backgrounds and education, albeit we are not Oxbridge, but we won't be treated like children or threatened. I have a terrible feeling that you want to clamp down on what we are doing and in doing so you are being very heavy handed".

"Because you have influence over all these people, they have followed your lead, and yes, we need to clamp down on this."

"We are not being followed." My turn. "We do not have followers. We were simply the first to do this and other people have chosen to do the same thing. We have simply enabled this and maybe allowed people to make the choices they couldn't make before."

"Exactly. And that gives you power and we cannot have you having this kind of power. It is undemocratic".

It had never occurred to me before that a body of people like those with the app could scare a Prime Minister to be this rash. I know we had the episode with Julian and his megaphone. This turn of events might merit some reflection in due course, but not now. "We have no intention of assuming any kind of power over anyone else. We are simply doing this for ourselves as are the others, I'm sure." This was a very interesting idea. I'd have to think more about it.

"Prime Minister, I think things have got a little heated. We'd be grateful if we could be taken home and if needs be, we can continue this discussion another time."

And we were back in the Jaguar on our way home. There were friendly handshakes in front of the cameras outside number ten and all was made to appear well. We didn't say much to each other on the way back for fear that the driver might be trying to overhear what we had to say and then report back.

Chapter 41

Julian

I quit the scene, man, it was too heavy now. I got back to the Big Issue, just to keep my head together. Bye. I might catch up with you later if I stay like, y'know, cool.

Chapter 42

Buzz

I have never worked so hard in my life, but this thing had taken off life crazy. I had half a dozen people working out of a rented office around the corner from my gaff. It was all a bit hush-hush as my Dad used to say because we didn't want to be bothered by the religious nuts that were standing outside Joe and Sandy's place. Luckily the phones were diverted to voicemail and all the emails were read by bots that looked out for keywords. Hate mail was binned, unread, nobody needs to read that shit. Orders were processed, money was taken and it was all done by the system but keeping up with the numbers was the biggest task. The website was taking thousands of hits a minute from all over the world. There were links to it from all the major media websites who were carrying the story, the telly, the papers, search engines were all driving traffic to us. We were all over Facebook and Twitter. Instagram had thousands of feeds of peoples' houses with signs showing their names. It was viral, proper viral.

There was an immense spike at lunchtime the day Joe and Sandy went to Downing Street. It was awesome. They were getting really famous, like celebrities, handshakes on the steps of number ten. You couldn't make it up. It was unreal seeing them there. I called early in the afternoon. "Hi Joe, man, you and Sandy looked great on the TV. What the fuck were you doing there?"

"They sent a car."

"I saw it. I saw the dude in the suit open the doors for you, the lot. But why were you there?"

Joe told me what the Prime Minister had made out, that we were an organised threat to the country. We weren't organised to do anything except sell the app but it did trigger a thought. "We have some great data." I told him. "We have email addresses, mobile numbers, post codes, data protection options. I can analyse what we've got and come back to you.

I called my mate, Fat Al, a marketing guy and asked him what we need to do. He told me to email him a sample of the data we had so he could get some analysis done. He also told me he had bought the app. A Chelsea fan he had Drogba's penalty against Bayern Munich and that Torres goal against Barcelona as his defaults and, he said, his mum and dad both had the app. He was well up for it.

A couple of hours later he came back to me with a report. It was quick because the person he'd contacted to do the actual work was a Sunderland fan with the app. He had told him that the only highlights he had were Bob Stokoe at Wembley in 1973 and Big Sam stopping them going down last season but he could watch them over and over and over. Any old hooey. What we had was gold. Pure gold. I'll give you some examples.

87% of the sample had degrees.

100% homeowners

65% aged 25-45

73% had children

93% car owners. 100% outside London.

77% took at least one foreign holiday a year.

They were comfortably off, professionals, largely white, although when we looked a little later we discovered the ethnic mix nearly matched the population of the country. This meant all religions were being impacted.

Top quality data by any standards. Powerful. I told Joe. He said he didn't want to use it. His worry was about this leading thing that had been suggested and he said he neither needed it or wanted it and didn't care for the idea that someone else might lead. "We might end up with another Julian. Let's just hold on to the idea that we have it."

I didn't object. I was happy doing what we were doing and making some serious dosh at the same time.

Every time Joe and Sandy were on the television, sales would spike. I don't know if 'they' were trying to persuade him to stop what he was doing but it didn't seem to work. Even my little knowledge about how things work could have predicted that. Put them on the television, increase their profile and more people will want a part of it. Simples.

Chapter 43

Sandy

A fortnight after the first visits by the religionists, as we had taken to calling them; there didn't seem to be a collective noun except believers but that infers non-believers in that there might be something to believe in. I'm wonking on again, aren't I? Any way we sat down with a nicer than usual bottle to see if we could make head or tale of what we might have to do, what we wanted to do and what might happen to us. Our preference was to have our own agenda knowing, or thinking through how it might impact on the children and grandchildren and, indeed, us.

We had started something of, what was that word, the one in the political comedy with the actor who became Dr. Who? That's it, a clusterfuck. Sorry about swearing again, I seem to have cut it out recently, but it is appropriate, if also inappropriate of you get my meaning. Sorry, at it again.

So, we had upset almost every religious group under the sun, we had apparently made the new Prime Minister feel threatened, the newspapers and the television people didn't know how to react but we had been on the TV and in the papers as had our history and backgrounds and we had made a lot of money in no time at all. Getting on for eight million pounds each for us and Buzz. He has worked hard and the website is going great guns.

We had paid for the house, paid for the cars and had a fairly healthy pension pot before this all started. Had we been complacent, I wonder. The girls were okay, reasonably secure, professionals with careers and successful husbands. They would be okay especially if the media would leave them alone.

Joe and I had each had all the time off work. Neither of us wanted what we had done to impact on our employers. That would be unfair. They had already had to fend off inquisitive reporters nosing into our jobs, how well we did them, had we been involved with co-workers, which co-workers we both might like to get involved with, had we turned up drugged or naked to work? Those tabloids have a lot to answer for. I never knew how low they could go. Apparently subterranean.

"If we retired, what would we do?" I asked Joe.

"Run the risk of drinking all day because we have too much time and money on our hands, like that couple in Spain who looked after that villa for us, do you remember?"

"Mmm. They sat in the sun all day, drinking from eleven in the morning till they collapsed. A waste of a life, if you ask me."

"And a waste of money. Could we be happy with our gardening and cooking? To my mind, it's not enough. The University of the Third Age holds no attraction either. I don't think I want to embark on a six-year open university degree course but we do need a focus."

"We haven't been to work these last two weeks and we've had plenty to do to deal with the nonsense that the people outside have created."

"It has to quieten down. The more people declare independence, the more they reject religion, the more targets for the religionists, the less attention we get. It makes sense."

"There's a part of me that worries after that load of supporters were here chanting LEADER at you that you might just be the person that attracts all the religious nutters."

"I've thought about that too. They might prove to be unshakeable."

"They're still there. I feel sorry for them."

"I feel some grudging respect. They've sat outside all this time because of their beliefs. Day and night, wind and rain, those camp chairs must be uncomfortable, teas and coffee from flasks is no way to live."

"But they do it."

"Gives me an idea. I'm going to call Buzz." Joe bounced out of his chair and I heard him on the phone. "Buzz can you email our database by postcode?" Seemingly the answer was yes. "Can you email them and ask them to join us outside St John's on Sunday morning, around 8.00." and then, "yes, a flash mob."

"What are you doing now, Joe?"

"Winding them up, give them a taste, what do you think?"

"I don't think you are going to do anything to improve the situation?"

"I don't think being non-reactive, passive, is the best way to deal with this. If we can get ten or a dozen people outside the church, with a few placards, peaceful, inoffensive, it might make that Vicar think twice about coming over here and cajoling his lot, who because of this cajoling gets more Catholics, Muslims and other ragbags outside the house singing songs and waving their placards. All they do is wind each other up and it continues to be a quest for whichever religion saves our damned souls. Pointless."

"It's all very childish."

Chapter 44

The Reverend Henry Tudor

Well, blow me down. I thought they were my lot at first waiting for the church to open for the early service on Sunday. But I didn't recognise any of them and then I read the placards. "*Have faith in yourselves*". "*Believe in yourselves*". "*you are not sheep, you are descended from apes*," That one from the writer, Huxley "*facts do not cease to exist because they are ignored.*" They all looked like slogans from a T-shirt shop and others. They had camp chairs like my lot and were drinking tea and coffee from flasks like my lot. I saw Mr and Mrs Quigley.

"I assume the mountain has come to Mohammed, Mr Quigley, Mrs Quigley".

"Hardly Mr Tudor, I think you are borrowing from the wrong lot there."

"Very funny Mr Quigley. And your placards, they are hilarious. Got them from a T-shirt, Mr Quigley?"

"Better than from a book of stories about an imaginary friend, Mr Tudor."

"I wish you well, but I think you are embarrassing yourselves here with these childish pranks."

"How come ours are childish but yours are not?"

"I have no wish to discuss this with you. Good morning Mr and Mrs Quigley, fellow atheists. Pray God saves your souls."

"Tricky, Mr Tudor, No prayer, no God, no souls. Have a good morning with your flock."

"I will Mrs Quigley, we will celebrate the Lord our God, give thanks to him and share in the body and blood of Christ." I knew I was on to a winner with that one. It is so joyful, so full of hope.

But blow me down again if they weren't there for the 9.30 service. I decided not to confront them again. It would do no good. We weren't going to change each other's' positions on this, but then I thought of all the evangelicals, those brave souls who go out on the street and praise the Lord our God to all and any who would listen. I walked up to the assembled group and asked "Would you like to join us, in the church for our next service. It is a full Eucharist, with some beautiful hymns and prayers and the church looks superb with the flowers from the ladies and God's glorious sun shining through the windows."

"God's sun, Mr Tudor?"

"Surely Mr Quigley, for he created the heavens and the earth."

"In six days. He must have been tired."

"And so he rested."

"I'll feed you the lines, Reverend, your timing is great."

Mr Quigley looked about at his flock. None of them were interested but a few were taking pictures of me remonstrating with them, pleading with them to save themselves, but nothing, not a jot. I was due to begin the service so I left them to their chairs and went inside. I was genuinely troubled for their souls and felt we should re-double our efforts.

After the service, I called the bishop and told him what had happened. He said we should re-double our efforts and I said I agreed with him and that I had thought of that already. He asked what the plan was and I thought I was rather quick with this. I said I would call Mr Corr, the priest and that Imam fellow at the Mosque, explain what had happened and ask them to make a joint effort on behalf of all our faiths to return the Quigleys and their hangers on to the way of our Lord, Jesus Christ or, for the Islamist, the ways of the Prophet. Strength in numbers. He agreed wholeheartedly and said I should visit him at Abbey Gate House. Could this be a promotion in the offing? I've done well here; attendance is down but not as much as the rest of the country and my reputation as someone who brings people together can only be getting better.

Chapter 45

Sandy

It was silly really. I felt a bit foolish sitting outside the church with Joe remonstrating with the Vicar. We didn't achieve anything the same as their lot weren't achieving anything. Stalemate. I said to Joe that we shouldn't do that sort of thing again. It only engages them.

He suggested lunch in the pub. I hadn't been out shopping for days and it was too late to get a delivery so I agreed. The Plume does a nice Sunday lunch and because the weather was fine we could sit outside and enjoy the view. Before all this brouhaha started we would walk to the pub and get a cab home, but this time we drove. I think Joe was thirsty after the morning's escapades.

We hadn't been there for a couple of weeks, not since that time with Buzz and we were both amazed to see a sign outside the pub saying "The Quigley tour starts here. Collect a leaflet. £15 per person including a pint of Aspall's". The bloody pub was trying to cash in on us. Normally it reads "three courses for £9.95 for the over sixties".

I confronted the barman, who, unfortunately for me and for their money-making scheme didn't recognise me as Mrs Quigley. So, we called the manager and I asked him to explain, to justify. This he did. Apparently, there have been scores of people visiting the pub wanting to sit in the seats where we had all had that first drink. I asked where the tour took people and it was the walk from the pub to our house, to the newspaper offices, finally the Campus and back to the pub, for more beer. It was clever, if a bit slight.

How could people be so shallow as to want to go on a Quigley tour? Do they not have lives and more interesting things to do? It seems that many of the tourists come from the pub's website having googled Quigley to get on the tour and these people were simply being led, like sheep, paying money for such little experience. Apparently sponsored by Aspall's.

We had a chat about whether we should go elsewhere but it seemed to us that it would only be another stop on the tour. We had one glass of wine each, to confound the Aspall's thing, ate roast beef and went home.

Chapter 46

Reverend Henry Tudor

I called Father Corr and the Imam and invited them round to the vicarage for tea. My wife, bless her, baked us a cake, a Victoria sponge with butter icing and strawberry jam. Delicious, one of her best. They arrived together, marching up the path in animated conversation. I invited them in, my wife made tea and cut slices of cake for all of us. Father Corr and Mr Butt complimented my wife on her baking skills which I thought was very gracious. She blushed a little and relaxed. She hadn't wanted them to come to the house; had felt it might be better if we met in a café but I told her the house was more welcoming and it represented the house of our Lord.

I told them what had happened that morning and they were aghast; it was totally out of the blue.

"How many were there, Mr Tudor?"

"A dozen or so."

"Is that all they can muster?" asked Father Corr.

"Perhaps, yes, although we don't know how they organised or where these people came from. I mean, they were taking photographs of me and the church. It was most perturbing.

"Cheeky eejits."

"But what are we to do?" Asked the little Imam.

"I spoke to my bishop after the eleven o'clock service and he said we should work harder to re-double our efforts. We should work as a team. His proposal, actually my proposal but one he believes is his, is that we all gather together as many of our people as can and pray and sing hymns to our Lord to convince them of the error of their ways and to try to get the Lord to speak to them, somehow, they should see the light, see the error of what they are doing. He also said he would be in touch with the Arch Bishop, in Canterbury, your Bishop of London and, I think he said, the Muslim Council of Britain.

"That is all very well for you Christians. Your prayers and hymns are all in English. My followers will want to pray five times a day, I will bring a muezzin, to call them to prayer but we will be praying in Arabic."

I had no problem with this. His efforts would be futile anyway. Were the Quigleys going to find God through Islam? I very much doubt it. "You should do all you can bring followers, bring those who will sing, those who will pray. We will make it a profoundly moving multi-faith moment for the Quigleys. They will want to thank us for it in due course.

Mr Corr too, was very gracious. "Mr Tudor, I take off my hat to you. It is a great idea, a great opportunity to show that God, whichever God, is greater than the sum of our constituent parts. I shall begin my prayers in earnest after mass this evening. Thank you for inviting us, and tell your lovely wife, the cake was a triumph."

Chapter 47

Joe

That Sunday outside the church was a bit of fun but it did show that we could, in effect, mobilise support. We didn't have many people there but it was at short notice and early on a Sunday when most people, unsurprisingly, like a lie-in.

We were amused that, on the following Monday there were more people than usual outside the house. They had fresh placards and were a bit more animated than they had been the last week or so. Mainly Christians and Muslims, the Sikhs had gone home some time ago, the Hare Krishna devotees had long since packed up and the Rabbi was nowhere to be seen.

The Imam had his phone held high and was obviously videoing the crowd and was soon followed by the Reverend Tudor who didn't want to be outdone, Father Corr, who struck me as being a bit less tech aware looked miserable and scowled each time he was filmed. I presume they were uploading their films to some Facebook, twitter or Instagram site to rouse support for their faith or to demonstrate that they were here, trying to save our souls from whatever damnation lay ahead. My word, can't they just bugger off and leave us alone.

We had long given up making them tea and Sandy no longer bought extra biscuits or cake. It only seemed to encourage them and we agreed it sent out a message that they felt they were welcome when all we wanted to do was get on with any kind of day to day existence.

I did notice that there again appeared to be a growing number of younger, male Muslims with long beards and the reports back from our insiders said they were getting a little more verbose, shouty, if you like. We still had the uniformed security guard on the gate and he was untroubled. He was barracked by the crowd and we heard him called the "Devil's stooge" which was a bit strong, but he said it didn't bother him. He'd been in Afghanistan with the army and had put up with much worse. He had plenty of tea and biscuits.

We did rather feel like prisoners in our own home but equally felt that if we went outside and asked them all to bugger off they would be inspired to send more people in in a war of faith based attrition. Neither Sandy nor I could be bothered. The press had lost interest which was good and the TV satellite vans had all gone. We were no longer news

Sales of the app were still going strong. Over two million. We were in the money, real money for the first time in our lives but we felt we couldn't spend any of it because it would upset the religionists if we flaunted new cars for example. I called Buzz to see how he was getting on.

"Joe, my man, how are you and Sandy?"

"A bit bored. We're not working and we feel trapped in the house."

"You can get your arses in gear and come and help here. We've started a market in re-feeding YouTube videos and we're making extra cash. That needs a bit of admin you can do."

"We would both really like to help but I worry that we would be followed and your place would be found out. We can't even go shopping without being heckled."

"Can't the police do anything?"

"We had that Constable Cross but he's gone. They say there are no crimes being committed. I just think they can't be bothered and have no interest in us. I don't blame them."

And then Buzz said something that worried me. "Joe, you know we filter the nutters' emails. We've added another filter to watch out for the key words including any work with 'fuck' in it and 'death'. There have been more than usual and they are increasing".

"I didn't know you did that."

"Your PR guy, that Simon dude, he called and suggested it. He said you were getting some security people in and he wanted me to watch your backs from this end."

"Thanks, Buzz. I need to make some calls. I'll call you later."

That worried me. Not so much the nutters, as Buzz called them, but the increase in the threats. I told Sandy, perhaps I shouldn't have done but she needed to know. She was angry and went out and had a good go at the crowd. I can't repeat what she said here but it was very profane and loud.

Almost immediately I had another call from Buzz. "Mate, you know we monitor Facebook and twitter, I've just seen and heard your Sandy outside your house kicking off and this is being re-tweeted all over the place. The number of dodgy emails we're getting is going up as I speak, get her back in, we need to make plan."

"I need to call the police."

They were worse than useless to start off with. The man I spoke to said he could do nothing for any of us who had declared independence. They didn't have the manpower to protect us all. He didn't realise that it was only me and Sandy that were getting these death threats. He told me he had seen the video of Sandy outside the house shouting and ranting and we only had ourselves to blame. Cheeky git wouldn't get me someone senior and said it was up to us to protect our own country if that was how we wanted to live. The idiot didn't realise that if something kicked off it would have kicked off from England and that the perpetrator would have been in England. Arse.

Chapter 48

Nick, the security guard

Morning. I'm Nick, the security guard. I get paid to stand here and look out for Mr and Mrs Quigley. It's a strange kind of job. Not one I have ever had to do before. I've done a bit of close protection, airport stuff; it's hard to find a proper job when you quit the army, nothing works the same way. Loads of temporary stuff, like this gig and until today it was simple. I stand by the gate, in my dark trousers, dark pullover, white shirt and wet weather jacket when it rains, do nothing and say nothing except when Mrs Quigley, it's always Mrs Quigley, brings me out a cup of tea and some biscuits or a slice of cake. She does look after me. She asks me if I'm alright, asks about the family; she's a real hun.

It kicked off a bit today. Mrs Quigley came storming out of the house and had a right go at all these people. She was effing and blinding like she was a squaddie and all these religious people were looking at her, mouths open, not having a clue what she was on about. Something about death threats. I pricked up my ears because that's part of my lookout.

I touched her on the shoulder and said "Mrs Quigley…"

She turned and looked at me and said "What! What do you want?"

I told her that I didn't think she was doing herself any favours by having a rant at these people. She calmed down a bit and said to me, "do you know we're getting death threats on the internet? These crazy, peace loving god-botherers are threatening me, my family and Joe. It doesn't make sense."

Thinking I should try and keep the peace, I said, "but it isn't these kind people who are threatening you." I'm quite internet savvy and I told her that all kinds of people get death threats from all kinds of nutters. MP's get death threats, celebrities, businessmen, footballers, anyone with any kind of fame gets it and there's nothing you can do to stop it. It just happens that people can say whatever shit they like without fear of any response. They do it on twitter using fake names. I told her they were all scumbags who should get a life, get a job, find something proper to do.

Mr Quigley came out and said Mrs Quigley should go back inside. He'd had a call from his tech mate saying Mrs Quigley was on the internet already. I couldn't believe how fast this was happening. Mr Quigley invited me into his house and sat me down in his living room. He said he wanted to get more security. He was worried. Did I have any friends or colleagues so we could have two people twenty-four seven. I was on a monkey a day and I did have a couple of mates who might like the same gig so I said "yeah, I can get you sorted." It would be a bit like we was an army for Mr and Mrs Quigley, in their new country. I asked Mr and Mrs Quigley if we should have some sort of uniform, fatigues or something and he thought that was a good idea. You can get this stuff on Amazon these days so me and Mr Quigley got on his laptop and ordered some gear. We got in some sturdy steel toe-capped boots, camouflage fatigues, gilets for when it was colder at night and some berets.

This was more exciting. I had been outside their house for a week, done nothing and now this was happening. I was a corporal when I was in the army and I asked Mr Quigley, "Sir…?"

"Joe."

"Sir"

"Joe, please."

I had to insist. "Sir. Would you like me to be in charge and do the rotas, make sure we have people in place twenty-four seven, brief them and so on?"

"Yes please." He said. I was made up. Back in the game alright.

"Do we need weapons, Sir".

"No. No. Nothing like that."

"Whatever you say, Sir." I thought he was wrong on that count but he was like my commanding officer. He was paying the piper so to speak. I called a couple of buddies who I knew were looking for work and asked them to come to my house. I went home later that evening and my wife told me she had seen me on the telly when they showed that video of Mrs Quigley. She said she thought I was dead handsome and what a good job I had done calming Mrs

Quigley down before she made a real mug out of herself. What a good day.

Chapter 49

Simon Cleve

Joe and Sandy had put me on a retainer to handle media relations. I had had a few celebrity clients recently so I was used to all this social media activity, the Twittersphere and so on. He was paying me a K a day and I was having to work for it. Buzz and I were doing the job of filtering the social media and emails to keep a handle on the negatives. We had added a media contact button to the website to stop the journalists getting onto Joe. We changed his phone number and put a voicemail on his old one asking people just to leave their names and a message and we would get back to them. We didn't ever get back, only spoke to those I knew would be positive about the turn of events but, like I said, we needed to keep a handle on everything. The poor people didn't know what had hit them. First the papers, then the TV, then social media, then all this negative crap from the religionists. A fair bit of it was a first for me too, but I wasn't going to let on. It's all a learning experience.

Part of the learning experience was all about keeping your head under pressure. I thought Joe would be the one to crack but it was Sandy. Someone outside the house had shot a video of her diatribe and posted it on YouTube. It didn't look too clever there and it looked worse when it was shown on the regional news and, again, with a piece on the television there was a spike in sales.

What was interesting was that there was a spike from overseas as well. The French, Spanish and German media were picking up the story as well as the people buying the app. We had got translators in to make the website multilingual and lawyers from around Europe to see whether declarations of independence were viable or not. It didn't matter whether they did the independence thing or not as long as they stumped up for the app and they were doing this by the thousand all across Europe and into the United States.

They were making a lot of money with the app and more with the tie-up with YouTube. It's ironic to contrast the Quigleys' lack of tech savvy with the amount of money they were making from it. I wish I'd had the idea but then I was equally grateful that I didn't have protestors outside my front garden.

It was a French TV news channel that made contact first and asked if they could have Joe and Sandy. They said they would pay all the expenses. The dichotomy for them was they would make money from the exposure but would get the attention from the church lobby. I called Joe and Sandy and asked how they felt.

"We didn't do this for the money", said Sandy

"We didn't expect this response, everyone said nobody would notice or really give a damn. But they do" said Joe.

"We didn't intend to antagonise but it looks like everything we do just winds them up".

I suggested they think about it and let me know. They wouldn't have to go to Paris for the interview. It could all happen over Skype or they could send a crew. On the other hand, a jaunt to Paris could be quite nice.

After a solid, hard working day with Buzz, keeping a handle on Joe and Sandy's situation I went home put my feet up and had a large glass of wine. The French news channel called to say they would pay a fee for their participation; five thousand euros. It wasn't much in the grand scheme of things but it was a gesture. I called Joe and Sandy who said they would do it but declined the fee. If word got out that they were being paid, things might not go so well.

I checked the filters on a laptop Buzz had given me. He had produced an algorithm that calculated a threat level. It was beginning to get worse not better.

Chapter 50

Sandy

I'm not usually impressed by what other people get up to or have. But this was a revelation. We were picked up in a car, nothing newly fancy there, and taken down the M3 to Farnborough. We had to produce our passports but it was into a lounge the luxury of which I had never encountered. The furnishings, the wallcoverings, the canapés the Veuve Cliquot all laid on, all for free. We hadn't had that with the British media and, unsurprisingly, it was more extravagant than number ten Downing Street. It was very modern, very tasteful; the leather chairs were made from the softest leather you can image, like rabbit or cat or something just very soft. The crystal glasses clinked as Joe and I toasted each other with the champagne. Simon seemed to take it all in his stride

A very, very beautiful woman came through a door that hushed open and invited us to the aeroplane. Joe, who was doing his best to avoid gawping at the steward informed me it was a Lear Jet, and boy, this was very smart too. We took off, over Hampshire, Surrey and Kent, over the channel and into France. I said to Joe, "England can look fantastic, can't it. Rolling hills, the greens, yellow, the villages", I came over all romantic. He looked out of the window, pleased to avoid staring at the steward and agreed.

"I know I wouldn't like to live anywhere else, except Hendrix, but you know what I mean, it's a beautiful country. Shame about some of the people, though."

Simon said, "when we get there, we need not antagonise the French. It is a Catholic country".

"But it does separate the state from the church doesn't it. Like, they don't allow religious symbols and they are doing their best to ban the hijab."

"But Joe, they aren't really enforcing it".

"I think I have an issue with the hijab and generally covering hair. Is it because they think we will be attracted to their wives? If I'm happily married, and I am happily married, do they think my values are not as deep as theirs about morality and attraction."

"Tell me Joe. Do you remember not so long ago you were dreaming of being on a nudist beach with Cameron Diaz?"

"Two points, my darling, firstly it was a dream and I have little or control over the content and secondly, we were discussing air cleanliness in the workplace, if I recall. Guaranteed not to excite."

"I believe you, just."

More champagne and these amazingly delicate canapés of crab, foie gras, various cheeses; it was a shame it was over in an hour or so. We landed at Charles de Gaulle but instead of going through arrivals and baggage with the hoi polloi, sorry forgive me, a bit tipsy, the scheduled arrivals, we were taken to one side, put in another fancy car and taken to a hotel in Paris.

It was odd having Simon along. I quite like him. I've got used to him, but Paris is supposed to be romantic and I didn't know how to ask him to dine alone that evening. Obviously neither Joe nor I are in the first flush of youth but it isn't every day you get this kind of treat, all paid for, no expense spared.

Later I discovered that Joe had had a word with him and Simon was relieved. He didn't want to be a gooseberry, as I'm not sure they say these days, and was unsure how to extricate himself from us. It appeared he knew some people in Paris and when we met him for breakfast the next morning, he looked as if he hadn't had much sleep. And, entre nous, as they say over here, Joe and I enjoyed the romance of the city, if you get my meaning. It was good to be away.

Another car, yes, another car, (am I getting a bit blasé about this?) came to take us to the studio. Simon explained there would be a translator. I volunteered my school girl French, Simon said not to try too hard for fear of being misunderstood.

Unfortunately, it was a similar line of questioning that we had had in England. Why were we anti-religion, we weren't. Why did we want independence, because, why were we upsetting the church goers and the Muslims, we didn't set out to, we can all just mind our own business can't we, it's our decision to be atheist, it is their decision to be Catholic or protestant or whatever. But they are born into a faith. No. they're not, their parents proscribe the faith group they will belong to and so on and on. We were well rehearsed; Simon had seen to that over the last few weeks and it was Simon who was switched on enough to contact Buzz to see what the appearance had done to sales of the app in France. A huge spike apparently and smugness is hard to conceal sometimes.

I called both Bec and Daisy who went to the French channel's website and watched the interview. They both called back very excited. Daisy using her best French to say, "Je suis trés heureux. C'était merveilleux."

"Clever girl."

The presenters had arranged to meet us for lunch. We drove there in another swish car to be met by the garcon, who, I felt, sneered at us. Was this just being a Parisian or were we being judged? This was modern chic and the menu looked awesome. I was salivating like, I don't know what, a drooling fool, and couldn't wait.

Chapter 51

Joe

And then a flash, blinding, a blam, a crash, the sound of smashed windows, creaking, groaning, screaming, alarms going off all around us. I looked at Sandy, she was on the floor. I fell towards her to cover her to protect her from whatever might happen next. I asked, "are you hurt?" She couldn't hear me. The blast had deafened us both.

"I don't think so, you?" I had to lip read

I noticed blood on my shirt and more blood dripping on to the floor from, I guessed my face. I picked up a serviette and Sandy grabbed it and shook it to get any glass out. I wiped my face, Sandy looked at me. The look of love was incredible. Then I saw the gash in her stomach, she was bleeding, the crimson was staining her dress, I grabbed and shook out another serviette and pressed it close to her. I called 911 thinking I was the only person in a position to do so but the sirens came, ululating until there was a cacophony of sirens with the alarms with the screams with the groans.

Sandy screamed and moved the serviette from the gash. The glass was still in place and I had made it worse. Fool, fool, fool. I shouted, help, help, louder, louder, aidez, aidez. I didn't know if I could be heard, I was still deafened. I stood, I waved my arms like a drowning idiot. A paramedic came over, I thought, to see us. He checked Sandy's stomach and my face, but bent over Simon. Fuck, I hadn't noticed, fuck, fuck, he was lying on the floor with the back of his head missing. I did all I could not to vomit. Grey matter spilled from his head and his face was in a rictus smile, left over from the story he was telling about a minor celebrity. I shielded Sandy from the sight, she pulled my arms away and saw him there, dead, lifeless, no patter, no smoothness, no advice on how to dress. Fuck, in an instant I missed him. I grabbed his arm and shook it. The paramedic gently removed my hand and covered Simon's face with a table cloth.

My head was spinning, the buzzing in my ears slowly quietened, my thoughts turned to Sandy. Survival instinct, I guess. "S'il est mort, attendez ma femme, s'il vous plait". I don't know if it was the right way to get him to see Sandy, but it worked. I didn't know if there were other casualties more hurt but I didn't care. I just got selfish for my interests, Sandys' interest, fuck the rest of them. Anyone would, wouldn't they? He pulled out a bandage and cut a slit in it to place it around the embedded glass and spoke into his comms. Another paramedic came over with a stretcher and they lifted Sandy onto it. She was taken to a waiting ambulance, I followed and climbed in after her. I looked around at the carnage, Bodies on the pavement, bodies in the restaurant, the car we had come in was blown apart. A burnt-out shell, smoke drifting from the seats.

We sped to the hospital. I didn't know which hospital or where we were going but wherever it was we were going there at a rate of knots. Sandy lay quietly. I was all over her. "How are you feeling? Does it hurt? Can I get you anything?" Blurting out any kind of stuff that I thought might be supportive. The paramedic was checking her blood pressure, and, I think, injecting pain killers, paying close attention to her wound, the bleeding and the bandages. It seemed like an eternity, but we arrived at the hospital, I jumped out, Sandy was offloaded onto a gurney and we were taken into the French for Casualty.

We were separated and I struggled to make out what the nurses and people seeing us in were asking. A lot of it was guesswork on my part. I have a little French, but the scene was controlled panic with a semblance of order. People were coming in ambulance after ambulance, some silent, some obviously in pain, struggling against their wounds, some came in, heads covered, obviously didn't make it. I thought of Simon for a moment. Our relationship had been short but quite profound. The thought that we were the targets began to nag at me. Our car had been destroyed. Who had known where we were going? Were we the intended target? I had no idea who we should ask, what we should do, what I should do, who I should ask. Sandy was in no fit state. I had to take responsibility.

A nurse approached me and in very broken English told me I should go into one of the cubicles to have the broken glass removed from my face. I had forgotten all about it, felt no pain, tried to brush her off, but she insisted. It took twenty minutes with a pair of tweezers and some stitching to my face before I could get out. Where to go? Who to turn to? Who to call? I had no fucking idea.

Somehow, I had to take responsibility, not doing what I was doing, which was close to panic.

I checked my phone. I had signal. I called Bec not knowing what I was going to say or what she would do. I told her about the explosion and I told her I thought her mum was going to be okay, she had been conscious, in pain but awake, Bec said she would call Daisy, organise their husbands and get to Paris. She asked me where we were. I had no idea. Like her mum she sounded like she could take control. I always fought the idea of giving control or decision making to the girls or their husbands; I could make decisions, but now my head was all over the place. I needed help. It was going to be a role reversal. I asked a nurse. "Ou sommes nous? A quelle hopital?" She answered in French too quickly for me to understand. I said I would call Bec back and she said she and Daisy would be on the next Eurostar. "Have you got enough money?"

"Yes, Dad. We'll be there soon. I'll call."

I asked at what appeared to be a reception for details of where Sandy was or how she was. They said she was in surgery and didn't have any more information. The not knowing was killing me. My face was covered in Band-Aids, my suit and shirt were torn and covered in blood. I looked a mess, I felt a mess. The nag in my head that we were the targets, that we were somehow responsible became a deafening roar of guilt. Everybody was busy, tending patients, tending those tending. I didn't know who to ask for information. I didn't know how to ask for information. I felt moronic, standing about helpless, vacant, vulnerable. To be crude about it, fucked, well and truly fucked.

Chapter 52

Giles Henshawe. British Embassy Paris

We were aware that Mr and Mrs Quigley were coming to Paris for the television interview. We were also aware of how they were coming in, where they were staying and their schedule. We check the manifests of flights in and out of all UK airports and Farnborough is no different. I watched the interview on television and, because I am paid to be a cynic, I could only see a downside. It doesn't gratify me for one moment when my expectations, perhaps that's a bit strong, were realised and the bomb went off outside the restaurant where they were going to have lunch.

A couple of calls and we knew which hospital they were being taken to and I made my way there. I had a photo of Mr and Mrs Quigley on my phone and recognised him the moment I stepped into the casualty area, the Service des Urgences. My French is pretty fluent. I have been on the embassy staff in Paris for four years. I know the people here and I know how they work. I have a fondness for them which is a little unprofessional but there you go.

I walked over to Mr Quigley, introduced myself and told him I was there for him and his wife. "Nasty business", I said.

"Worse than nasty," he replied, "it's monstrous, my wife is somewhere in here, in surgery, having a large shard of glass removed from her stomach and I haven't a clue how she is doing."

"It's being removed from her liver and she will be fine. It will repair itself but leave her with a scar that will fade in time. She should be out of surgery within the next thirty minutes."

"How do you know this? I can't find out a thing. And where are we? I need to call my daughter."

"We are at the Saint Antoine. One of the better hospitals and one used to dealing with this kind of situation."

"Tell me. What is this kind of situation? No, don't tell me yet. I need to call my daughter." He made the call and half way through, started sobbing. He could hardly talk, hardly breathe and collapsed onto a chair. He told his daughter the information I had given him, told her he loved her very much and would see her when she got here. He also warned her that he and her mum weren't pretty sights.

He looked a mess. I looked him up and down and called the office to get them to go out a buy the man some clothes. Marks and Spencer. I sat down next to him. "You are in shock, Mr Quigley. I am here to help you. I represent the British Embassy. We recognise that you have chosen to secede from the United Kingdom and have encouraged others to do so, but we see that as no more than childish petulance. Can I get you a cup of tea? Have you eaten?" He shook his bandaged head at me." Tea?"

"Yes please".

"A sandwich?"

"Yes please".

"Anything you don't eat? Are you veggie?"

"No and no".

It did seem a lot of effort to get an answer from him. But then he is sixty plus and now looked much older, pale, grey and shattered. I went to the cafeteria and bought him something to eat and went back to where he was seated. I gave him the tea and sandwich, he managed to get it down, eventually. Shock does parch the mouth. "Let's go and see if your wife, Mrs Quigley, is out yet, shall we?" He nodded at me. I put out an arm to help him up but he didn't take it. Perhaps he was more robust than I thought.

We went up a couple of floors to intensive care. At the nurse's station, I asked for an update on Mrs Quigley and translated for Mr Quigley who was looking increasingly desperate. "Your wife is out of surgery. She had a general anaesthetic and is sleeping it off. The doctors will bring her round in a couple of hours and assess the damage done and make a plan. In my view, we need to get an air ambulance to get you back to the UK as soon as possible, back home and in a hospital closer to home. Yes?"

"I guess so. I don't really know what the choices are."

"We should start by getting you back to your hotel and getting some sleep so you are fit to travel, fit to help later on. Let me make a call." I called the office to chase up the clothes, no one had been out yet so I told them to forget it, but I did ask for a couple of security guys to come to the hospital to accompany Mr Quigley and stand outside his room as well as two more to stay with Mrs Quigley.

"Was this our fault, Mr Henshawe? Were we the targets?"

"We believe you were. I'm sorry." He collapsed to the floor and beat his bloodied head with his hands.

"What on earth have we done? How many casualties are there Mr Henshawe?"

"We believe there are six dead and thirteen wounded enough to be in hospital. Those seated towards the front of the restaurant were worse affected and I'm afraid your Mr Cleve was one of them. Do you know if he had family?"

Mr Quigley shook his head. "I never asked. He did all he could for us and I didn't have the manners ever to ask him about himself. What an arse I am."

"You are not responsible for this, Mr Quigley. The perpetrators are. The scum that did this are."

"And do you know who did this?"

"No group has taken responsibility but we are sure there will be one soon. It will be seen as a victory by those twisted individuals. There is CCTV outside the restaurant, the police will soon know what's what and who is who."

He sat in stunned silence, processing the information I had given him. The security guys arrived and accompanied him back to his hotel.

Chapter 53

Joe

Here are some of the questions I was trying to resolve.

How responsible was I?

What could have been done to prevent the bombing?

What were the threats to us now?

What were the threats to the girls and their families?

Will we have to live in a permanent state of threat?

What was going on back home?

How were the media reacting?

Where was blame being apportioned?

Who was outside our house?

Was the house itself threatened?

Was Nick, the security guard, and his friends come to think of it, okay?

Would they stay on duty?

Would I have to get more security for the girls?

I don't know if this happens to you, but the thinking had me asleep. I had lain down on the bed, too tired to shower and change and gone to sleep. How could I when my wife was in hospital having been blown up. I had got away lightly. The cuts on my face were an irritation and would soon be gone. The injuries to Sandy would take much longer and would be an ever present for the rest of our lives.

I showered and dressed having thrown my old clothes on the floor for some poor chamber maid to dispose of tomorrow. I am not normally this unthinking, but this wasn't normal times. We had been in a restaurant when it had been blown up. Fuck, it doesn't bear thinking about. The embassy representative, Giles I think his name was, can't remember his surname. Did I have his card? He had given me his phone number so I called him to see what was what. He told me that Sandy was going to be brought round in about half an hour and the girls had arrived at the Gare du Nord. He had arranged a driver to collect them. He was efficient. Cold, but efficient.

I arrived at the hospital at the same time as the girls. We wept together and hugged, happy to see each other. Sandy was on the ICT ward and we went up. She looked peaceful, coming round, but there was no evidence of her wound under the blankets. It looked out of kilter. Why was she lying in a hospital bed when she looked as though nothing was wrong?

The girls embraced her and when they finally let her go, I went to her, asked her how she felt and hugged her. She asked me what had happened. What did I know. I said, "not much. We are waiting for the police to identify the bombers from CCTV". I told her what the embassy man had said, that they thought we were the intended target. Her face crumpled.

"I thought we might have been. Lying there on the floor of the restaurant it occurred to me that there were people who would like to see us ruined, or dead, or see us getting a comeuppance for our lack of faith."

I said we should think about that later. More important was how she was feeling. "Sore", she said. I told her the embassy chap was going to organise an air ambulance the next morning to get us home after the police had interviewed us. She smiled, and we sat in quiet contemplation for half an hour or so. All of us had questions flying around in our heads but none of us could provide any answers. The questions went unasked.

Sandy dropped off around sevenish. The embassy chap, Giles, I'll call him Giles, called to say he had confirmed bookings for the three of us at the same hotel. There would be security for each of us and we should go and eat. With my face covered in stitches and plasters, I felt conspicuous. We went back in the car to the hotel and ordered room service. I turned on the television and there was a shot of Sandy and I, a still taken from the programme that morning. I hadn't seen it yet but the girls said we had done well.

Buzz texted. I called him. He wanted to know the answers to the questions we were asking ourselves and didn't have the answers for. He did tell us that sales of the app in France had rocketed. It was little consolation in the grand scheme of things. He wished us well.

The girls phoned their husbands to reassure them that all was okay, relatively okay and to let them know we'd all be home the next day.

The change in security was profound. The room service we had ordered arrived and the guys on the door checked it out, checked the ID of the room service waiter, sniffed at the meals and let him in. He was duly humble and apologised on behalf of Paris for what had happened in very broken English.

Daisy checked her phone for the internet and the BBC. We were on the news channel, presumably having been on the main news. We were all over their website, the ITN website, Sky news, everywhere. Facebook and twitter were fizzing with input and contributions, messages of support and ominous messages saying we had got what we deserved. "Heartless fuckers", I said out loud and the girls stared.

"Dad, you don't swear. Mum does but we don't hear it from you".

"If you'd heard me earlier or my thoughts had been out loud you would have had no doubt about my depth of feeling towards the people that did this".

The media was full of speculation, predominantly that it was a Muslim faction of one sort or another that had done it. Witnesses said they had heard someone cry Allahu Akbar but that might just have been an easy answer, the expected answer, the predictable answer. We tried the French news channels and blow me down if there wasn't a vigil going on with people bearing placards and wearing T shirts that read "Je suis Joe", "Je suis Sandy" and, sweetly, others with "nous sommes Joe et Sandy".

I thought again of Simon. Our advisor and guide through the shit storm of the media. We'd paid him well but that wasn't the point. He was on our side, had died for what we believed in and didn't deserve it. Didn't deserve it. Poor sod.

The girls wanted to go and be part of the vigil, to see what was happening, to share what was happening but the security guards advised against it. We were told it was unlikely that anyone would have a second go quite so soon but the threat couldn't be ignored and we were safer in the hotel; in one of the rooms that didn't face the street.

The girls went back to their room. I brushed my teeth, put on my jim-jams and missed Sandy terribly. I have no qualms about letting you know I sobbed myself to sleep. Great retching, heaving sobs. I missed her so much. I felt I had let her down. I was her husband, I was the man. It was pre-historic. I should have been able to prevent it. I should have been able to protect her. And I failed. Miserably.

Chapter 54

Sandy

I could guess how Joe was feeling. His masculinity had been impugned. I like the fact that while he is a bit "new man-ish" he does lapse into the old ideas of protecting his woman. He did it once before. We had been out in London, in the eighties, when Thatcher was in power and crime was on the up. We had been stopped by a youth wielding a knife, demanding Joe's wallet and my handbag. He prodded the air in front of us with his knife and said, with no attempt at originality, "Give me your wallet and your purse. Now."

Joe simply stood up straight and said, "Fuck off, mate, fuck off back under the stone you crawled out of." And we walked away. He did, indeed, fuck off.

"Where did you get that from?"

"I've no idea. But I thought that if I out-harded the hard case, he would back off. And he did".

Joe had a smile on his face for days after. I think he ignored the fact that we might have been stabbed, how close we had become to being a crime statistic. I knew he would feel guilty this time because of what he did then and couldn't do about the explosion. The mugging attempt was thirty years ago, he was thirty years younger, we didn't have the girls, he was out to impress. He couldn't fight and wouldn't fight. Didn't have a clue. Hadn't had a brawl since he was thirteen at school and then he lost.

As I said, this time was different. There was nothing he could do. I knew it, he knew it, but the guilt might well last for years. Perhaps the onus is on me to get better soon. During the night, I had been woken by a doctor who spoke English. He explained that we would be flying back to England the next day. I had a tear, quite a deep tear in my liver and had had my gall bladder removed. He said there would be some post-operative care in the UK but that there would be no long-term complications especially if I ate properly, "no fats", he said. I missed the idea of cheese, with the wine in the evening, but now, perhaps there were bigger fish to fry.

I went back to sleep and woke in the morning to see the enormous faces of Joe, Bec and Daisy huddled around me. Blurry eyed, we greeted each other and kissed and hugged and then a man in a white coat came in carrying a breakfast tray. Croissants and Orange Juice. "No chance of a coffee?".

"Pas du tout, Madame, je regret".

"They took out my gall bladder, apparently. It seems we don't really need it." I said. Joe slumped in the chair. Another slap in the face for his ability to keep me safe.

"Did you hear about the vigil last night?" Daisy asked. "There were hundreds of people showing their support for you like the Charlie Hebdo lot. Je suis Joe and Je Suis Sandy and Nous sommes Joe and Sandy. It was so touching".

"Have you had breakfast?" I asked.

"Yes mum, all kinds of croissants, pains au chocolat and pains au raisins. We need to be able to do that in England."

"You'll put on the pounds."

Another man, in another white coat came in, presumably having had his credentials checked by the guards outside and in very good English, "We must start with some physiotherapy before you leave. It is important to start exercise as soon as you can." He helped me from the bed, I groaned in pain, the anaesthetics having worn off, and he put me in a wheel chair. "Simple exercises. Lift your legs, one at a time and try to breathe in as you lift and out as you rest your leg." He also had me walk a couple of steps before I could get back into bed. It hurt.

Shortly after that, Giles, from the embassy came in and said the ambulance was ready to take us to the airport and there was a car for the girls for a Eurostar back to London. A porter helped me into the wheelchair and we made our way to the lift and then the lobby escorted by the security guards. What was interesting was that these burly men were in suits, not uniforms, expensive and professional not cheap, at all.

I got another hug from each of the girls as did Joe. It was prolonged and tight and tearful. The doubt about the future was intense in the short term and indeed in any term. We still had no answers to the inevitable questions and we hadn't had the time to check the news on the French TV or on the BBC web site. So we blanked any discussion until we could be more sure and who knew when that might occur?

The contrast between the flight in and the flight out couldn't be greater. On the way out we were all up, laughing, joking, chatting, the three of us in sponsored luxury. The air ambulance was clinical, cramped, with a bed for me, a seat for Joe and a nurse, with medical kit attached to the walls of the aircraft. And of course, no Simon. It hit home. I hadn't taken to him at first but he knew how to do his job and he had some good stories to tell. He had been very supportive and always on hand. He opened up about his work, not, however, his domestic life. Perhaps there were dark things going on there, but I'm not going to judge.

Joe sat close by me all the way to Luton airport. Holding my hand until both our hands were sweaty and his attention was in the way of the nurse trying to check my blood pressure. We had more security at Luton as we disembarked the plane into a waiting private ambulance. The subject of money hadn't come up yet. I guess we were going to get a bill from the French embassy but I was in hospital in Stevenage, the nearest one to Hendrix, in half an hour. I had a private room with another couple of security guards outside. It was like I was in a movie. Scary stuff, the implicit threat worried me and Joe.

Joe stayed a short while and then said he would pop home to get a change of nightie for me, bring my phone, some make-up, some sweeties. A doctor came into to see me. He name was Mahmud; he approached very sheepishly. "I am very sorry for what happened to you. Please do understand that, if it was Muslim perpetrators, not all we Muslims are the same. We believe Islam is a religion of peace and the ways of these people are errant".

"I am sure you are correct. Unfortunately, in my current state of mind I am not yet open to forgiveness, if that is what you are looking for".

"No, Mrs Quigley. I want you to understand that you can trust me as your doctor. My intentions are medical, I swear by the Hippocratic oath, albeit that oath is sworn to the Gods of healing and you have no faith in any god."

"Please do not judge me, Doctor. I am the patient, I am the victim and I am sure you will do your utmost to make me well again."

"Then we are agreed. Differences aside, as they say".

Chapter 55

Nick, the security guard.

We had our rotas in place. We had our uniforms and the peace had been kept well. After the explosion in Paris, though, things got a bit heavy. The religious lot outside the house separated. The Christians moved away from the Muslims as if they were distancing themselves physically, spiritually and morally but the numbers in both camps swelled. To match those increased numbers, we had hundreds of supporters of Joe and Sandy come and chant their names with that French slogan on T-shirts and placards.

I took it upon myself to recruit some more former squaddies from the regiment. I knew, well, I hoped and believed, Joe would see it as a sign of me taking the initiative, not taking the piss and not make me take a hit for the money. I also got a couple of guys into the daughters' gaffs. You never know what might happen and for the sake of a couple of quid they could well afford, it was a no-brainer.

The day after the explosion there was still no concrete news about who had bombed the restaurant. The suspicion was always that it was the Muslims, that terrorist group ISIS or whatever and that little man, Imam Butt was doing all he could, telling everyone he could that his religion was a religion of peace and they all disowned violence. I, for one, was doubtful. You know what they say about all terrorists being Muslims and so on and I had done a tour in Afghan, Helmand and they can be a vicious bunch of bastards. They don't seem to care who they bomb, what with their IEDs, or shoot, take that girl, Malala, they tried to top her didn't they. And them medical people with the polio jabs. They don't give a flying fuck unless they live in a world ruled by that Sharia law. Honour killings and all. I find it hard to understand what they want.

There was a pretty heavy presence from the police as well. They organised the crowd into three groups. Christians. Muslims and non-believers with a line of coppers between them. Didn't stop the shouting mind. I think it would have been better if they put the Muslims at the end, not in the middle. That was just asking for trouble.

You can tell how hypocritical they are when tempers flare, as they did. The baiting the Muslims took from the Christians was dreadful. The shouting, the finger pointing, the waving of those bloody placards they carried and what was written on them. There seemed to be an endless supply of white painted hardboard and multi-coloured board markers like we used to use in training. The Muslims responded with equally strong messages about Sharia law and how western civilisation will be crushed. I couldn't believe they had the balls to be so obvious.

The little Imam was running around trying to pull some of these placards down but he was not successful. The men in dark robes and some in balaclavas where shoving him around, pushing him to the floor. The police seemed reluctant to get into the crowd to help him. Were they scared of physical harm? If so we could get in there, me and my boys and show them who is going to be crushed. I lost sight of the little fellow for a minute and he re-appeared with a bloody nose. Nobody did nothing to help the little bugger so I went in shoving, pushing my way through to help him get out. I got hit round the head with a placard but it was only a bit of card. I lifted him up and carried him in Hendrix, you know, the Quigley gaff and sat him down.

"I promise you, Islam is a religion of peace." He pleaded.

"I believe you mate, but the evidence isn't on your side."

"These are hard liners. They come here from Luton, from Finsbury Park, from Birmingham. I have never seen them before."

"What do they think they're going to achieve. They aren't going to crush Western civilisation. Not with placards and explosions in restaurants. I reckon we should bomb them back to the fucking stone age they want. Then see what they get with no internet, twitter and Facebook to recruit. It'll be fucking pigeons."

"Please mind your language. My ears are very sensitive and there may be children here."

"If your children go to any school like my kids, they'll know this language alright."

"It is why many people send their children to the free schools and the madrassas. To avoid exposure to that kind of talk".

"If you ask me, they can avoid that kind of talk by not coming here in the first place." I never thought I would do a "go back to where you come from" rant but I was well wound up. I stepped back, took a couple of deep breaths and found myself apologising to the little guy. He was gracious enough to accept the apology without over-egging it but I wasn't convinced by what he'd said.

The non-believers, that lot that had came could have had a field day taking the piss out of the Muslims. There were more of them and they didn't have a peace thing to keep to. It wouldn't have done them any good to kick off. It wouldn't have surprised me if they did.

I reckon we was doing a good job keeping the peace. We did still have a couple of guys dressed up like a Muslim, listening out for trouble-makers. They had told us there was a bit of noise from some the hard liners so we was ready for it. We'd told the police what we'd heard and they were on board. I reckon some of the anti-terrorist lot were in from five watching, listening, it was all getting a bit heavy.

Chapter 56

Joe

I left Sandy in her room with a couple of heavies on the door. Again, they wore suits and had those windy cables into their earpieces. They looked like they knew what they were doing. I tried to figure out who was paying for them. Nobody had asked me for any money for any of this. I would have been quite happy to pay for any of it, but I didn't know who organised it, where the bill might come from.

My bigger concern was Sandy, making sure she was comfortable. There's no way she was going to be happy with this lot going on so I settled for comfortable. I got a taxi from the hospital back home and the bloody car couldn't get anywhere near the house. The driver was from Stevenage and didn't know what was going on. He, too, looked like he was a Muslim but he didn't recognise me and didn't say anything until we got into Blossom Avenue. "Goodness me, what's going on here?" He patently knew nothing.

I had to walk the last five hundred yards. Past the Christians who shouted and blessed and said they were praying for Sandy. Then past the Muslims with their western civilisation crushing cardboard placards, and then past a new bunch who chanted my name, chanted support for me and Sandy. I say bunch but there must have been a couple of hundred of them and these three groups were being kept apart by columns of police officers.

The media were there in all their satellite glory barking questions at me that I had either no inclination to answer or no ability to answer. I got indoors went upstairs to change but sat in a chair and found myself weeping. There was a big Sandy shaped hole in the atmosphere and I couldn't help wishing I knew more about Simon. I wanted to write to someone, a note, a card but I didn't know who I should send it to. I could have phoned work to find out who had found Simon but I didn't want to involve former colleagues and fail to answer their questions.

I've never been given to depression but the tears fell from my eyes and the, sorry about this, the snot ran out of my nose. I was slumped in the armchair in my bedroom looking at the indentations in the pillow where Sandy's head had been, wiping my nose on my shirt sleeve unable to muster the energy to find a tissue, unable to muster the energy to pour myself a whisky or pull myself together.

I've never been a control freak; I've always liked some order in my life but the entire edifice was falling down. Work was always a stabiliser; it defined me. Sandy was always a rock, a regular rock, went to work at the same time, came home at the same time. I did my nine to five thirty. We changed our cars every three years, had a holiday of some sort in France every year. Now I have no work, no definition that I was accustomed to. Now I was an agitator, if you like, a rebel, or, as the newspaper said, the most dangerous man in Britain. I had never had to question what I did or what I do and now I was being smashed around the head by questions like a boxer's haymaker. And feeling selfish, indulgent. This self-pitying was pointless. My beautiful wife was in hospital, albeit out of danger and my, I don't know what to call him, colleague, mate, associate, conspirator, friend, perhaps, was dead. The back of his head missing in a Paris restaurant.

I had just about convinced myself that my lot wasn't as bad when I heard the key in the lock and both Daisy and Bec crying "hello-o. Are you there?" I blew my nose on a hastily retrieved handkerchief, rubbed my eyes to hide tears and make it look as though I had been sleeping, disguise the truth, put on a solid parental face for the vulnerable kids.

"Down in a second." I tucked in my crumpled shirt and, thinking I looked like a dad, went downstairs to see the girls. The façade fell away like the ephemera it was. I crumpled at seeing the girls and they both met me on the semi-landing, where the stairs turn at a right angle, with an immense hug. My sobs wracked my chest. My girls' arms wrapped my head and shoulders and we sat there, on the stairs for a good five minutes crying together, wiping snot together, trying to console the inconsolable.

"Come on Dad, have shower, I'll put the kettle on."

"Have you eaten?"

What good girls. There must be a time in the life of a man when you realise that your little girls, your offspring, your progeny have got all grown up. Role reversal takes place. We've had friends for dinner and I know colleagues at work who won't make a decision about a holiday, a carpet, a car, a plant for the garden without either the advice or influence of one of their children. I had tried to fight it. Sandy and I knew more about cars, plants, homes than they did but now it felt like they were the parent and I was the child. I could fight it, I could go with it, I could pretend to go with it. I pretended. Fake to the last. "A cup of coffee and a couple of eggs would do the trick."

Chapter 57

Daisy

It was a shock to see Dad like that. You never see your Dad cry, do you? We heard him but never saw him when Steffan died. He's always there, always in control, unless he's had a little too much red wine especially when your Mum has had a little too much too. He looked dishevelled and while he is not always well turned out, he looked like he hadn't slept or changed his shirt in days, which, come to think of it, he probably hadn't.

Me and Bec had gone to the house to see if there was bread and milk and stuff in the fridge so we could do a shop if needs be and the plan was to go on and see Mum later. But what a shock. I said to Bec later it was a real surprise to see Dad like that and she said it must have been the pressure, getting to him like pressure hasn't before. We all had a good cry although I'm not sure we were all crying about the same thing. It felt cathartic, like we needed it. So me and Bec took control of Dad, made him have a shower while we knocked up some scrambled eggs and toast and some strong coffee.

There wasn't much to say, I mean, there probably was but where do you start. If Dad had known who did the bomb thing, I'm sure he would have told us and better that than finding out he doesn't know and him thinking he should. Understand? All the various godbotherers were outside but there was also a group of people with their own placards in support of mum and dad. It still seemed to me that the godbotherers weren't going to give up their fight for the redemption of my parents and the supporters weren't going to give way until the godbotherers did. This was all ramped up by the bloody telly people now hanging around, who knows what for. I guess it was lucky they didn't see Dad all crumpled on the stairs.

The reporters and presenters were walking round with those long fluffy microphones interviewing all and sundry and all and sundry were doing their level best to be the interesting ones who might appear on the telly later. Man, these people were competitive.

We all had some eggs and toast and coffee. Dad looked more composed with a clean shirt, socks and I daresay, pants, hair, thinning hair, combed. I didn't need to say that did I but he was looking his age more so now than ever before. Spruced, we left the house and walked up the street to my car past the crowds. They were emphatic in their beliefs.

"We're praying even harder for you Joe."

"God will see you don't suffer."

"Join us in prayer for your wife".

"Our God, the one true God will redeem you".

"God forgives you, Joe and Sandy."

"Islam is peace".

"God loveth not transgressors".

And I wasn't sure who the "transgressors" referred to were. Were they the people who blew up the restaurant or was this another dig at my parents. When we got to my car, there was graffiti on it. Someone had sprayed "all sinners will burn in hell" to which someone else had added, in a red paint "for eternity".

I lost it. "Which of you fuckers did this? Come on, don't fucking hide, own up, admit it, be responsible, you pricks." There were no hands raised, no one fessed up. Cowards. I ran over to see Nick, the security guy and asked him if he had seen anything. Nothing. Dad said not to worry, don't take it personally but I couldn't help it. Dad said he had the money to get the car sorted out and that was the irony. I asked him what he meant. He said the more the godbotherers do to hurt us, the more people buy the app. He was being very calm.

He walked over to where the telly vans were and grabbed one of the presenters, that Jemima Bunn with her morals and big hair and dragged her over. "Look what they've done to my daughter's car. First the bomb in Paris and now this and they all claim to be religions of peace".

"But do you know who sprayed it, Mr Quigley?"

"No, I don't, Ms Bunn."

"Then how can you accuse anyone of perpetrating this act?"

My turn. "Are you defending the perpetrators of this act, Ms Bunn?"

"No, not for a moment, but it could be one of those people who seem to be on your side, trying to focus blame on those who believe. I do think we should have a round table on this. Perhaps you'd like to come to the studio this evening?"

"No", was Dad's instant reply. "We have more important things to do like go and see my wife, try to find out who was responsible for Paris and who was responsible for murdering Simon Cleve and let's not forget the five others and the thirteen who were wounded. Come on girls, we'll take my car."

We walked back to house with the amusing sight of Jemima Bunn waddling after us with her too tight pencil skirt and heels. Jemima Puddleduck more like. Dad opened the garage door, we got in the car and he reversed out. The car hadn't been used for a couple of days and the driveway was blocked by some elderly Christian ladies who had to shuffle in their camp chairs to let the car out. As they shuffled they knocked over picnic tables and thermos flasks and a couple of old dears fell over on their arses. "Have a care!" One of the godbotherers shouted. I'm afraid I stayed in the lost zone.

"Just fuck off out of the way. Now!"

Bec put her hand over her mouth to stifle a laugh. She's always been a bit more prudey than me. We had a bit of a laugh in the car. "Did you see that old lady's bloomers. I haven't seen big knickers like that, ever?"

"it's not funny", said Dad.

"Or the one with the wig. When she fell over the hair fell about all over the place and she panicked trying to keep it in place. It seems to me there's a lack of honesty in that woman."

"But still, it isn't funny."

"Yes, it is. They sit there all self-righteous, full of self-belief, no doubts, no questioning, not allowing seventy years of misguided belief to get in the way of some serious thought about what it is they tangibly believe in."

"The more they think, the more they believe. Some will choose to believe that Simon Cleve and your mum were victims because they don't believe and the work was the work of the devil. They will think it should be a spur to our re-belief and deep-down inside they will think it is a good thing the bomb happened."

"Fucking twisted."

"Calm down on the language, Daisy. Please!"

We arrived at the hospital and were taken to mum by a security guard wearing a suit and an ear piece. There were more telly vans and more reporters there all after a gobbet of news. As we were. Mum sat up in bed and smiled. She reached out her arms, grimaced a little but gave us a cuddle in turn. Dad last. I didn't want to say anything about how we had found Dad; we didn't want to worry Mum but Dad said, "the girls have really been good. I was on my knees when they came. I miss you so much and I'm so sorry for what has happened to you and to Simon."

"It isn't, it wasn't your fault. We are both in this together and you're not the only one who feels responsible for Simon. I had got to like him. He was on our side."

"But as a man, I have a duty to take care of you." He looked as though he were serious.

"I am not some poor defenceless woman needing to be cared for by an alpha male with genetics issues. I may not now have a gall bladder but you have too much gall to believe you have any more responsibility than I do for anything that has happened."

Mum coughed and held her bandages. "You're not the only one who has had time to think about what has happened. We need to make a plan of some sort and not be reactive to this stuff. We need a strategy".

Then one of the men in suits came over and asked Dad to go with him. Mum said she had been interviewed by the police, by MI5 and Interpol. They were all as clueless as she was but apparently, some distant offshoot of ISIS had claimed responsibility. There was a video on YouTube with some bescarfed youth going on about the prophet, Allah and death to infidels. Why can't they think of something new to say?

We stayed with mum for a couple of hours while dad was questioned about anything he might had said, seen or done and then back home.

Chapter 58

Nick, the Security guard.

I saw Mr Quigley's Honda come round the corner towards the driveway. The old ladies had re-established their positions where they had been earlier and were in the way again. "Come on, ladies, out of the way please. Mr Quigley has every right to park his car in his garage on his land".

And still they went on about God and prayers, and redemption and apostasy. I had to look that last one up. I didn't want to engage in conversation with any of them. I don't much believe in any higher thing although my Mum and Dad did. I didn't want them thinking I could be like a conduit, a way into the minds of Mr and Mrs Quigley so I just stayed schtumm. Even when they goad me and try to wind me up by telling me I am working with the devil to defend sinners I let it pass. It's my professional training. I can't let them get to me otherwise I won't be responsible for my actions. That was why I had got my discharge.

I had taken responsibility for the girl's car, Daisy I think she is, and called a mate to get it out of the way and to the bodyshop. I know I didn't have a key but some of my mates can do shit that you wouldn't want to know about and we got the car there in one piece. Mr Quigley asked me if I could get the car moved and I told him it was all taken care of. He looked like I was a moron then I explained that I thought it was better if it was done before some other numpty did something worse.

Joe asked me if I knew anyone who could drive. Not just drive, but you know what I mean, drive. I said I did and he said to get him on board, we'd be needing him. I was beginning to think why doesn't this bloke and his family just get out. They had the money now and didn't need all the shit that went with it. I managed to keep quiet because me and my mates were on a monkey a day and we didn't know what the next gig was going to be.

Mr Quigley, or Joe as he wants me to call him but I can't, I just can't; he's like my commanding officer, and the girls walked up to the front door and I walked behind them, like trying to provide cover. As I said before, I had done a bit of close protection in the past and instinctively felt I should be between them and the crowd and it was lucky I was. It was me that got splattered in fucking rotten eggs, all down my back. I couldn't see who done it. I couldn't react but the girl Bec, looked at me, smelled me and asked what had happened. I told her I'd been egged by someone in the crowd and she turned around and shouted. "Leave us the fuck alone. Go away. Go home. Haven't you got anything better to do?"

And one of them said, and you wouldn't believe this. "We have got nothing better to do than save your souls." By throwing fucking eggs at us. My life.

I went in to the house with the Quigleys to get out of my uniform and change into a spare. I put the smelly one in the washing machine, found one of those detergent things in a cupboard and put the wash on. Don't tell my wife. I've seen her do it a few times but it is part of what she does that I don't want to get involved in.

Mr Quigley asked me if I would like a bit of lunch. I asked him what he was having, nothing poncey I hoped and he said he would call the Chinese and get a take out. Good man. I do like a king prawns with oyster sauce and asked if that would be okay and he said, yes Nick, not a problem, he said I deserved it more than I could imagine.

While we waited for the Chinese he had a call, it must have been from his mate with the IT skills. I only heard one side of the conversation and it went.

"Yeah. Yeah. Uh-huh, mm, right, who? Yep, no, okay I trust you Buzz"

I was curious and Mr Quigley said we would be getting some visitors that afternoon, maybe quite a few but not to worry. They were harmless and on our side. I had no choice but to believe him and then the Chinese turned up. The girls, good girls, got plates and spoons and forks and we had a lunchtime feast.

I said I had to get back to work and thanked Mr Quigley and the girls and went back to my post. Something was apparently going to happen that was good or at least not against Mr and Mrs Quigley. I had no idea what was going to happen next.

There was a bit of scuffling going on along the road between some Muslims and some supporters and the coppers were doing nothing about it. I felt rising tensions and told the copper, Cross his name is, not to be an effing chocolate teapot and to do something to quell the disturbance. He said he was waiting for orders from above waiting for guidance from the Home Office or some such bullshit. Me and the boys stepped in and slapped a few of the fighters, put them in their place and said simply, "Stop, stop now. Or there'll be more of where that slapping came from". Fucking filth, teapots the lot of them.

Chapter 59

Daisy

First mum and dad and the PR guy get it in Paris. Then my car is graffiti'd and Nick the security guy gets egged. Fucking godbotherers and their hate. I thought all this 'God is Love' stuff led them in a direction they were okay with and was the basis of their belief. But some of them are fucking twisted. I'm having this rant because I am fucking livid.

Nick was outside trying to sort out some of the demonstrators who had kicked off and a man from one of those delivery companies walked up to the front door and left three boxes, unmarked boxes mind, in the hallway. (It was open because Nick had hurried out). He then got out a penknife and opened them up.

And do you know what some bastard had sent us. Fucking live locusts. A plague of fucking live locusts, the kind people buy to feed snakes and lizards. Hundreds of them and the delivery driver must have been in on it to have opened the boxes.

They flew into the house and landed everywhere, filling the rooms downstairs and then upstairs. All me and Bec could do was waft our hands at them to try and kill them. I didn't want to stamp on them to kill them because that would have mucked up the carpets.

I shouted for Nick to come and help and he did with a couple of his mates. He got out the Dyson and sucked them in one by one by one until the chamber filled with buzzing insects, whole or in parts and put them in the recycling bin. He did this twenty or so times until, we hoped, they had all been vacuumed and put in the bin.

It could have been funny. We were trying to catch the bloody things and they just bounced everywhere. They were quick, they didn't want to be caught and they were noisy, scary noisy, that scratching, buzzing noise you hear on holiday. We thought we had them all, but over the next few days they kept appearing. We even got one out of the fridge. It was dopey as fuck but had gorged on the lettuce in the salad tray. Horrible little fuckers.

We got onto the delivery company but they denied any knowledge of what had happened. The delivery note on the box was from livelocusts.co.uk so we called them. They traced the order back to an address in Welwyn Garden, at the end of Dad's road but the house number was too big and it didn't exist.

Looking back, it was funny. Was it desperate Jews, feeling left out of any process trying to persuade us that we were denying people a homeland or encouraging people to want their own homeland. I don't know and there was no one taking responsibility that I could ask. It would be even funnier if four people dressed up as war, pestilence, famine and death, mounted on horseback came down the street. Then we could all have biblical analogies to draw on. Luckily, the police only ever came in cars, never with horses.

It was weeks later that we finally got rid of the last one, well after mum came out of hospital. We told her about it before she came out and she laughed, laughed like she wondered how low or desperate the people who didn't like what we were doing could get. I swore that if the rabbi showed his face again I would confront him. I know I've jumped to a conclusion and, like as not, he will deny everything, it pains me to know scum could be so, I don't know, scummy.

Chapter 60

Buzz

After what happened in Paris, and it still blows me away to think about it, I had grown to like Simon. We had nothing in common but a desire to do the right thing for Joe and Sandy. They are weirdly inspirational. I don't know whether it was principle or money that drove him but he worked hard, endlessly helping to refine what we were doing with the app, with the website and with social media. He took calls when he had to, pointed us in the right direction with comments that we posted on Facebook and twitter. He was always of the view that we should be reactive to whatever happened. I didn't always agree but his point was that neither Joe nor Sandy were going to be the instigators of any of the shit that was happening.

We got messages of support as much as we got grief from the religious nutters. I say nutters because they were so far off the mark they can only have come from nutters especially the ones that sent the locusts.

We were all very down about Paris, I mean, who the fuck would bomb a restaurant and kill so many people because somebody didn't agree with their faith. Arseholes the lot of them. But we had a post from a woman who was part of a large group of people, who made me smile. I knew it would have made Joe and Sandy laugh out loud; we all needed a laugh, and she wanted to show some support for Joe and Sandy but didn't know how to. We exchanged a couple of emails and made a plan. She assured me what she was going to do would be supportive and peaceful and there would be a couple of hundred people in the group.

Meanwhile the money was pouring in for the app from all over the world. Interestingly we were getting orders from Catholics who simply didn't want to see Muslims on the telly, Hindus wanting to block images of beef being cooked and Presbyterians not wanting images of alcohol consumption. I had a team of twenty kids searching YouTube and every other video library for the stuff people didn't want to see. It was getting very weird.

I also had a call from a colleague of Simon's who said he would like to be part of the team, didn't want to intrude on Joe and Sandy's grief and could we meet. We arranged to meet in a pub, a busy pub in case he too was a nutter, for a beer and a chat.

I called Joe to let him know something was about to occur, that is wasn't a scary thing, he had no need to worry, the outlook was warm and he would enjoy it and that this guy had called wanting a meet. He said he would send Nick, the security guy to sit in the pub and make sure everything was as it should be. I thought this was a bit of paranoia but Joe reminded me that was just forethought.

Chapter 61

PC 'George' Cross

After this member of Mr and Mrs Quigley's almost private army had gone in and assaulted some of the believers and non-believers I was stumped. I had orders from above who had received orders from further above that we were to keep the peace and have as small a number of arrests as possible. We didn't want to be seen to be being racists and getting the Muslims and no-one else. We didn't want to be seen arresting the Christians and not the Muslims and we didn't want to be seen just getting Mr and Mrs Quigleys' supporters. We were left with no recourse to the laws of the land and all these fraying tempers. Add to this the fact that the weather was unseasonably balmy, people were hot and bothered, they had been there for some time and there were some veterans who had been there since the start. We had long ago given up on the Summerhouse agreement, especially since Paris and you can't just stop people being where they want to be particularly if they are not breaking any laws. It was a right old two and eight.

And it got worse. Just after three o clock, marching down Blossom Avenue came a group of around three hundred naturists. All stark bollock naked as the day they were born. Carrying placards as well saying "naturists for Joe and Sandy", "Joe and Sandy's nudey army" and the like. Singing and chanting they were. All sizes, skinny, fat, tits wobbling all over the place, more bingo wings than a night out at the Gala, more knobs dangling than B and Q could dream of, bare-arsed, not a care in the world.

You should have seen the others. The Muslims shielded their women's eyes while the women themselves looked determined to peak. The old Christian ladies turned their backs, covered their eyes and many scuttled off into the distance leaving a trail of discarded thermos flasks and half empty packets of biscuits, chairs and tables scattered in their attempt to distance themselves.

The naturists sat themselves down on the verge outside the Quigley's house and started eating sandwiches, drinking beer and wine, laying on towels and rubbing sun cream into each other. It was a proper party going on. Some of the supporters, who had been taken aback by these events took off some or all their clothes and joined in. What a turn-up this was. It was the quickest way to disperse the crowd I had ever seen, but we had seen one set of fanatics replaced by another set.

Father Corr came over to me, demanding the arrest of the nudists. "Can't you see what these sinners are up to, displaying, indeed flaunting their private parts for all to see. This must be against the law." Now, I'm not an expert in this but I was buggered if I was going to arrest a few hundred people for taking off their clothes when no previous arrests had taken place for any slogans, chanting or scuffling. "I insist action be taken against these exhibitionists. I am offended. Therefore, it is offensive."

I asked him, "why does it offend you father? Do you not have your own nakedness at times? In the bath, the shower?"

"But I do not flaunt it in public. Popes past have taken to removing the genitalia with chisels from the statues in the Vatican in order to preserve their modesty. I think modesty here should be preserved".

"You're not suggesting we take chisels to the private parts of these good people are you. Is that Christian, Father Corr?"

"I'm not suggesting that for a moment..."

"Good, because that would be incitement to violence."

The naturists sat on towels on the grass verges of Blossom Avenue, enjoying the sunshine and the free expression, knowing there were too many of them for the limited numbers of Officers on hand. The telly people and the journalists swarmed around them with little or no consideration for the content they would get. I assume the more salacious excerpts would go to the porn channels for other sad people to look at. The supporters of Mr and Mrs Quigley were filming with their smart phones, again I would assume that the films would be posted online. I have no idea what the policy is on YouTube for male and female nudity be it what my colleagues call T and A or a little more, how can I say, front garden.

Father Corr was buzzing in my left ear. Mr Butt was at in my right ear. All I could here was "disgrace", "offensive", "shouldn't be allowed". "outrages public morality", "praise be to God, the lord will protect us", "make them put it away". I called the station and asked The Sarge what I should do.

He said, "leave them be, it'll get cold soon enough and it'll be over in a flash, so to speak, if you get my drift." Sarge was a proper comedian. Not. I tried to explain to Mr Corr and the Imam that there was little I could do but they went on and on. I wasn't going to disobey my guvnor so I said if they didn't like it, to move around the corner where they didn't have to look at what they considered offensive.

"And then the sinners will have won, Officer. And that cannot be." He sounded like he was that old Paisley fella.

"Officer Cross, you must uphold common decency, common values of what is moral and what isn't."

I was going to reply that blowing up restaurants in Paris wasn't common decency and writing graffiti on a young girl's car wasn't moral but I didn't want to make the situation worse by engaging with them. It is what we are trained to avoid.

The religious demonstrators did, indeed, retreat around the corner. The Quigleys' supporters joined the naturists, not in disrobing but in congregating in a peaceful way, and, as the Sergeant had predicted, come the early evening they all got dressed again. Many sauntered off to the pub and the religious lot assumed they previous positions in the road and on the verges, armed with blankets and thermos flasks. There was one thing about those thermos flasks that puzzled me. I never saw them being replaced or refilled.

Chapter 62

A meeting of COBRA

"I've asked you here today because we really do have to address this issue of all these people seeking independence, we are now at over five hundred thousand applications. The Home office cannot deal with the number of people seceding should I say, the assumptions being made that once you have written a letter and placed an advertisement in the local newspaper you can be on your own. We also need to look at what went on in Paris and the almost private army the Quigleys now have at their disposal. What are the figures now Home Secretary?"

The Home Secretary shuffled some paper and said "I'm not sure what the current figure is, Madam Prime Minister, but I believe you are correct in saying we have had close to half a million applications. It is our estimate that the Quigleys have earned well over five million pounds, a sum matched by their technical support."

There were gasps around the table. "Almost as rich as your average Tory minister then", quipped a senior civil servant.

"That's not very helpful, is it," warned the Prime Minister. "But what do we need to do? This is a movement unheard of in history in any developed country in the world. They don't seem to need to worry about important things like healthcare, education, roads, policing."

"Strength in numbers." interjected the Home Secretary.

The Cabinet Secretary made a valid point. "These people are generally white, middle-class and middle aged and homeowners. There might be a large constituency of renters, either social or private, who share their views but are not in a position to act. What I am trying to say is that they are potentially Conservative voters who are leaving", and at this point he did the bunny's ears thing, "the United Kingdom. You are losing votes in marginals. We have carried out a brief survey and you stand to lose maybe two dozen seats if these people can't or don't vote."

"So" sighed the prime Minister," we can sit around and do nothing, lose the next General Election, be the laughing stock of a Europe that laughs at us already or make some changes. Do we have any figures on what is going on in Europe and elsewhere?"

The Foreign Secretary too, shuffled paper. "I have spoken to my counterparts in the major European economies and while we are taking the greatest impact, there have been one hundred thousand or so in each of Germany, France and Italy that have disassociated with their respective mother countries."

"Are you introducing a name for this activity? Disassociating?"

"I believe I am, Prime Minister. And in the smaller countries the proportion of disassociators is no less".

"Disassociators?"

"Yes, Prime Minister."

"And do each of these countries have leaders, focusses, such as the Quigleys?"

"No, they don't and apart from a few people who have attempted to make capital out of the situations, such as that nutter, you remember, the fruitcake that got himself on the television."

"You cannot say 'nutter', Mr Foreign Secretary, or 'Fruitcake'. It is not acceptable to this face of Conservatism."

"I'm sorry, Madam Prime Minister. I mean there are no focal points, no opinion formers we can approach to form some opinions that they are being very childish, very spoilt and they should bloody well grow up and take their responsibilities to their countries seriously."

"Mr Foreign Secretary. This may appear to be an easy decision for many to make and act on, but I remain convinced there is an underlying motivation for their actions that we need to address before the country implodes, and implodes under our watch."

"You're not thinking of inviting that man and his wife to Downing Street again with a view to negotiation. Surely what they are doing is akin to terrorism and we do not negotiate with terrorists."

"It seems to me that after Paris, you recall that their PR man was murdered, that these people are more likely to be victims of terrorism than most. While they have this apparent private army, they may deter any direct activity, we cannot have acts of blatant terrorism perpetrated in our country."

"Okay, let's run a few flags up the flagpole", interjected the Defence Minister. "What can we offer, strictly entre nous."

"I've given this some thought," replied the Prime Minister. "We can take away, the charitable status of faith based religious education establishments, we can reduce the funding we give to the established church, we can take measures with VAT, we can provide a few inducements to see if we can't stop this disarray. I'll call the Quigleys and invite them in. Can someone see if Mrs Quigley is out of hospital, or what her condition is? Thank you."

Chapter 63

Joe

That was fun, the first bit of fun I've had in ages. Nearly three hundred naturists turning up outside the house, scaring off more of the godbotherers in one fell swoop than I have been able to do since this all kicked off. I went out and met a couple of them who said they were chuffed to come and show solidarity. They tried to persuade me to get naked as well but I declined. I didn't want any more focus, any more pictures in the papers, any more film in situations that I wasn't completely happy with.

In the evening Sandy came home in an ambulance and was wheeled up to the house by a couple of paramedics. She had a bag of medication and some bandages and we were told a nurse would be out the next day to change her dressings. I would have cooked something for her after she had had to put up with hospital food but I hadn't had time to go shopping. So we had a takeaway from the local Thai. Two takeaways in one day was a bit extravagant but the girls came over and we had a good catch-up.

I know we were all relieved that Sandy was home, and making satisfactory progress. We didn't talk much about the attack and we didn't tell Sandy about Daisy's car, we all tried to keep everything on an even keel. We watched the news that evening and some of the footage from outside the house was funny. The naturists marching down the street with their own placards, the godbotherers scuttling off not wanting to see naked people, knocking over chairs, tables, thermos flasks. The amount of pixelisation was incredible. The attention to detail. I wonder who has the job of identifying peoples' parts so they don't appear on the television. Much the same as our app, I suppose.

The house felt better full of people. A little life, a little laughter, more lights on, the pop of an uncorked something French, background television noise. All of it louder than the twenty or so people that were still camped outside the house every night.

We made up the bed in the spare room downstairs for Sandy, the girls went home and we got an earlyish night. I kissed her goodnight and we hugged. We hugged reassurance and love and support back into each other. I knew we would be back into our old routine sooner rather than later and it felt fantastic. I told her what it meant and, good old Sandy, she stifled a tear, and said how pleased she was to be home. I checked outside for one of our lads standing guard at the front gate and he was there. All was calm for the first time in weeks.

The next morning, I got up early and did a big shop at Waitrose. There were sideways glances and a few people nodded at me in a kind of subdued greeting but it was uneventful. I looked forward to a quiet day but my phone went off while I was at the fish counter ordering some cod loin. I thought with a plain lemon, butter and white wine sauce. Back in the old routine. I looked at the caller ID and didn't recognise it. I left it but it rang again.

There's barely a rude bone in my body, as you know, I dislike swearing more than Sandy, so I answered the thing to be greeted by a pompous man calling himself the Prime Minister's Private Secretary telling me a car was being sent for me at eleven to take me to Downing Street to see the PM. I didn't have plans for the day, but I told him I did and that I wouldn't be free until the afternoon. The line went quiet and he came back saying the car would be here at three o'clock. Was that okay? I said it would be.

I apologised to the young girl at the counter for having taken the phone call and finished the shop. I drove home and at the gate was Mr Butt, the Imam. I said, "good morning".

And he replied, "good Morning Mr Quigley. How are you today?"

"Very well, thanks."

"And Mrs Quigley?"

"Improving every day." I didn't want to go into any detail.

"I hope you understand Mr Quigley, that when I say how very sorry I am for what happened to you and Mrs Quigley and your colleague, I mean it as condolences, not as an apology for what happened, taking responsibility."

It riled me. "Are you speaking then as a human being and not as a follower of Islam?"

"I am speaking as a follower of Islam, Mr Quigley. It is, as you know, as we have maintained all along, a religion of peace."

"Unbelievable, Mr Butt. The attack in Paris was not a gesture of peace. It has been claimed by some Islamist sect that I had never heard of before. It killed my friend and it maimed my wife. I would be very grateful if, when you want to offer condolences, you do not offer them qualified. Good morning." Unthinking fool. I couldn't believe he was so blinkered to believe that his faith, his prophet, his Allah hadn't had responsibility for this. I was furious and I didn't want to be. The day had started well and now the pressure was on again.

I popped in to see Sandy who was awake and listening to the radio then I unpacked the shopping and made her some breakfast. Creamy scrambled eggs with a little grated truffle on the top. Beats hospital food any day and told her the news about Downing Street. I told her I would do it alone, that I didn't want her exposed to any grief and she willingly accepted my decision. Still not better.

I made calls to and fielded calls from Sandy's friends. Julie, Susie and Cath. They were all keen to know how she was. I told them a little knowing that Sandy would tell them more of the truth in due course when I was out. The phone rang again. Buzz. "Man, how are you? Did you have fun with the naturists yesterday? I see you didn't get your kit off and it was a nice warm day."

"Morning Buzz, how are you?"

"Good man, good. How's Sandy? Home?"

"Yes. She came home yesterday and she's doing okay. I think she has been hit hard by what happened and it'll take time for her to get back to where she would want to be. Still, early doors."

"I have news. You know I had a call from a PR guy who said he knew Simon and would be interested in helping. I went out for a beer with him last night and he seems okay. He is aware of what happened to Simon, says he is prepared for anything and keen. I gave him your number so expect a call."

"I will. What are the numbers like this morning? I've been summoned to Downing Street this afternoon. I don't know what for but I can guess it'll be about Paris, people seceding and all that."

"I'll email you the detail but we have sold close to eight million copies of the app, ninety-five per cent cutting out religion and we have them from all over the world. We are working on a software only solution so I can email the thing to people that want it, cut costs and be faster. I should have it in a couple of days. Yeah, and you're still trending on twitter and making a load of noise on Facebook. Instagram is full of shots from your house of naked people as are some of the porn sites. Not that I'd know of course. I think I may have got myself a girlfriend.

"Good news, thanks mate, you're doing a sterling job."

"I'd much rather do this than go through what you and Sandy have done. Respect, man."

"Thanks Buzz. We'll have to meet up soon. It's been an age since we had a beer and a chat and I miss it. You can tell me about the girl."

"Cheers, mate. Ring me when you've done the Prime Minister."

I turned on the television and there was more footage of yesterday. The Home Secretary was on saying she thought I should stop what I was doing, settle down, stop being childish, disband my private army and re-join the United Kingdom. So that's what the Prime Minister wants. Forewarned, forearmed and so on. She also had the balls to say she offered her sympathy to me and Sandy and to Simon's family for Paris. What a mendacious individual she was. I sometimes used to struggle to understand just how low someone can go and this plumbed new depths. It was a shame. The day had started so well.

The next call was from this new PR man. He introduced himself as Johnny and asked if he could come over for a chat. Excellent timing, so I said yes, can he come over this morning? See you in an hour.

I helped Sandy out of bed, we dressed her to make her presentable and I went upstairs to shower, shave and get ready. This new man, Johnny, didn't know about the plans for the afternoon, I would hit him with that later, but out of some strange respect for Simon I put on the chinos, shirt and shoes that he had had his stylist bring on that first occasion.

I had a look outside to see what Johnny would see when he arrived. The old biddies from the C of E were there, but no Mr Tudor, I hadn't seen much of him lately. Butt was there with a group of bearded men in kurta pyjamas and jalabas, huddled around each other, some smoking. Father Corr was there, standing on his own, seemingly, at this time of day, unable to muster a following. Around fifty people were there, still, after all this time. My word, weren't they bored.

I had long given up any attempt to engage them. It had become attrition and I was sure, as the naturists had given up when it got cold, that this lot would cave in when the weather turned colder and wetter.

Johnny arrived wearing a formal suit and highly polished shoes. He had a soft leather attaché case and looked like the kind of man that didn't feel pressure or heat. Short blond hair, steel rimmed glasses, a youthful complexion, possibly borne of facial scrubs and a morning regime, slim, well turned out. He shook my hand warmly and we went inside. "Let me introduce myself, tell you something about me. I have worked in reputation management for a number of years, not as many as Simon, but I knew him well."

I interrupted. "Did he have family? We never knew, he never spoke of any."

"He was divorced from his second wife, no kids, which saddened him, and no immediate family. His clients were the closest people to him and he did tell me that he had great respect for you and Mrs Quigley. I worked in tabloid journalism for a number of years so I know how they work, I worked on television news as well. I am younger than Simon but I have worked in each of the areas where he had expertise. I am also a humanist. I want to offer my services to you because I believe in what you are doing, I share the values you have projected and it is a very interesting challenge, big, changing. We've never been here before."

"Let's get the grubby question of money out of the way. How much," asked Sandy.

It took me aback but Johnny said, "One thousand a day, on a retainer, shall we say for the next month?"

It was a lot of money compared to our previous lives, but not so much now and we could afford it. We shook hands again and I told him about the summons to Downing Street and what the Home Secretary had said that morning.

Johnny said, "the media has been full of the same arguments that have been going on outside your house. Some in favour, but most against and I guess that will happen until the market changes. Media owners always back the winner and they believe the winners will be the status quo."

"I don't see this as a win lose situation," I told him. "We weren't expecting a fight of any sort. We weren't expecting to have to manage public opinion or manage our own reputation. You know this started as a laugh, fuelled by more than one glass of wine and a desire to be rebellious."

"But it has turned out to be one. You have shifted public expectations of nationhood, of patriotism and while it may or may not be about you, it is about the State, it is about power and maintaining power. Think of that bastard Assad in Syria, clinging on to power like a man having second thoughts about jumping off Beachy Head. Politicians don't embark on a career for the simple pleasure. It isn't show business for ugly people, it is about power and reach and you are diminishing it. You are threatening it."

"Serious stuff then."

"Absolutely, Mr Quigley".

"Joe, please."

"Joe. I fear that the visit to Downing Street may be tricky. But shall we go and find out."

I called Downing Street on the number in the call log on my phone and told them I would be bringing an advisor and that my wife wasn't well enough to travel. The pompous man who had made the call sounded sniffy about me bringing some support but did pass on sympathies for Sandy.

The same driver arrived in the same Jaguar and Johnny and I were whisked to Downing Street. The media were outside, the now familiar whizz and clicks of cameras, shouted questions that never get answered and I wasn't about to start. Johnny walked confidently through the glossy black painted door and we were met by the pompous guy from the phone calls.

"How do you do. My name is Maxwell. James Maxwell. I shall take you through to the Prime Minister." We were led down a corridor and into a larger room than before, populated by the Prime Minister, the Home Secretary, the Foreign Secretary, a man in a suit who wasn't identified and secretaries for each of them.

"Good afternoon," I said "Are we in trouble? This is some turn out."

"Would you like some tea, Mr Quigley and perhaps you could introduce us to your colleague." The Prime Minister started proceedings.

"This is Johnny Marsh, he has stepped into Simon Cleve's shoes. Tea would be lovely."

"I was terribly sorry to hear about Paris. How is your wife?"

"Improving. We think she'll be fine. It was obviously a terrible time and it will take time to get over it."

"Yes, I'm sure. Now to get to the point Mr Quigley. What is it you want? What will stop this silliness that you have started?"

"To be fair Prime Minister, this all kicked off when your predecessor said he thought we should live in a Christian country, as I'm sure you know. Mrs Quigley and I chose not to be part of that. It was a personal act of defiance based on increasingly strongly held views about religion. None of which have been changed or challenged by what has happened recently."

"But if you re-join the United Kingdom, then everyone else will follow suit, surely."

"I fear not Prime Minister. I have no influence over these others who have parted company from the UK, I do not attempt to sway them one way or another. I think you need to accept they are free thinking individuals who want to do more than cock a snook at the establishment."

"Listen, Mr Quigley, we are here to offer you a number of concessions if you can persuade your followers to stop this agitating."

"I appreciate it may be hard for you as the daughter of a churchman to accept my position, but I do not want you to offer me things that I cannot possibly accept on behalf of anyone. I do not have influence. I do not hold sway".

"But if I said we would rethink our policies on, say, faith based free schools, would you support that?"

"Of course I would but it is for you to do that without using me as a conduit. Unlike you, I seek no power, no influence. I can't even tell you how many people have left the United Kingdom as I did and what will persuade them to come back."

"We call them disassociators."

"You've invented a word for them?"

"After a fashion."

We didn't have time to finish our tea or the biscuits that came with them. The Prime Minister stood up, was followed by her team and the unidentified man spoke for the first time. "This private army you have. It needs to be disbanded. We can't have uniformed thugs patrolling the streets."

"They are simply doing what the police are failing to do which is keep some sense of order and to protect my family and my house from people who choose, noisily and violently, to disagree with us. As long as they are on my land, they will be employed. As long as there is a threat to me and my family and my house they will make themselves obvious in the United Kingdom. If they break the law, arrest them. If they do not break the law, treat them like the police have treated the godbotherers and do absolutely nothing about it. Good bye."

We stomped out and took the driver by surprise, jumping into the Jaguar while he finished a cigarette and waiting for him to catch up. He did and we wafted our way back out to Welwyn Garden.

"I didn't say much in there, did I?" Johnny said.

"Not to worry. I was a bit wound up. These bloody politicians simply do not understand where we are and how we got here."

"I think I learned a lot. Thanks for that. We should expect some flak from them for not playing the game their way. They will react, either by doing something about state ties to religion or attacking you for not co-operating. Let's see what's on the news."

Chapter 64

Sandy

I didn't let on to Joe just how I felt. It would have demoralised him. But the restaurant in Paris and my injury had hit me like one of Vic Reeves and Bob Mortimer's' giant frying pans, but for real. I was shaken, I was miserable, I lacked energy. I had come close to death. The image of Simon's head, minus the back of his skull wouldn't go away. The pain in my stomach was a reminder of how close I had come to death. An escape from death that six others hadn't had.

An escape from death that Steffan hadn't been able to get. I know Joe and I think of him every day. We don't always talk about it because it only serves as a reminder we don't need but there are times when it hits hard. And this was one of them. Joe had had the opportunity to be busy with this new man, Johnny. I had nothing to do but dwell. And I did. My head was in turmoil, my stomach was sore, I could barely move. I just stared out over the garden, looking at a middle distance while terrible thoughts swam around my head.

Was there a God? Had He done something? Had we caused something? Was this a consequence of our actions? No, no, yes, yes. I struggled to get my head sorted out without thoughts of a possible God creeping in to my consciousness before I could kick them back in to the pile of crap they were.

Having security guards outside my hospital room reminded me of the persistent threat and coming back home to see those bloody men and women outside still going on about the kind of sinners we were was all too much. I tried to stay jolly for Joe and the girls and we had a nice takeaway but when they had gone to bed, I, like Joe had before me, cried like a baby. Being back in the security of my own home was better than being exposed away from it; it was more familiar, more comforting but still I felt vulnerable.

I tried to focus and ignore what had been going on but the girls came around in the afternoon to see how I was and persuaded me to watch some of the YouTube footage of the demonstrators. To borrow from Smokey Robinson, outside, I was masquerading, inside my heart was breaking. I chuckled at the footage, it was funny seeing all this going on outside our house, instead of those bloody godbotherers with their *Kumbayas* but the whole thing was becoming a drain. I know we now had millions in the bank and I should have been pleased, excited, ambitious, grateful but I had no motivation to try to enjoy the money.

The girls waited for Joe to come back from London. Daisy asked if I thought it had all been worthwhile. I said there hadn't been a plan to do anything that would get this kind of response so there was no benchmark for it being worthwhile. I tried to explain that we had had a perfectly good way of life before this all started, we had been content, settled, getting older with the certainty of funds to do so comfortably and now we had no idea what the future held.

"Any regrets?" asked Bec

"Plenty. I regret what happened to Simon. I think I regret not being able to be flippant any more. I can't say 'it must be fate'. I can't say anything about ying or yang, or the stars. But that's me being silly. I really regret what happened to Simon, he didn't deserve it".

"You didn't deserve being hospitalised."

"Some people would disagree with that." I thought I was being empathetic.

"It's not fair. You're not trying to impose a view on anyone but this lot outside and that lot in Paris are trying to impose on you."

"We all believe we are doing it for the best intentions."

"Mum. I've got an idea. Why don't we make some placards and go and sit this side of the hedge and just ask them to go home. Politely."

"We could try it, try something at least."

We made placards for each of us. There was some board in the shed and a long bit of wood. Daisy did woodwork at school and made them up for us. Mine read, "*please go home to your families*". Bec's read *"Be warmer at home"* and Daisy's read, "*You will not win us back.*" Not very inspiring I know but we got three chairs and went down to sit at the gate, at the border.

It was like we had kicked a hornet's nest, but hornets resembling agitated old ladies with tinted hair and agitated men with beards.

"We are doing this to save you from the error of your ways".

"Repent now and share God's love."

"Drive out the devil, come pray with us."

"Glory be to Allah"

And more and more. Could they not simply go away.

I countered in a different tack. "We don't deserve your prayers. We are apostates, we are sinners, we have no love for your Gods, your Gods have no love for us."

"But they do, God loves all his children and he will welcome you back into his flock. Once you repent, He will redeem you," came the booming voice of Father Corr.

"So does God love me even though I do not believe he exists?" Asked Daisy

"Of course he does. That is the beauty of Christianity..."

"And Islam", piped up Mr Butt.

Joe and Johnny arrived in the Prime Minister's Jaguar. I felt as though I had been hostile towards Johnny when we first met and I apologised. "I haven't really got my head around the idea that we are now very comfortably off and that you probably deserve your fee. Simon certainly deserved his."

"Let's see what happens and how I can help. Perhaps some more inspired banners. I'll work on that tomorrow."

"Let's go inside", said Joe, and have some tea.

Joe told me and the girls about what had happened, that the PM had expected Joe to be a leader of some sort, able to influence those who head seceded from the United Kingdom. We chuckled at this new word, disassociators, and at how far off the mark the politicians had been. Johnny explained that this was the mindset of all politicians and it was difficult for them to understand the position we had taken.

Johnny also said he had thought about a media strategy. I asked if we needed one and he said he thought we run the risk of being sucked in deeper being responsible for all that had happened unless we took control of the message. Having met Buzz, he said he understood why he had been exonerated and agreed that he should be left to get on with what he was good at and not trained to handle something he would undoubtedly baulk at; media appearances. Johnny's plan was Radio 4, Newsnight and the broadsheets. That was where politicians still got their thoughts from. For them social media was something that they needed to be aware of but they didn't know how to control.

Johnny suggested dinner out so Joe called the Tilbury, a very good gastro pub out in the country where we were unlikely to be recognised. I thought I should make the effort, got dressed, put on some make-up and we took a taxi. Johnny was great company. Perhaps it's a gift for PR men, but he had stories to tell that kept us entertained and our minds off the recent events in Paris. It was fun and I got to laugh out loud for the first time in a while.

The next morning, I confessed to Joe about how I felt and said I wanted to see a doctor.

Chapter 65

Joe

It was no surprise that Sandy wanted to see a doctor about her depression. I had seen enough and read enough in my years to know that survivors feel guilty and depression can follow. I don't know how shallow I am or whether it would hit me later, but I felt I needed to be strong but empathetic, supportive but coping. I guess this was a price we had to pay for the money that was collecting in our bank account. Something for nothing? No chance, it had never occurred before, perhaps this was the quid pro quo. If it was, I would have paid the money back in a heartbeat.

I noticed this morning there was a chill in the air and the number of people sitting outside was lower than normal. The ones who said they were our supporters had generally all gone now. I thanked them for their show of support and equally I thanked them for not hanging around. And you may ask why. My neighbours. For weeks now they have had to put up with these demonstrators, their noise, their singing, chanting, bells and cymbals, their very presence blocking the road, blocking their driveways and none of them asked for this.

I did put a note though each of their letterboxes apologising for the melée and hoping it would die down but this was a set of circumstances that I couldn't control. The newspapers and the television channels were discussing why I had been seen coming out of Downing Street again and this time with a well-known PR consultant. They wanted to know why I was being seen, what it was that I wanted with all kinds of speculation. Some of that speculation can only have come from other people at the meeting suggesting I wanted to break a link between education and faith groups.

I called Johnny. "Bang on. Exactly what I said they would do. Some spinning from them to make it look like you were the bad guy."

"What're we going to do?"

"We're going to get you some serious exposure as I suggested and finally put an end to this idea that you are leading a revolt against religion. Once that is clear, all those people outside your house will have to dissipate and you might get back to an ordinary life."

I was prepared to accept this at face value but my experience of any kind of publicity was that it attracted the godbotherers to my house and increased sales of the app. Buzz phoned. "You're not going to believe this, man."

"Yes, I am."

"But that lot this morning was another three hundred and twenty thousand copies of the app. Luckily we're all set-up to respond automatically. They choose the footage themselves, we load it onto the copy of the app we send them. We're minted from this and YouTube is coughing up the dollars too."

"Thanks Buzz. Listen. I want to tone all this down and the new PR man has a strategy to do so. Are you okay with a reduction in the money you get from the app as a result?"

"I am richer beyond the dreams of this particular Croesus. No sweat. But we are getting more and more non-religious stuff being asked for."

"Like?"

"From the USA, we're getting people who want to block Clinton and Trump. Spain gives us Barcelona fans who want to block Ronaldo in news programmes and likewise Real Madrid fans who want to block Lionel Messi. Now we have an on/off switch to differentiate between news footage and film, football, documentary, we are getting more sophisticated requests from more sophisticated customers. You'll have to come down and see what is making you and Sandy and me and mill a day. I've got thirty people here, day and night churning out apps to customers."

It was beginning to sound like we were becoming big business, we were on a treadmill that we couldn't get off. As Sandy got out of bed, I looked out of the window to see a large group of people walking down the street. There seemed to be some agreement in that there was Father Corr leading a band of pious looking old ladies. Mr Tudor, leading an equally pious but better dressed group of old ladies. Mr Butt ahead of his men with beards, a group of men and women, the men with kippah hats and sideburns to their collars, a Sikh group and a rag tag of others all with fresh placards. *"Our schools teach morality". "There is no room for blasphemers in our children's education." "Free us from the sinners who hate". "Give us only the teachings of our Lord." "Do not deny the Torah".* And more.

They had obviously read their papers, watched their televisions, contacted their Facebook groups, been to B and Q for the boards, gathered somewhere and decided upon a show of combined strength. Silly Buggers. It was later that I found out that this was all being escalated to a higher level, Bishops getting involved and they had taken it upon themselves to display a show of unity in response to what they saw as our challenge to their right to worship. Silly, silly buggers. I thought they were given to understanding and empathy. Patently not.

I went out to get the leaders and invited them into the summerhouse. I made tea, had biscuits on a plate and settled down to what I hoped would be a chat, eventually some kind of agreement, as before. But they were genuinely angry such that tea and biscuits would not calm them. Like a pack of agitated teenagers, they made their points about exam results, inclusion, having the families of non-believers in the school because of the quota system, shouting over one another to the point where I heard nothing. I put my hands up to quieten them, successfully in the end and said, "I am no threat to your schools. I was invited by the Prime Minister to a meeting where she said there would be things she could do if I stopped people seceding from the United Kingdom. I said it wasn't in my gift, that I wasn't a leader and I wanted nothing. This is the politicians spinning you and you have been taken in."

"We have been taken in by the voice of the disbelievers", started Father Corr.

"There is no one more wicked than he who lies against Allah, may peace be upon him."

"You come here in a funny kind of peace, Mr Butt. I am not the liar. I have not lied and to accuse me of doing so is very hypocritical."

The otherwise quiet Sikh spoke up. "You will not find peace as long as you lie."

"Shall I tell you how much money I have made today, in the face of this spinning against me. Over one million pounds. Every time I am on television or in the papers people buy the blocker to block the hypocritical nonsense you speak. Every time they see you coming down the street, I make money. I'm not proud. I didn't set out to make money but I do."

"Then you must disperse your funds correctly. The International Red Crescent does very important work."

"As does Save the Children."

"As does CAFOD," barked Corr.

Now they were after the money they were making me make through their own lack of understanding.

"The Shri Venkataswara Temple of the United Kingdom is a very worthy cause, Mr Quigley".

"The who?" Why was I engaging?

"It is a very important distributor of funds to further work in the community to support the disadvantaged, Mr Quigley".

"I feel very disadvantaged by having you lot outside my house and my neighbours' houses all hours of the day, making the noise you make. How much will it take to make you go away?"

"We cannot be bought, Mr Quigley."

"Are you trying to tell me that the very decorative church you, Mr Tudor, run, the establishment you preside over and your church Mr Corr are not built from funds from people who wanted to buy their way into heaven?"

"That is not how it works, Mr Quigley. Pious people donate as much as they can in praise of our Lord."

"I'm thinking of camels and needles and rich men here Mr Corr, Mr Tudor. I'm sorry Mr Butt but I do not understand Islam well enough to find an appropriate analogy".

"I will consult the Quran and find a passage to help you. If indeed you would like to know more about the words of our prophet I would be more than happy to guide you."

"Gentlemen, thank you for your time this morning. I do hope we are agreed that you will reduce your numbers and make less noise and I will do my best not to upset you. I will do all that I can to have you understand my position as I understand yours."

Chapter 66

BBC Head of Religion and Ethics

I knew what was going on, I did. I was fully aware of this blocking thing but hadn't had a plan about what to do with it. We knew that people were actively switching away from our output to images of their own choice. Now, what I also know is that we are not supposed to be in the business of chasing ratings but they are important to us.

Our research told us exactly who was opting out. We contact thousands of people every month for a record of their viewing habits in addition to the BARB data. What the BARB data doesn't give exactly is how many people are switching off *'Thought for the Day'* in the morning on Radio 4 to listen to something of their own choice. Anyone that listens to the Daily Service does it because they want to and those figures didn't move. As you would think.

'Songs of Praise' has always been a bit of a duty. We are required to transmit so many hours of religious stuff, mainly Christianity and for years we've just gone to a church, told people we were going to be there and they all turn up, best Sunday clothes, coiffed, made up and in hearty voice. It fills the gap between the Sunday afternoon and the evening when people eat but leave the television on. On the ratings, they say they've watched it because it is the right thing to watch and bingo, it continues without much effort. We have tried to modernise it, footballers from Hull, rappers

and the like but each time we do there are letters to *'Points of View'*. You can't win.

My dilemma is that, for example on Saturday and Sunday mornings on the Breakfast News we often have a Vicar or an Imam review the papers. People have been switching their app things on and killing other viewpoints at the point at which they are being made. They don't get to hear the views; they don't get to know what it is they disagree with. Ignorant fools. If you don't agree with something philosophically then you should have an idea what it is you don't agree with. All this blanket switching off because of the way some people dress or look, it's like a kind of fascism.

There are more people who want to hear the compassionate voices of their local religious leaders than don't. There are more people who respect the role religious leaders play in community life than don't and I firmly believe the majority should prevail. As more and more people have these blocker things, the greater the majority of people left who are, perhaps, comforted by what they see. It's a no-brainer.

I was due to have a meeting with my counterparts at Sky and ITV but they don't have the same obligation that we do. It goes all the way back to Lord Reith, our first Director General, a man of some faith I tell you, who decreed that the BBC should entertain, inform and educate and particularly that programmes on a Sunday should not begin before 12.30 so that viewers could attend church. Now I know we are more diverse, more multi-cultural than we were in the 1920's but I believe that legacy should remain. We must educate people about religion. We must inform people about religion and we should entertain them.

I wasn't going to be cowed by the activities of this man and his wife. I was going to do the complete opposite. I was going to film a documentary about them and the impact they had had on religion in the UK.

I got the number from BBC London who had had Mr Quigley on a couple of times and I called him. "Mr Quigley, I am the Head of Religion and Ethics at the BBC." I waited for a response. Response came there none. "I would like to discuss with you the idea of our making a documentary about what you have done and the impact you have had on religion and religious broadcasting in the last few weeks." Still silence. "Are you there Mr Quigley"

"Yes I am."

"How do you feel about the idea?"

He said he would call me back. Most people would jump at the chance to be in a documentary. They all have a point to push, an agenda. I don't know why he wouldn't.

I waited five minutes, ten minutes. This was unheard of. An hour later he phoned and dismissed the idea in two words. "No thanks." And he hung up. Who doesn't want to be on the television. Who doesn't want their fifteen minutes? He might have had some time in the spotlight, but to deny the opportunity of a documentary. Beyond me. Even the Scientologists let us make a documentary even if they prevented its broadcast later. We even got into the

Finsbury Park mosque. Not to get into the Quigleys was a defeat that I wasn't going to broadcast.

My colleagues from Sky and ITV arrived for the meeting but I cut it short. As I said, they don't have the obligation we do.

Chapter 67

Sandy

We decided to let things take their own course for a few days. Both Joe and I were tired, exhausted, it had all been out of our comfort zone and I was still in recovery. There was a physiotherapist every day who came to the house with a regime of exercises to help me recover. The community nurse came every other day to change my dressing. (It seemed that the idea that we continue to pay our taxes is respected and we weren't asked to pay for these things. We would have done had we been asked). I wanted to see more of the world than our house, than Hendrix, but I couldn't walk far.

While there had been this time when Joe and I were recognised in the local Indian restaurant and Joe had been nodded at in Waitrose, we didn't know how much we would be recognised a little further afield. Dinner out at the Tilbury had been successful. Lunch out was an option but Johnny had said we might get a call anytime to go on one of the programmes he had shortlisted to make our point to other opinion formers, as he called them. This meant no booze during the day for Joe and I wanted to be supportive so no booze for me.

Perhaps this could be the start of at least a reduction in the amount of alcohol we were drinking. My healthier diet, because of my gall balder might have seen us on a, to borrow from the bible, a Pauline conversion on the road to a longer, healthier life.

Free from the strictures of work we had to work out a plan for the short, medium and longer terms. Assumptions we would have to make included a permanent threat to our lives, a threat to our daughters and their families, more money than we ever dreamed of, no more privacy, media attention at all times and perhaps a sense of isolation.

I phoned the girls, not my daughters but our friends some of whom we had known since before we got married and we planned a dinner. These were important people and if I couldn't get out to them they could come to us. I wanted to know how they felt. Typically, dinner parties over the decades had involved plenty of booze, good food, the occasional joint and, as we have mentioned before, perhaps a toot. I think we were way past the cocaine and I didn't need the idea that there would be anything else there so I called them, invited them round and told them to be on their best behaviour. I forewarned them that there might be a line of godbothering pickets but to ignore them, not to engage them.

Joe cooked and cooked well. He made a beef wellington lined with mushrooms, Parma ham and a pancake to absorb the meat juices and make sure the pastry was crisp all round. His speciality pudding is a rhubarb crumble made with rhubarb marinated in dessert wine and a crumble topping of semolina, porridge oats, flour and brown sugar sprinkled over the top to keep a little bit of crunch.

I guess what you want to know is not so much the cooking but the advice of our friends. One of the girls' father was a vicar and her views on religion were that she felt there was a higher being and was unable to believe in the idea of a big bang. Joe piped up about the flying spaghetti monster and how that was just as valid. I told him to shut up, we had invited our friends over to hear what they had to say, not to repeat what we had said or done.

They all thought it was typically us. I was a bit confused because I had thought we were entirely normal but apparently, the nudist beach thing separates us and our longer- term travels. I think I was pleased to find out that we were not as normal, or can I say as boring as we thought.

Joe and the men talked about football, work and work intrigues and as the evening went on one of our friends, Gordon, asked what Joe does about not getting an erection on the beach. He was sure he'd get a stiffy. Joe explained that it simply doesn't happen, it isn't about perving at the women on the beach, unless you are sad, lonely and single, it is about the sense of freedom, of being unrestricted, of not lying around in wet shorts. "What about when you come out of the sea and your bits are all cold and shrivelled."

"If someone wants to look and judge then they can, but everyone goes in the sea at some time to take a leak and therefore everyone has to come out of the sea at some time. Why don't you try coming with us the next time we go on holiday? Give it a whirl."

"No chance, mate, You're weird."

We chatted, bantered, laughed, drank too much and it was good. At around twelve a posse of adult children arrived to take their parents home. Joe and I did talk about Steffan. Maybe it was the wine but we talked about "what ifs", "what might have beens" and got absolutely nowhere but to a place where we both felt better.

I had been prescribed Prozac by the doctor but it just made me feel slow and not functional. I stopped taking them and thought I should just try to get my act together as my mother would have suggested, in those good old bad old days before anti-depressants and talking therapies

With millions in the bank Joe and I both formally retired. We chose to abstain from workplace parties, carriage clocks and warm white wine and the unspoken words of disdain or agreement from colleagues. It was a little sad, to have spent so much time in one workplace and to not have made an event of finishing was a bit of a damp squib but we had the money, we had each other, we had the family.

Chapter 68

Johnny

It took about ten days to get the media strategy in place. The longer it was left the less relevant it became but we all agreed we need to finalise the situation. Most of the godbotherers had run out of stamina and had gone home. There were probably twenty or so diehards there on a rota basis, something about a summerhouse agreement and they were mainly reading books and magazines or swiping their smartphones to pass the time. I had watched old footage of the demonstrations, especially the nudists when it was enthusiastic, lively and seemed to mean something but now it was just sitting in a chair, getting uncomfortable because you don't want to let your religious leader down.

To make it relevant again we organised a street party of non-believers and supporters in Blossom Avenue to celebrate the fact that it had all died down. Of course, it hadn't all died down and we wanted to whip it up again.

We used social media to let it out that we were going to have a party, laid out trestle tables, put up some especially made bunting, baked cakes and made it look like a typical street party celebrating something royal or commemorative. I know it's a bit cynical but we were fighting fire with fire and maybe a little oil.

On the day, we had a bunch of caterers lay out the tables, chairs, food and plenty to drink in double quick time, like a flash mob with food before there could be a reaction. We needed footage of the party. And then, bang on cue, the religionists came down with their banners. It couldn't have worked better. The TV cameras were there and we had coverage on local and national media. Joe and Sandy were interviewed and they explained that it had been such a challenging time, unable to leave the house, unable to have friends and family over, the neighbours being put out that it was time to celebrate the end of the faith led protests. It was a cause for celebration.

The media had only one question. Did Mr and Mrs Quigley believe they had won? The well-rehearsed answer was that they hadn't set out to fight anyone, hadn't set out to have any kind of contest and while they had some respect (actually, very little but 'some' can have a very broad definition) for the views of the faithful they were pleased they had dispersed.

Buzz, as usual, called in with the numbers. Where they had been slowing down for the religious lot and growing steadily for the football, for the politicians, there was a real peak. Those who chose not to have religion in their lives, (see how I can temper my words to fit the message) bought about eight hundred thousand copies of the app from all over the world. Likers and followers swiftly saw the party trending on twitter and Joe and Sandy had another couple of million pounds in the bank.

Call me cynical, and many people do, but this was playing them like puppets on a string and it did occur to me that we could do this as long as the faithful had faith that they felt was being threatened. Joe said he didn't want to play that game and that he hoped once would be enough.

As we expected, there was a call from a producer on Newsnight. Would we like to come and talk about what we thought we were celebrating? There would be a representative of the Church of England and someone from the Muslim Council of Great Britain. As we had predicted. Joe, Sandy and I had rehearsed for hours the questions, the postures. They were both good, Simon had worked well with them and we were ready. After the party had subsided at around two in the afternoon, I sent them to bed. As surely as day follows night, The Today programme would call for a follow up interview and they would have to be up early in the morning.

We also had requests from the Sunday newspapers and we chose one to have exclusively. Web sites, such as the Huffington Post and other media outlets called for an interview, but we turned them down. We wanted control. We wanted to communicate with the politicians who were ramping up their output about disassociators. We had talked at length. If Joe and Sandy wanted to make millions they could antagonise the faith leaders, sell more copies of the app and have the merry-go-round continue. Our plan was to mollify, settle things down and lead the discussion. As they have said countless times before, they were not in it for the money.

They were the first item that evening. The skinny presenter in his skinny suit introduced Joe and Sandy, the Right Reverend somebody or other and a bearded man with no moustache (I never thought that was a good look, the chinstrap) and the discussion ensued.

This wasn't so much like a string puppet but more like a glove puppet. I could have had my hand up the faith leaders' arses and mouthed off for them. This is just a brief snippet.

The reverend. "You have upset so many people, people of faith with your antics, your sinful ways, your disregard for God."

Joe. "We didn't intend to upset people. This was a personal thing, for the two of us."

The reverend. "But what you did, you did in public. Many people came to your house to pray for you. They believe you had lost your way and were there only to help you, to save your souls."

Sandy. "But we don't believe in the concept of souls therefore we don't believe there was anything to save. And surely it is our own private decision."

The Imam. "Well you should have kept it private, shouldn't you? Not putting advertisements in the paper proclaiming your lack of faith and encouraging more people to do so."

Joe. "I think, if I recall, Mr Butt, the local Imam, came to my house and launched the demonstration, on his own, until joined by the Catholic priest, Father Corr, then I believe they were simply being competitive in trying to redeem us."

The Imam. "I can assure you, Mr Quigley, Mrs Quigley, there was no element of competition."

Joe. "On the contrary, we had to have what we called the Summerhouse Agreement to limit the numbers to minimise the disturbance to our neighbours."

The reverend. "All you had to do was repent and you would have been redeemed."

Sandy. "We were not looking for redemption. We were looking for peace and quiet. Your groups came down in their droves. As there was more of one group, the other groups called for reinforcements, if you like, more people to come and chant and sing and pray. My recollection is that it started because there were more Hare Krishna devotees than either Christians or Muslims."

The Imam. "But they are a joke, Mrs Quigley. They are not serious."

Joe, having fun. "Is there a scale of seriousness in religion, Imam?"

The Imam. "You are taking me out of context Mr Quigley. You are using words to distort my meaning."

And with Joe, simply saying "pot calling kettle black", the presenter rounded off the discussion and thanked everyone. Joe and Sandy, more used to the process, went off to the green room for a glass of wine and some sandwiches. The reverend and the Imam were discussing their performances as they left the studios and that was the last Joe and Sandy saw of them.

The next morning on The Today programme, Joe got the slot at around 7.45am and was interviewed by the ageing male journalist/presenter.

"Good morning, Mr Quigley".

"Morning." Apparently pleasant exchanges but then.

"Mr Quigley, tell me why it is you wanted to offend so many devout worshippers, what did you want to achieve, apart from the millions you have in the bank?"

"Mr Humphries (I had told Joe to use his name as he would use Joe's to buy time and make it more emphatic) I shall set out to provide answers to your questions, and not try to obfuscate or simply reinforce a point. We didn't set out to achieve anything, we had no objective. It was a personal move to distance ourselves from religion. We don't believe and we don't want it thrust upon us. You know this because we have said it time and time again".

"Come on, the money you have made from this project."

"Is that a question, Mr Humphries?"

"You know what I mean, you have made millions from this exercise."

"Ironically, every time we are questioned by you or your peers more people buy the app. If you could find it to be less confrontational, we will make less money. So please, let's play nicely."

"Play nicely? You have upset countless thousands of people with your antics, your private army, your nudist friends, your supporters all in the name of making money."

"Is that also a question, or an opinion?"

"What I'm trying to get across to you is that even the Prime Minister has found herself having to react to your silliness. The leak from Downing Street this morning is that the Lords Spiritual are going to be disestablished. What do you think of that?"

"it is entirely the decision of the Prime Minister. If that is what she feels she must do, then so be it. I'm not sure of her motivation?"

"I believe it is to influence you to persuade your fellow disassociators to come back into the United Kingdom."

"Disassociators?"

"Yes, Mr Quigley. There is a desire for you to lead you fellow disassociators back into the United Kingdom and this is being offered as an inducement."

"Why can't people listen. Mr Humphries? I have no influence, I have no desire for influence, your putting me on this programme is giving me a status I do not, one, covet, two, deserve, and three, welcome."

"But will you talk to the PM?"

"No! She has been told how I feel, and if she or her acolytes are listening to this then they need to stop and think of alternative ways to achieve their objectives rather than use me as a conduit."

Joe was emphatic. I had told him he needed to steer the interview in this direction and make this last point. This was the one that would finally take the pressure off.

"Thank you, Mr Quigley. And now for Thought for Day". How ironic.

Chapter 69

Joe

Phew, that was heavy going. Johnny had done an excellent job preparing us. Now I know why celebrities and business leaders pay them so much money. We had breakfast in the green room at the BBC and caught the train back to Welwyn Garden. I have to say, the unpredictability of the faithful is beyond belief. They were all there again, like they had never been away. Fresh placards, full thermos flasks, Tupperware containers full of sandwiches and apples and all set for a long-term show of faith.

The Catholic's were there with Corr, the Muslims with Butt, the C of E with Tudor. I can't remember the name of the Rabbi or the Sikh, I guess he was a Singh but it was like old mates come to haunt me. They all got on with each other perfectly well and for them it was a party atmosphere. For me it was a snub, Johnny was supposed to have strategized them out of the way. We both looked up and down the street, I don't know what for. It provided no answers.

We went into the house for coffee and to muse over the outcome. Johnny thought it was a rekindling of their effort to gain the redemption to beat all other redemptions. I had no real thought to offer bar the disappointment that they were there still; again. The third part of the media strategy was to have one of the Sunday broadsheets come to the house for a long interview with both Sandy and me. I was in two minds. The more we do the media the more the crowd outside but the more we sell of the app. We didn't need any more money.

"Johnny, I don't want to do the Sundays". I told him.

He was deflated but held his ground. "I do feel that one final in-depth interview will set the record straight. It gives you the opportunity to put your case fully in a controlled way."

"But I'm not sure what the outcome will be. We've spent the past few weeks trying to give our side of this bloody story and no matter what we say, they still believe we are attacking religion and they feel they have to come to its defence. I don't know how to make it any clearer that we are not attacking."

"Shit or bust Joe, Do the Sunday then knock it on the head."

So, this was a Thursday afternoon and the interviewer from the Sunday paper was due at three in the afternoon. The girls came over to help with a bit of hoovering and dusting; we didn't want to be judged on the quality of our domesticity. We abstained from a glass of wine and, at three, she turned up.

I'm not going to recount the entire conversation here because I was making the points you have read so many times already and for you they don't bear repetition. You know the arguments, unalloyed, uncorrupted by wishful interpretation, unblemished by pre-disposition. You know I have never set out to win an argument, never set out to offend. Sandy and I, as you know, just want to live our lives as we want.

What she did do that was different was ask about background. She looked at the pictures on the wall, a couple of Klimt prints and a Modigliani nude. The bookcases contain literature as well as easy reading. There is a copy of Roget's profanisaurus in the toilet with a couple of books on cats and renaissance painters. Nothing flash, nothing pretentious, nothing to judge us by.

By five it was all over and she left. She shook hands and said she understood what we were trying to do. I said I hoped that she did and looked forward to seeing the article in print. I held out no real hope. Her view might become tainted by the needs of an editor or a proprietor who wanted to put a spin on things.

At the risk of poking a stick into a wasp's nest we had tried Johnny's media strategy. So far it hadn't achieved the objective of silencing the crowd outside. We didn't know the effect on politicians from the Humphries interview but hoped they were shrewd enough to work out there wasn't much we could do, or indeed wanted to do to help them recover from the ignominy of losing half a million residents. It was up to them to pursue their own agendas. Shrewd or otherwise.

We now had even more money in the bank and I thought it was time we spent some of it. Not a substantial sum, in our current context, in our previous life it would be substantial but we had put up with enough crap in the last couple of months we deserved to blow some of the proceeds.

I asked Sandy where she would like to go, to go and spend some money. She ummd and ahhd for a good five seconds and blurted out "New York. I want to go to New York, I want to stay somewhere flash, I want to shop at Bloomingdales, I want to go to MOMA, I want to do the tourist thing, up the statue of Liberty, up the Empire State Building I want to go on the Staten Island Ferry, all those naff things people do. I want to be naff."

"You've thought about this haven't you?"

"I haven't finished. I want to go to Madison Square Garden, I want to go to the Metropolitan Opera House."

"How long are we going for?"

"Let's decide. Have a look and let's see what's on, what we can see, what we can do."

She told me she loved me for having had the idea. I asked her how she was feeling. Was she better with the Prozac and she told me she had stopped taking them after a couple for days because she felt dopey. I hadn't seen her happy for some time and this cheered me. I didn't think she was faking it because I was buoyant at the prospect off a trip. Straight upstairs, onto the internet, what can we see?

I booked flights, I booked the Waldorf Astoria because I had heard it was flash and we were due to go in two days. Impromptu spontaneity you could call it. Quite unlike us and it was an expensive throwback to our unsuccessful visit to the Cotswolds.

Chapter 70

Sandy

We left on the Saturday before the Sunday interview was published. We decided not to wait for it, we could always read it online and we paid for the access to the newspaper just in case it was something we wanted to do. The airline provided a limousine to the airport; first class is a wonderful experience and we had champagne in the lounge once we had gone through passport control. On the flight, we had these bed things and televisions and unlimited champagne and we both conked out and slept until we landed.

Groggily, we joined the queue at passport control and edged our way to the front. We went together to the booth and the customs official looked at us long and hard and appeared to check and re-check our passports and our faces. He said nothing but two burly men in uniforms approached us, were given our passports and asked us to accompany then. "What's the issue?" I asked. There was no reply as they walked either side of us and steered us to a windowless room away from the main concourse.

"Please take a seat and make yourselves comfortable, sir, madam".

There was a desk, four upright chairs, a window disguised as a mirror, you see them on every spy movie, and a blinking red light on a half spherical closed-circuit camera, the kind we had at work in the reception area. The room was a sterile, functional holding unit. Joe and I sat on a chair on either side of the table and waited. And waited. And waited. On many occasions, I tried the door to find it locked. I don't know why I tried it more than once, I think it was out of curiosity, then frustration and then anger. More puzzling was the fact that our phones were not working, not even for the emergency call you are supposed to be able to make.

I asked Joe what time it had been when we landed and got as far into customs as we did. He said it had been nearly four hours. That was four hours when we should have been luxuriating in a bath for two, drinking more champagne, thinking about what we were going to have for dinner and getting dressed to go out. I had bought several new outfits and was waiting to try them and I'm sure all the women out there reading this will understand exactly what I mean.

There was a rattling sound of a key in the door, I hadn't heard one when we entered which was curious and a man in a black suit and tie asked if we would like something to drink. "What on earth are we doing here?" I asked, I demanded.

The man looked blank and said "I'm not sure I know, Maam. I was simply just asked to organise a hot drink for each of you. Now what would you like"?

"I'd like to be out of here and enjoying my stay in your supposed big apple."

"I'm afraid I don't know nothing about why they are detaining you, Sir, Maam."

"Well can you please go and find someone who does know. I don't think we'll be here long enough anyway to enjoy your American hospitality". Joe joined in.

"That'll be fine. We'll get back to you." He left and this time I heard the door being locked.

I needed a pee so I banged on the door. The young man in the suit came back and told me he would let someone know. I went all clichéd. "I am a British citizen. We have applied on the Visa Waiver Programme and were never told that we could not come. We have not been told why we are being held up. I have not threatened a bomb. I have not said we engaged in acts of terrorism".

I tried to cover all the reasons why we might be being held up, but the man's only response was to say, "I'm afraid, Maam, that I do not have the seniority to answer your questions. I am simply doing my best to make sure you are both comfortable and would ask you to respect me trying to do my job under the duress you are creating".

In the style often seen in American movies, I put the middle digit of my right hand towards his face and said, "Respect this dumbass". I can't remember where I had seen or heard that but it made me feel much better. I didn't get to go for a pee and Joe said he thought it hadn't been the wisest move I had ever made. I apologised, he opened his arms for a hug and I gratefully fell into them. Joe said he could guess why we were being held and he thought that they were taking advantage of any security scare. I said we were no threat to security and we had spent thousands in preparation for the trip.

Chapter 71

Officer Knudsen

I thank the divine Lord that he presented me with the sinners Mr and Mrs Quigley. They came up to my booth and I crossed myself raising my eyes towards the heavens before I handled their passports. They had the gall to look me in the face and smile as they approached as if a smile from these devil-struck individuals was going to make any mark on me. No, Sir, I am emboldened by the Lord our God and would not, could not waiver in my faith because these dark individuals had tried to enter my heart.

I praise the Lord that they were taken to a holding room where they would be given every opportunity to think about their sins and to consider the effect they intended to have on my fellow God-fearing countrymen. Do they not know that we sing "God bless America" and we are rewarded with his blessing? Do they not know that when we swear the oath of allegiance we finish it with the words "So help me God"? We are a God-fearing country and these people, these sorry, sorry individuals have taken it upon themselves to corrupt the minds of our children and our citizens with their hostility to our Lord.

Coincidentally, our Pastor took it upon himself last Sunday in chapel to remind us of the work of these sinners. How they had denied the Lord our God, how they had nearly killed worshippers gathered outside their house in the United Kingdom of England when they sped off in their automobile, how their private army had attacked lovers of God as they prayed for the souls of Mr and Mrs Quigley. How they had encouraged millions of people throughout the world to renounce God. I understand that renouncing all other faiths in favour of our Lord God would be a good thing, but their actions were against all faiths.

Then we were given news by Homeland Security that they intended to come and visit our country so I was on the lookout. I was watchful. I was on guard. I was rewarded.

I sent an SMS to my Pastor and said that I had been blessed with the opportunity to have them re-think their ill-done deeds and he replied that I was doing God's work and how I would be blessed and, more importantly, how he would pray for me and mention my actions in his sermon for the following week. My heart was full of joy.

I sent a further SMS to my wife and she replied saying that she would hasten her way to the airport with fellow Congregationalists to pray for me as my soul might be tainted, might become prey to the wickedness of the Quigleys. I was heartened by her love and messaged her again to tell her so and that I would meet her once my shift had finished.

Little did I know that by the time I had finished my shift, with no apparent feeling that my soul had been touched by my proximity to the sinners, that I went outside to see hundreds of Christians being confronted by hippies and other miscreants debating the Quigleys. I took off my uniform, found my wife, checked that she was okay and took a banner and waved if, forcibly in the direction of those disbelievers who dared to question us.

You would have been proud of us. We stood firm, we stood tall, we sang beautifully the words of "*Amazing Grace, how sweet the sound that saved a wretch like me. We once was lost and now we're found, once blind but now I see.*" How appropriate those words are, especially as they were sung by some hippie woman in the sixties. There are not that many people who can sing the whole six verses in their entirety but we were practised and polished. We turned those sweet words back on those sinners with a holy vengeance.

I must tell you at this juncture that I did not believe myself to be a wretch. I had never been miserable or unhappy. My upbringing by my devoted, devout parents had been blissful. We had gone to church every Sunday and Wednesday and I took bible class on Tuesdays and Thursday all the way though my teenage years. I had never kissed a girl and I had never seen fit to sow my seed on barren ground, unlike many of my classmates.

I met my wife at bible camp one Summer and we did no more than hold hands. I swear to you I did not even imagine what delights might rest under her pullover for fear that I might disgrace myself in her eyes or the eyes of the Lord. As time went by, we were able to see each other without the need for a chaperone and when we first did kiss, the day I proposed, it was as though the Lord had entered my heart and kick started my adult life.

This twitter app my wife uses was bipping away and hundreds of people gathered at the airport. We received messages the of support from Seventh Day Adventists, Southern Baptists, Plymouth Brethren, Anabaptists, even the Charismatic movement sent video footage of themselves speaking in tongues in worship of our Lord. Now I admit I think that is a bit too far out there, wacky you might say, but the support filled out hearts with joy. I was conflicted by the attendance of both Jehovah's Witnesses and the Mormons. They are not true Christians but are known as cults. They twist and distort the bible to their own ends. I guess I will eventually have to accept their support with positivity and good grace.

      Sinners also came in their droves and the competing crowd hustled and bustled all the while, while TV crews appeared as did the police who tried to break up our peaceful gathering. Our Pastor had warned us about the faithful gathered outside the Quigleys house in the UK of E, how the TV crews gathered and filmed and interviewed. We were ready and when I saw a microphone thrust under my chin, I proclaimed as loudly as I could. "I am the follower of the Lord who was blessed with the chance to help the Quigley sinners see the error of their ways. My name is Bill Knudsen and I am proud to be a Christian, proud to be an American and proud to keep our borders safe". And do you know what happened. Later that evening when we got home, there I was, on national TV, my phone didn't stop ringing. I nearly committed the sin of hubris my heart was so full.

      Neither my wife or I drink alcohol, tea or coffee but we have a malt drink before we go to bed. We pray at the bedside and we go out like lights. Snap, just like that. In the morning, the phone didn't stop ringing. It was so much I had to put it on to the answering service. I'm sorry, friends, but we just could not take all your calls even though you were wishing us well. I had my breakfast with a glass of milk and went to work as usual, but with a spring in my step and when I took my place at my booth, I saw the Quigley sinners being taken to the departure lounge for a flight back to the UK of E as you call it. My work was truly complete and we were once again safe.

Chapter 72

Joe

Eighteen hours we were held in that bloody room. As time went on they bought in what they called cots, we would call them camp beds and allowed us to go to the toilet and brush our teeth. It was an absolute disgrace. While we couldn't use the phones as phones we could use them to video the conditions. We shot footage of each other knowing we would upload it as soon as we could. We were going to take the fight to them.

Apparently, we were on a watch list and considered dangerous. Why they couldn't have done this when we applied for the visa and saved us all this time and money and aggravation, I don't know.

During the night, we had a visit from a be-suited embassy official called Matthew, irony of ironies, who said the embassy had been told about our impending arrival in New York. The British embassy in Paris had sent over their file about the bombing in Paris and this informed the New York embassy who collaborated with the US Immigration service to have us denounced as dangerous. Matthew from the Embassy reminded us that we had seceded and were not wholly entitled to representation but the embassy seniors had decided to try to help. What help? There was nothing.

The Americans decided that our drug use, occasional smoking and the fact that we had demonstrated outside their embassy when we were young made us undesirable. Add to that the fact that we had been bombed and they just did not want us on their soil. We learned later that the assorted godbotherers of the United States claimed a victory was won in our not being able to get in.

I repeat, why they couldn't have done this before we left home, when we applied for the visa waiver, I do not know. You may have noticed, earlier in this recounting of events that I am normally quite relaxed and easy-going. It is Sandy who does the swearing in our house but I was fucking furious. All that money wasted, no refunds coming our way for the hotels booked or tickets reserved. Sandy was the calmer of the two of us by some measure. I don't know how she did it, but she said later that one of us had to be thoughtful and she was happy to see me let off steam and get angry, as long as I didn't burst a blood vessel, have a heart attack or stroke in the process.

We were effectively frog marched from this holding room along corridors and onto the plane. We were given economy class seats because our reservations were on a different flight and there were no first-class seats available. I'm ashamed to say we rather cowered on the plane. All that had happened, especially with the uniformed staff escorting us to our seats and making a show of our not being allowed into the US was a bit difficult. I think I now understand how a bearded Muslim or a turban wearing Sikh might feel with judgemental Christians judging whether he has a bomb or not to blow the plane out of the sky. We were made to feel like terrorists. We kept our heads down, reading, snoozing, just wanting to be home.

At the airport on arrival we were greeted by a demonstration populated by more Christians, Muslims, Sikhs, Hare Krishnas, Buddhist monks all with their bloody placards and across the road a show of supports from fellow atheists and humanists, all with their own placards. The media were there in droves with reporters reporting and trying to get a few profound words out of us. We, however, were just fed up with the attention. We were bored of the same old toing and froing, the same old arguments. Again, I will repeat, we had asked for none of this. We hadn't set out to achieve anything like this.

There was no limousine to take us home so we jumped in a taxi and even he couldn't help himself. "You set off quite a shit storm over there, didn't you? It was on the telly and everything." We didn't say a word. Anything we might have said might have been given to the media so we decided to stay silent. "So, how much moolah have you made out of all this? You must be loaded, eh?" Ongoing silence from Sandy and I. "Come on, you must have something to say, think of all the children who are being brought up with morals to believe in God and you are destroying all that effort". It was hard ignoring him; he just wouldn't shut up. "What about them poor old ladies you nearly killed. Haven't you got anything to say, to apologise?" Trust us to land ourselves a godbotherer for a driver.

"Stop the cab. Now." Sandy had had enough.

"I can't stop on the hard shoulder. It's against the law."

"I don't give a fuck what you can and can't do. Stop the cab." He did. We got out of the taxi, the driver unloaded our bags and we were stranded on the M25 and it began to rain. A traffic officer pulled up about ten minutes later and asked what we were doing on the hard shoulder, where was our car, had we called the AA? We explained the circumstances and, with unexpected charity, he said he could take us to the next junction, for our safety. Thanks.

We were offloaded again. I called Daisy who said she would come and collect us. We stood, in the rain, getting soaked for half an hour and then she arrived. I felt hollowed out. Sandy burst into tears' shivering with cold and shaking with anger. Daisy turned up the heating in her car and another half an hour later we were home. To something of a surprise, apart from Bec, waiting with tea in the kitchen, there were just a few people there.

The place was littered with apple cores, banana skins, tissues, paper cups, sandwich wrappers, takeaway cartons, abandoned chairs and umbrellas, a couple of gloves and a soaked scarf in the gutter and discarded placards looking every bit as sorry for themselves as they should. I called the Council hotline and said they should get someone round to clear up before there was an infestation of rats. The jobsworth answering the phone replied that if we wanted it cleared up we should do it ourselves. I told him to fuck off, I'm getting angry with these people, and we all spent an hour litter picking outside. I filmed a part of it and posted it to YouTube. I was getting good at this.

Bec told us that there morning current affairs programmes had been full of our story. There had been a couple of Bishops, an

Imam and a Rabbi on television all saying they now understood what had happened. Time to turn the other cheek, one of them had said. I was puzzled. Did they now realise they were responsible for the furore? Did they now realise that the escalation of the problem was down to their need to compete for a redemption that was never going to come?

Buzz rang. He'd seen our arrival at the airport. "I am so sorry, mate. It's all my fault. If I hadn't go so pissed that day at the pub and uploaded the footage, none of this shit would have happened".

I wanted to agree with him. I wanted him to feel guilty, to feel responsible, to feel as bad as we did but he interrupted my train of thought. "The website crashed last night with orders for the app. I got it back up again, we had to get new servers, but we had sold over thirty-three million copies in the thirty-six hours you have ben away. Ninety per cent of them in the good old US of A. We are fucking awash with money and I don't know what to do with it".

I guess there is a philosophical argument about how much money is too much money. I have never been one for deep thought, not like a Wittgenstein or Sartre, pretty shallow is my watermark but how hard should one work for the money one earns. We had done very little actual work. There must be a difference between the person in the factory standing there all day, pushing a button on a machine having to work out what he is going to have to go without in order to stretch his wages, all those Polish girls who come and clean our houses for a pittance and people like Bill Gates and that Facebook man who have made millions and seem driven to want more. We, Sandy, me and Buzz had all this money in a matter of six weeks or so. It was life changing and I had no answers. I wasn't even asking questions. Just thoughts rambling about in my head.

Did those religious leaders finally get the point that the more they objected to me and Sandy, the more they all shouted and argued, the more money we made. No separation of God and Mammon, except Mammon was on our side. Perhaps they had. Perhaps it was the money motive that made them shut down the protests outside our house. At last.

As the rest of the world was unable to accommodate us, we booked a cottage in the middle of nowhere for a month to go away, do nothing but try to figure out what we should do with the rest of our lives. Off-grid was what Daisy called it. No mobile phone, no internet, a generator and log burners. The only people who knew where we were, were Daisy and Bec and we thought we had better let Charlie, you know, the Solicitor know, in case something happened.

Chapter 73

Imam Butt

That Sunday morning, I was attending the peaceful gathering outside Mr and Mrs Quigley's house with my fellow theologians, Mr Corr and Mr Tudor. There was something of a hoo-ha going on, we were all very animated by the news we were getting from America about how they had upset so many millions of people as they tried to enter the country. We thought we should join with our brothers across the ocean and make a further effort to convince Mr and Mrs Quigley of the error of their ways.

Mr Tudor approached me when I was at prayer with my congregation and had the bad grace to interrupt me. He said he had received a message from his Bishop that while he had done very well in organising the multi-faith protest, it was time to go home and get on with their lives.

I argued for a moment that it wasn't a multi-faith protest, it was a protest I had started and a bandwagon on to which he had jumped along with the Catholic and all the others. He said it was no longer a time for arguing between the faith groups and arguing with the non-believers. I wasn't sure that it was his decision to make but he told me the Archbishop of Canterbury, no less, had called his Bishop in St Albans who in turn had called him and explained that there was a school of thought that thought the protest was self-defeating.

Father Corr approached the two of us with a very solemn look on his face. "Do you know what?"

"What?" We replied in unison.

"I've just had a call from the Archbishop of Westminster, would you believe and he is asking me to ask my fellow Christians to cease the protest telling me it causes more harm than good. The church has calculated that the Quigleys have made many tens of millions of pounds and that each time we, or they, are on the television or that Facebook, they make more money."

"Then perhaps it is fine for you Christians to give up and go home, defeated. Buy my efforts shall not diminish." And then my wife, who recently had come to understand why we were protesting as we were, came down the street. I wish she wouldn't call me an old fool in front of the others but she did. I had left my phone at home and missed a call from the leader of the Muslim Council of Britain. Would I call him immediately?

You can guess the conversation. Apparently on the television that morning there had been a discussion about the Quigleys and the events surrounding them sparked by an interview they had given to one of the Sunday papers. I learned later than the politicians had got in on the act during the programme and the Home Secretary had made a hasty appearance shortly after the theological debate and almost instructed the attendees to call their respective leaders in the country to get the demonstrators to stop and go home. It seemed, and it is obvious now, that the more they were on television, the more support they got. I recall Mrs Thatcher in the 1980's calling it the "oxygen of publicity". The more we protested the harder we made it for ourselves to succeed.

Tudor, Corr and I talked with our followers and persuaded them to go home, have a warm drink and get back to their daily lives. I think many of the Christians were relieved. They packed up so quickly, scuttling around with their chairs and thermos flasks they couldn't get away quickly enough. Of course, many of my fellow Muslims wanted to stay and fight the good fight and it took a good ten minutes to bring them round to the Council's way of thinking. There would be other ways to bring them to Allah in the future.

Chapter 74

The Prime Minster

I'm not going to stop for long. You will appreciate that my job is a very busy one what with Europe and everything else, Grammar schools etcetera. But you deserve an explanation. We had to come to a decision about these disassociators. How I hate the word. We had another meeting on the Saturday night after the Sunday newspapers had published on the net and came to the conclusion that this was not a fight we were going to win. How can you fight without an opponent? We were so used to fighting amongst ourselves, to fighting the opposition, to fighting the Europeans that we hadn't made the philosophical jump that we needed to make to, shall we say, overcome, the Quigleys and their actions.

We were in danger of destabilising the country ourselves and losing our parliamentary majority so, with the help of Government lawyers we figured out a quick settlement. Those who had seceded, I shan't call them disassociators again, would be allowed to dis… sorry secede and we would accept their decision. In a show of magnanimity, we decided we would let them have the vote in all the elections they could previously have voted in. It was their choice as to whether they chose to accept it. We were back on the front foot so to speak. Majority assured, all things being equal.

They could have their silly little protests. We were not going to bother bothering with them. We would ignore them, not make a fuss and that way it would all go away. We called the production team for the next day's morning current affairs show and offered up the Home Secretary to make the announcement. I wasn't going to do it. Not my bag. We were offered a five-minute slot on an otherwise busy programme and we briefed the Home Secretary on what she was to say. We also called the offices of the three religious groups that had been making the most fuss but all we got was the voicemail. Useless people, don't they do twenty-four seven like the rest of us?

Chapter 75

Sandy

Like Joe, I was taken aback by the absence of noise outside our house. Their leaving might have been seen as a victory but we didn't feel victorious. That episode with the taxi driver and the traffic officer just cemented in our minds how much we had appeared to upset people. We were recognisable, our faces had been all over the news and the papers and social media. Quigley is not a common name and we were now branded, and I am sorry if there are other Quigleys out there who have been mistaken for us

What was especially disconcerting was the demonstration outside the airport, having been noisy and coming home to silence and litter, just less than an hour later. How fickle people can be. Either that or they were looking for permission to stop the protest and get home to their families or back to work, either way, somewhere warm and dry. But, mustn't grumble. All quiet on the hedge row front. Johnny's strategy had finally worked. I called him to thank him.

We packed our bags for the sojourn in the country and off we drove. It was going to be a leap into the unknown with just Bec and Daisy with the address able to contact us if needed. The sat nav took us to the edge of a wood, with the cottage standing in mature gardens, surrounded by a more impressive hedge than ours in Blossom Avenue. The owners had left a bag of groceries but it would do only for a day or two. We decided to head out to the shops to stock up for at least a couple of weeks hoping not to be recognised, hoping not to be followed. And we were lucky.

The shops didn't have a great selection of the kind of food Joe likes to cook but it didn't matter. We had food, we had some wine, a bottle of single malt, some gin and mixers. We were all set up.

We also enjoyed an Indian Summer. Although it was September there were a few sunny days and in the isolation, we got undressed and sunbathed naked. You need to be reassured that we checked for paparazzi, reporters and nosey neighbours. There were no cars down the lane and you hear about these drone things being flown over peoples' gardens. We made sure there were none of those around as best we could. We even had some al fresco sex. Naughty or what?

Most of the time and especially in the evenings, it was chilly outside and we spent hours huddled over books and magazines on the sofas in front of a fire. It was bliss. Joe even grew a beard. I don't know if it was recherché of temps perdu. When he was a teenager he had some bum fluff but this time it suited him. He looked good, the sun had coloured his cheeks and the top of his head and the lines and bags that had grown under his eyes gently receded.

We used the boots and sticks we had bought in the Cotswolds and walked through the woods. We found a quiet pub that did nice enough food and we weren't recognised as we enjoyed a pint or two of some locally brewed beers, Cobblers Knob or some such. The seismic change from all that had gone before to this bucolic easiness was lovely. I could get used to it except we both know that boredom would come crashing down on us. Joe had had all these thoughts about race horses, camper vans and so on but they were not realistic. This, he recognised, thankfully.

For a couple that have been together as long as we have, we think we have done pretty well. We were able to spend a month in the country without boring each other, not saying too much or too little, a bit of walking, some cooking, some sitting, some reading and just simple pleasures. We didn't miss the television, we did take the last series of the West Wing with us, but didn't miss the news or phones or the internet; we were happily cut off from the outside world. I know that in a lot of books, the reader might be led to believe something drastic was about to come along and spoil this contentedness, but the month went by without incident.

We enjoyed the garden with late flowering roses and clematis, the woods were beautiful with the leaves changing colour. The cottage was gorgeous, we had no visitors and no need to contact the girls. You know that cosy feeling of warm pullovers, scarves, hats, chunky socks, red wine, beer, shepherd's pie, you know it as well as we do. We had it. I can't tell you how good it was.

There was one idea we chatted about which had legs. We talked a while and questioned it to make sure it had a chance of working. We needed to talk about where we were going to live, how we were going to live, how we were going to be fulfilled and active.

We eventually returned home to get on with life. We couldn't ignore it indefinitely. Blossom Avenue was populated only by the people that live there and a few supermarket delivery vans. It was clean and tidy as it should be in that part of Welwyn Garden City. Back to some semblance of normality except for the fact that we had two hundred or so million pounds in the bank as did Buzz, although he must have had expenses. It was like some huge lottery win, doubled, even trebled.

Chapter 76

Buzz

I was happy that Joe and Sandy had got away for the month. I felt so guilty about all the shit they had put up with. The Paris thing was bad enough but for the septics to do what they did, that was shitty too. They are a pleasant, unremarkable couple except for the size of their bank balance and that too, is my fault. Does one balance the other out? I don't know but I guess in time when the pain of the last few months has died down then the bank balance might be considered an upside.

While they were away we were still getting money for the app. The process had been automated, we had upped the levels of security because we had heard fundamentalist Christian hackers were trying to get in to both us and our users. Around a third of our customers were buying the upgrade with the on/off switch and our income stream from YouTube was looking good but dying down as the volume of new sales declined.

I was loaded. I had more money than sense but no time to blow it. I was working twenty hours a day, seven days a week organising staffing, fulfilment, keeping the web site going, keeping out the hackers, developing a firewall that was impenetrable. I could have done with a holiday, a month in the country, any country to chill and drink beer, smoke a joint. Colorado perhaps.

At the peak, I had twenty or so kids in here developing systems, writing code, managing payments and got my friend Drew in to develop the system that prevented anyone from siphoning off the funds that were pouring in. I paid him a small percentage but a big enough sum to motivate him to do the right thing.

But I couldn't believe the money, Apparently, we were the fastest selling app of the last three years, worldwide. Us, me, me. I developed it and now I was minted. That's fair, but what to do with it. It doesn't seem right to be sitting on a pile of dollar like this and not know what to do with it. I haven't had time to think. A house, a car, a boat, a razor, some new clothes, a cleaner, a girlfriend. That would be nice, rewarding, I could spoil someone rotten but not a gold digger. Fuck, that really does create a problem. Who's going to go out with me, long term, for the right reasons, for me, for my intellect, good looks, charm, cleanliness and not for my money. I'd have to start out on a lie with someone, say I'm okay for money, go to a decent restaurant, but not be a meal ticket for some lazy money grabber wanting all the flash stuff and put no effort into it and then throw me away like some old smelly banana skin.

I'm going to be well out of my comfort zone if I have to change who I am to suit my new-found wealth. I don't want the flash gaff, the flash motor, the flash clothes; it isn't me.

Joe called and said I should come out to Welwyn Green City; have lunch with him and Sandy. We hadn't seen much of each other yet we had so much in common. It was a good idea. A couple of days later, I was on the train and got collected at the station by Joe and Sandy in their Honda. Nothing new and flash for them either. I liked Joe's beard. It suited him. I asked him if he thought it was a disguise and he couldn't quite answer yes or no. No, he thought, he'd grown it because he was lazy at the cottage.

We drove out to a village outside town to a pub he knew did a decent lunch. As we walked in, people stopped eating and sneaked peeks at Joe and Sandy followed by knowing whispers. Joe said, out loud, "it appears the beard as disguise isn't working" to which an old lady replied.

"After what you have done there will be no escaping the wrath of the Lord".

"I thought your lot had reached an easy peace with what has happened. You know, the more you fight it the more you lose"

"There will never be an easy peace for you, young man." She must have been in her eighties if she was a day.

Joe called the waitress over and asked if we could be put at a table well out of earshot of the old crone, and that was the word he used, and she heard it. "Old crone, you call me. At least I have lived a life of virtue."

"Hate and intolerance" helped Sandy. "Come on, Joe, Buzz, let's go and sit over here and not wind up the old… lady".

We talked about their time in New York and the cottage and the fact that I needed a holiday. They offered the cottage but I said that brought into the light other thing I needed; a good woman.

They like a drink and I like a drink and after bottle two we decided that a taxi was the better idea for getting back. No point in bringing further grief down on us. Joe said that he and Sandy were working on an idea and would I like to be part of it?

Chapter 77

Charlie, the Solicitor

Good afternoon. Remember me. I was the one who said that no one would notice, no one would care. And here we are. Joe and Sandy have achieved their own nation state and helped five hundred thousand people in the UK do the same thing as well as countless thousands or even millions around the world. I think I should have been paid a licence fee each time someone seceded from their given country but I didn't raise it as an issue.

We met and Sandy looked great. Joe had a new beard which I think made him look a little scruffy. I did ask him if he would like to join the Rotarians but he had other ideas, he said and that is what they wanted to talk about. It seems they had amassed a huge amount of money from this unlikely venture and wanted to do something with it. I was all too glad to help. To be honest, the younger chaps and chappesses in the legal business were quicker than me at conveyancing, more understanding of divorce laws and family courts and my work was not as abundant as it had been.

To do what they asked me to do I would have to bring in some expertise and that would cost them, I told them. It was not a problem for them and I realised this was something they were going to take seriously, which was good. While Sandy had always been unshakeable I still had doubts about Joe. I don't know why, not jealousy or anything, of course.

Once the idea was established, they asked me if I wanted to be a part of it. Because it was based on atheist principles, I wasn't sure. I can't let go of the idea that there is a higher something, something that might have formed us and I know there is no basis either in science or theology for it, but it makes me feel secure. I had to promise not to make the Rotarians any part of it even though there were shared values. Joe said he felt the Rotary Club was just networking for middle-class men at golf clubs and I must admit it, it was hard to deny. Sandy simply had no interest in golf or the Rotarians, bunch of overgrown school boys, she described it. Masons without connections.

Part two

Twelve months later

Chapter 1

Joe

As Johnny told us, the media intensity died down. As it did, so did the attention being paid to us. The Christians and Muslims, because they were the die-hards, finally left the camp they had made outside the house. A team from the local council came along and finally cleared up the mess after we had done the lion's share. One might have thought that the godbotherers outside the house might have been inclined to tidy up, but they left chairs, blankets, food wrappers, empty soft drinks bottles, a camping gas and kettle and so many crisp and chocolate wrappers. It was a disgrace really, but with the new peace and quiet, I wasn't going to make a point.

The TV vans had left shortly after we had come back from the states. We were no longer the story. A hurricane up the east coast of the United States had caused, forgive me, a storm, that diverted attention from us. Curiously, we didn't see a vicar or pastor on the TV this time. Had we made a difference? A drone attack on a wedding in Yemen, killing 200 Muslims gained no attention on the

TV that we saw. We were seeing less and less of the Sheringham and Solskaer goals, Rafa Nadal's chest or indeed, Jamie Lee-Curtis. There were always celebrities and sports stars seeking attention and all this was now more important that Sandy or I. Good thing.

There were still nods of acknowledgement every time I went to Waitrose. We were stopped and our hands shaken every time we went to a pub or restaurant in and around town but that too, died down over time. Even Wayne Rooney must be able to go shopping these days without clamour from the press. We had time on our hands and, to be brutally honest, we were getting bored. We had scores of millions of pounds in the bank but little idea what to do with it.

I think lottery winners go on a spending spree; house, cars, holidays because that is why they do the lottery. We all used to talk about what we would do if we won and we all had fantasies but for some reason, and I can't quite put my finger on it, we had no motivation to buy tangible stuff with the money we had. We were comfortable in the house, our cars were newish, we had taken decent holidays. I didn't want a Rolex watch. I didn't want a jet ski, I didn't want a Porsche. I am not a man of taste as evidenced by the clothes I had to change out of when Simon first met us.

I didn't read *GQ* or *Esquire* to get hints and tips on how to dress and what to buy and what to do and places to go to be seen. We felt hemmed in in the house, perhaps too introverted to go out and run the risk of being feted, arms around the shoulder, high five or hand shake. I cooked a bit, looking up recipes for inspiration on the internet. We shopped on the internet to save going out and the delivery drivers soon became on nodding terms. I had to watch out for the one who did the locust thing with us. That was bad at the time and we still find the bloody things from time to time, under the sofa, in a drawer and I stepped on one I found in my slippers. It wasn't nice.

We did keep in touch with Johnny and we still had Nick, the security guard at the hedge. We didn't want to let up on security, we didn't want to become an easy target. The guys who had mingled with the crowd had gone; there was no longer a crowd.

Buzz came over frequently and gave us the numbers and had a chat. We were pleased that he had found himself a girlfriend but I guess you want to know how much money we had made. It seemed important to the papers and you are the people that buy the papers. We had over two hundred million in the bank, as did Buzz. Like us, he had no idea what to do with the money. He had taken driving lessons and was now on his sixty-fourth, having failed the driving test three times. I'm sure he will tell you about that in due course.

The girls were carrying on with their lives. It was pleasing. They could have asked for some of the proceeds of our activities but never did. I think either Sandy or I told you before that they were both fairly successful in their own rights as were their husbands. The money stayed in the bank, not doing anything.

Of course, the bankers and advisors who called us with their banking skills and their advice were offering all kinds of opportunities to further enrich ourselves and most probably themselves but we were not in it for that. These greedy suits were on the phone day in day out and seemed to creep out of the woodwork with earnestness and faith in their own ability to help us make more money. It's all understandable. They care more for the idea of money and wealth than we do, but we are the people with the big bank balances.

Chapter 2

Buzz

Joe has told you about my girlfriend, hasn't he? She is fantastic. She knew Johnny and he introduced her shortly after the first time we met. It was a little like the time when Johnny and I went out for a beer in an effort to kinda, vet him before introducing him to the Quigleys. He told me he knew this girl, Sally, that she was great, he said, that she was pretty, lively, not interested in money, had quite liberal views about politics and wasn't religious, as far as he knew.

We went out in a group made up of Johnny's friends and me, and he introduced us. I was daunted, I have to tell you, she was bright, sparky, quick witted and I wondered if she would ever want to go out with me, a geek who spent too much time playing games and writing code. We had the "what do you do?" conversation and I managed not to put her off with tales of IT daring do. She is a nurse, with a specialism in intensive care, which makes her a good person, in my book, I couldn't do that job not with the blood and pain.

We shared a taste in music; we had both been to the Springsteen concerts at Wembley and been equally impressed with the ageing Bruce's ability to play rock and roll at that tempo for three hours. We didn't stop chatting, she was brushing her hair back behind her ears. I found myself sitting opposite her in the same position, if you get what I mean. I invited her back to my place after we had been out together on our own and she wasn't put off by my "student" look. We smoked some of my better weed and went to bed.

I told her about Joe and Sandy and she looked at me as if I was a celebrity. I had to put her right and persuade her that I didn't need any spotlights shining on me. I did feel I might have trusted her too much at the beginning, but you know how it is with secrets. Once you have one you can't help telling people. Luckily, and I thank Johnny for this, the secret stayed secret and she didn't ever blurt it out and she didn't ever ask for money. I paid for dinners and stuff but that was just me being old fashioned, old school. For a couple of weeks, I was wary that she might out me to the press if we had an argument. We didn't argue because we didn't need to and the idea of outing me as the richest non-entity in the country never arose.

I've had three driving tests. I just can't get the hang of this shit. I used to be very good on Super Mario Cart and Rally Cross in the arcades, but I couldn't get a handle on the other people on the road and the need for spatial awareness. (I kept hitting the kerbs). I took a course in a week in Devon, where there are no people or cars but still blew it. Fuck it, who needs a car when you live in London anyway?

As you would expect, traffic to the site died down. Anyone who wanted the app already had one and there were others on the market. The big Internet companies, you know who they are, had 'emulated' our software and integrated it into their own social media products and developed it so you could stop images of religious faith, or footballers, or politicians, getting on to any of your devices. It must have cost them a lot of money to do such a big job, sums of money, that even I didn't have. But then I had had my adventure, made a load of money and was content.

    I introduced Joe and Sandy to Sally. They were a bit like my mum and dad and I wanted them to meet. I think, I suppose I wanted approval from them, letting her closer to the money we made. We could all have been dead flash and gone to wherever was fashionable in London at the time and rocked up in a rented Roller or even bought one just for the sake of it and been grand fromages but it wasn't like that. We went out to The Plume of Feathers, where we had gone that first time we met and drank Aspells, in a kind of replication after the event. We all got pissed again. Sally loved the Quigleys who loved her in return. Sandy appeared happy and healthy and said she was content. We laughed at the antics Joe and Sandy had endured, the protestations, especially after the naturists had done the "Joe and Sandy's nudey army" thing. This was when Sally told me she too, was into naturism and we should try it some time, perhaps on holiday. I gulped, metaphorically and literally on a mouthful of Aspells.

    But I did. We went to a place in the South of France, a naturist resort and I walked around and lay on the beach and swam in the sea stark bollock naked and it was good; liberating as they all say and I didn't get a stiffy at all, in public. In private, man, Sally was fun.

Chapter 3

Sandy

We had travelled a bit over the months with no problems with the passports. We had been to Italy, to Morocco and spent three weeks in Brazil. That last one was incredible. From the frantic excitement of Rio to the Iguacu waterfalls and of course the rain forest. We got in and out without hassle from any Border Security and had a fine old time. Have you ever drunk a Caipirinha? Delicious.

All the travel was great but it wasn't what we wanted to do for the rest of our lives. We had both formally retired from work and were getting our pensions. Not as much money as the salaries but that was a side issue. We were rich anyway but didn't want the accoutrements of money. Like Joe, I didn't need stuff. I had all I needed with Joe. The more time we spent together the more I liked him and the more I liked him, the more I loved him. It was like that first flush when you meet and you know you have met the one. We were like kids, holding hands, taking photos, selfies and yes, posting them on Facebook. We had started a private Facebook where people have to be invited and join on the basis that nothing gets re-posted. So far it was working, nothing viral. Buzz had sorted the one out for us.

Retiring was odd. Joe had worked at his place for twenty or so years and I had fifteen years at my job. We worked with a lot of people but for all of them we had just disappeared from the workplace and ended up on the telly or in the papers. There was no announcement, thank goodness, no party, shame, and no clock, good.

We were rootless. Organisations and institutions kept asking us and offering us large fees if would speak at conferences on atheism or humanism but we turned them all down. The publicity attached to us had died down to a trickle and we didn't need more of that or more money. Joe had had those ideas of hobbies he told you about earlier, you know, the race horses, camper vans or sailing and I had rather pooh-poohed them. I still wasn't keen because they didn't provide an answer to our lack of focus and lack of ideas about what we wanted to do or achieve.

It was on the plane back from Brazil that my next big idea started coming together. You know that Rio is as famous for its favelas as it is for the carnival, the Olympics and the World Cup and we hadn't seen such poverty in all our travels. Poverty combined with an air of menace; drugs and guns. We talked about how we could make a difference, could we sponsor a school, could we award bursaries to universities and soon realised we didn't know enough about how to address issues such as these without throwing away money; without risking it getting into the hands of those who would continue with a status quo because it suited them. We were happy to distribute funds but didn't want them getting into the wrong hands and didn't know how to go about it. So I phoned Charlie. I wanted some concrete thoughts before I told Joe what my idea was.

Chapter 4

Charlie. Solicitor

I made the appointment with Sandy and, as before, she surged into my office chockful of enthusiasm for her latest wheeze. I alluded to it earlier. She talked at me at a hundred miles an hour, a barrage of questions that I couldn't answer but promised I would try and get the information that she wanted. As I said before, most of my work is in Magistrate's Court, conveyancing, wills and leases and employment law. I pointed this out to Sandy but she said I was the only lawyer she knew and she didn't want to risk going elsewhere.

I had no experience of this whatsoever; I told her so. She said she respected my integrity and was sure I could do as good a job as anyone and it would be an intellectual adventure we could both go on.

This was a much bigger fish to fry than the last episode and I told her it would cost an unknown sum to make it happen. I think she thought I was trying to take advantage of the money that they had accrued over the last year and a bit. I told her the hourly rate I would charge and would give her a breakdown of the hours on whatever basis she wanted them and she could stop me whenever she liked. I don't want her to think of me as an opportunist.

She told me that she wanted to put her and Joe's around two hundred million pounds into the project and my fees wouldn't make a dent in even the interest the money was earning. It was a bit of a put down and I was ashamed of having brought it up thinking my value was still higher than hers, you know, as a Lawyer.

It took me a couple of weeks to get the information I wanted and make it coalesce into what Sandy wanted with the detail she needed. It was a great idea, but I will let her tell you about it. I'll also let her tell you about the other news they have that I got involved in. It gave me a real sense of pleasure, a sense that I hadn't had since I became a solicitor. I was doing something good. I was going to be a part of something that would make a difference, not joining in something for the sake of show and networking. (I'm not going to be negative about the Rotarians but Christmas collections in town centres can only do so much).

Chapter 5

Sandy

I met with Charlie and he appeared to have come up trumps with the plan. I presented it to Joe. I had hated keeping the idea from him and wanted to tell him every day. I knew that he would like the idea but I wanted the details pinned down.

We don't have to go for fancy meals or flowers or good Whisky as a precursor to a thought shared but I booked a table where it would be possible to get a bottle of fizz if he liked the idea and wanted to do it. I was confident and my confidence wasn't misplaced. I said, "do you remember that day when I told you I was working up an idea?"

"Yeeeees."

"I've got another one."

"Please, no."

"You'll like it."

"Go on then."

I was bursting to tell him. "I think we should set up a charity to disperse our funds to do good things, to do good things with no strings attached."

"What do you mean?"

"What we saw in Brazil, what we see on the news in Africa, the poverty, the lack of educational opportunities, the hunger, the disease."

"We can't eradicate those things."

"But we can make a difference. If we choose activities carefully, maybe on a small scale at first and do it with no angle."

"I see your point. When I was talking to Corr, Butt and Tudor, they said we should donate money to charities, charities related to their faiths. I just thought they were being hypocrites and they were. So your idea is to find and fund projects that have no religious angle?"

"I'm not sure. Do you remember those women in Morocco, begging on the streets and you thought there should be a man or a family taking care of them? What if there was no man or no family and they were destitute, what if they had no angle based in religion. They were just poor, on the edge".

"I'm not sure we should get involved. What if someone objected to our giving funds to these women and punished them for taking money from apostates."

"We would need to look on a case by case basis but I think we can do good things, be busy and make a difference".

"I like the idea."

"Good."

"But we have no expertise."

"You might eventually guess this, but I have had Charlie take a look at the options. We can either set up a charity or a charitable foundation, or both. With the foundation, we can donate to organisations that share our values but have experience and knowledge on the ground, in each of the areas they work, in each of the countries they work."

I knew Joe was testing me to see how far I had thought the idea through. He told me he was thinking similar thoughts but had done nothing about them. "Shall I order some fizz then?"

"Yeah. Let's do it." I think Joe told you at the beginning he wasn't one to make a hasty decision but he did it again. I was so pleased. "Tell me how we're going to do it."

I spent the next twenty minutes telling him what Charlie had told me about setting up a charity, or a foundation, the need for trustees, the need for a broad range of skills, the need for financial responsibility. He asked me why don't we just give the money to a charity like Oxfam. I said their heritage was Quaker and that I wanted, and hoped he wanted, was our money to not have any religious affiliation whatsoever. He agreed.

"What about trustees. Any ideas?" he asked.

"I've spoken to Charlie, who has done a lot of groundwork and he would be happy to continue to provide legal expertise."

"Does he have any expertise. I thought he just did scumbag burglars in court on a Friday morning and a couple of houses a week."

"What he does is limited, I know, but he is a solicitor and he is capable of doing things we ask of him. As evidenced by the information I've got from him."

"But isn't that just a job creation scheme of his own creation?"

"Now you're being too cynical. I know he has always fancied me but it doesn't mean anything. You don't need to be jealous."

"Jealous? Get out of here."

We opened the bottle of bubbly to celebrate the birth of the idea. I say birth because up until then it had been a gestation if you get my drift. I'm back to waffling, aren't I? That's a good thing. I'm happy again.

Chapter 6

Joe

It was a good idea and, like she said, she had done far more work on making it happen than I had. We needed a name and went through that whole process again. The initial idea was for the Quigley foundation but it sounded over pompous. A bit like the Bill and Melissa Gates Foundation and we weren't going to be on the scale. We thought about calling it Hendrix but dismissed the idea. We decided we were going to have to be serious if what we were going to do was going to be seen as serious and that name didn't work.

We went through the whole thing we did last time but this time we had to exclude any references to Gods or any kind of deity and not to any name anyone else had. But we finally hit upon it. It was obvious really. My idea. The Steffan Foundation. We were going to do the work in his name. It made Sandy cry. She blubbed like a baby and thanked me.

We spoke to the girls about the idea and they loved it too. In fact, they both wanted to be a part of it and that suited us. We hadn't wanted to ask because we hadn't wanted to impose our will on them. Bec said she was bored at work and wanted to learn new skills in new environments and Daisy hoped we would get involved in educational projects that she could lead. Fine by us.

The discussion about the objectives of the charity or the foundation went on for some time. There would be a flood of demands for money and we would need a set of principles. These were the ones we decided on. We weren't going to get involved with war zones. It would mean the possibility of taking sides and as most wars were fought by religious zealots, look at Iraq, Syria, Kashmir, we didn't want to appear to support one or the other. We weren't going to get involved with famine relief. It was too big and corrupt. There was no way we were going to pay despots for the privilege of feeding people and the other charities had a foothold there anyway. We weren't going to become an NGO, attending conferences and events and splashing money around at dignitaries. This sounds like a lot of what we weren't going to do. We decided to focus on education which would be on IT, mathematics, engineering and science. The rational subjects.

	We asked Buzz if he would do the IT. Neither Sandy nor I had sufficient knowledge of contemporary systems albeit I had been effectively supervising them at work for years. I didn't need to confess that it was all above me, especially the social media side. Buzz, blew us away when he said he would give us half of his fortune, around a hundred million pounds and set up the IT. We couldn't thank him enough. He said he would have given more but that he and Sally had been working on similar ideas for a charity and he wanted to get involved in start-up IT ventures in Africa to do with healthcare. We were all as one. We had more money than we could ever dream of and it seemed blasé for Buzz to simply give us that much money. But he did. He also became a trustee.

Johnny joined us. Not on a full-time basis. Not on a retainer, but because he wanted to do good, worthwhile things and he didn't want to be paid. I looked this gift horse in the mouth and asked if he would be as committed as he should be if there was no money in it for him. He said he would do it for the memory of Simon Cleve and that touched us all. You don't expect PR men to have a heart for anything other than money.

We briefed him about the balance of publicity we wanted. We didn't want to raise merry hell and have all kinds of godbotherers outside the offices, offices we were yet to find, with placards, noise, chairs and thermos flasks. But we didn't want to have to be secretive. We weren't going to be blowing a trumpet about the ability of the faithless to do morally acceptable things but we needed to manage the volume of publicity and its location. He was game, he said, it would be a challenge and he would do it to balance his work with vacuous celebrities and their drugs issues.

None of us wanted the money but we didn't want it to go to waste. None of us wanted tangible blingy things, or not much. We talked though the concept of whether we were going to do what we were going to do to seem somehow better than the religionists who did things with a "I want to get into heaven" motivation or a "look at me, look what a good person I am" viewpoint. There was an element of wanting to be seen as having a moral compass but not in comparison with the religious charities; simply because we could.

There was still money coming from the app. It trickled in, I say trickled, at the rate of nearly a million pounds of revenue a day from all over the world. It's like people still support underdog internet ideas like Yahoo! and throw a little money their way. We had no direct connection between the app and the charity, we didn't want people buying the app as a way of supporting what we were doing. Our efforts would be based on what we could earn from the money we had, not on new revenues but we weren't going to turn down any money so long as it came from the right place.

Chapter 7

Nick, former security man

I was well made up when Mr and Mrs Quigley asked me to work with them, or more accurately for them, in their new charity. The explained to me who Steffan was and I thought it was well sweet what they were doing with the money. I had no idea how much they had made but when I went to their offices they were getting on with a load of stuff. They had a building on an old industrial estate in Welwyn Garden. There was an open plan floor and a couple of offices including a meeting room. There was loads of IT stuff and what looked like a studio with some black geezer talking to the camera and fiddling with some piece of kit. I don't know what it was but I found out later., I never knew I had it in me to say something like "It's a PLC, no not a business you numpty. A programmable logic controller". Look at me.

I've never worked in an office before and I didn't know why they had asked me in the first time. I was still doing a bit of security, you know, nightclubs and such, but it wasn't much of an earner and, believe you me, it was dull as fuck compared to the army or protecting Mr and Mrs Quigley's house from those religious nutters.

They wanted to know if me and my mates wanted to work for them. I had no idea what we could do but Mr Quigley explained that they were going to be building schools across Africa to teach IT and engineering and he needed men who could build. My army training was more than how to shoot an Iraqi or an Afghan. I learned electricals, Pete did plumbing and big Jacko was a dab hand at carpentry.

So, a few months on, we find ourselves out in a relatively peaceful Rwanda building what they call a Steffan school. It isn't that fancy. A couple of classrooms but Buzz, the IT geek, it was weird meeting someone looking like he does with the amount of money he's got, coming out to install the routers on the satellites for the internet and plugging it all together. Man, he works quickly. Two days it took him and he had it all up and running. The charity has developed what they call distance learning modules to bring these skills, that are basically beyond me, to the kids in the most far flung places.

Me and the boys are having a good time. We sleep in a tent and cook on a billy, no comforts, a bit like being out in the army. We get up in the morning, build, have a lunch with the locals, they love us and love what we're doing, do some more work and then they teach us stuff in the evening. We are made to feel welcome. I learned how to cook millet. If ever my missus saw me doing some of this stuff she'd laugh her tits off but we put stuff up on Facebook for the schools to show what progress we're making and back in England they love the pictures and put them all over the charity website.

This is the third one we've done. We did two in Burundi where we had a local fixer help us get the materials. It's cheaper to source locally than to get them shipped over, but the IT stuff comes in a crate a day or two before Buzz gets here and bingo up it goes.

The locals organise who goes to the school and what they learn with, programmes set up by one of the daughters, the one that had her car graffiti'd. Daisy, that's the one. She was out meeting locals finding out what it is they have, what they need, finding locations, getting all the right permissions. We would have done a few more schools but the dignitaries, chiefs or whatever, wanted money to let them do it and, to be fair, the Quigleys are true to their word. No backhanders.

    This is good work. When I was at home, me and the missus, love her really, got on each other's nerves a bit. I was used to postings overseas whether it was training in the Artic or shooting towelheads in the middle-east. Can I call them towelheads? Is it okay? I get home for a few days after each school, we go out, have a drink and a laugh together, take the kids to MacDonald's or the football and then I get all itchy. This gig is perfect.

Chapter 8

Former PC George Cross

I bet you didn't expect to hear from me again but after all the noise died down outside Mr and Mrs Quigley's house I was at a bit of a loss. I had enjoyed trying to keep the peace outside their house although I hadn't been that successful all the time. Afterwards I was on the beat and doing paperwork back at the station and it wasn't much. I was bored so I retired hoping I might find something more interesting to do.

I had a retirement party, after all I'd done over thirty years, man and boy and that girl from the local paper, the one who did the Quigleys at the beginning, she was there with a photographer and I got a piece in the paper. Imagine, my ugly old mug staring back at me on page five.

And blow me down. Didn't I get a call from Mrs Quigley. Come and see us, she said, come and have a cup of tea and a biscuit. I always liked her, and him, both of them, so I went to this place of theirs, a scruffy old building and they told me what they were up to. Nice idea, really.

Did I want to do reception and security for them in their office. I was delighted and said yes please, like a kid. They got me a uniform, black trousers, white shirts, black pullovers and a couple of ties and I sit in reception checking visitors in and out, checking parcels in and deliveries out. I manage the CCTV, a system that that Buzz man put in, very good it is, state of the art and I answer the phone. I've got a computer to log calls and visitors and parcels and I do the rotas. You might think it isn't much but we have to watch out for cranks and assorted nutters. We haven't had any because we keep a low profile but they wanted my nous, my nose, my ability to sniff out troublemakers.

I get on well with the girls and the others who work here and it is easier. All those youngsters in the force, sharper than me, quicker on their feet than me. I couldn't chase a runaway burglar if you put a rocket up my arse. And it's indoors, warm. I've got a card for the coffee machine and I can help myself whenever I want. Makes a difference from having to cadge off the local caffs on my rounds. I'm happy.

Chapter 9

Buzz

My news! Well, me and Sally are engaged and we're going to get married soon, out in Africa. Fuck me, it is a big place and hot and not like England at all. Very few nerds to talk shit with. I've been out quite a few times with Sally to look at healthcare projects we can fund and to do the Steffan schools.

That Nick, he's a good find. He and his team turn around the buildings in no time at all and he's a big bastard, so's his mates, all ex-squaddies. They have fun with the locals and it's good to see them joining in but they don't take any shit from anyone who objects to what they're doing. I know Daisy paves the way for the school with the local dignitaries so there shouldn't be any trouble but there's always some chancer trying it on. They get short shrift from Nick.

So far, we've done three schools and there's plans for at least ten more. It's funny because sometimes Charlie, the Solicitor comes out to have a look around to make sure the money is being well spent, trustee function of some sort and he can't cope with the heat. He walks around in khakis like he is some colonial and he shouldn't but you can't see him in anything else. He has sweat patches all over, holds a handkerchief to his nose to avoid breathing in the dust and fumes. He looks like he should be in a 1920's Tarzan movie.

So far me and Sally have got a project getting antidysenterics out to remote areas where the water isn't too good. We are working with Joe and Sandy to develop water systems from underground aquifers in Tanzania. We want to get the systems in and that is where the next school is going to be, Dar-se-salaam, to train up the students and engineers to be able to stand on their own two feet. First, we identify the problem and go in with a clinic and the drugs. Sally is great at this. We have scores of people coming in weary from the shit that pours out of them and we put them on drips and give them the drugs they need until they are, well, solid again.

The clinics are permanent and we work with locals to make sure demand is met in the right places. Then we plan to send in a geologist and we do some aerial mapping to try to find the water that's clean and extractable. It'll take a year or so but we're making good progress and it's nice to have a plan, a focus. I haven't worked this hard, ever, even when the app was pulling in all the money but the beer, when we stop for a bit, is delicious.

I have to have a driver still, a guide, a fixer, I can't get the hang of it even when there's no people and no kerbs. Sally thinks it's funny. I think there might be something wrong with me. It isn't coordination. I can put a system together in one of the schools in no time. I don't know, I'm not going to dwell on it.

Sally didn't want any of the money but I had to insist she gets paid. I've got enough to do whatever I like but she needs to earn. She said we should get Charlie to look at a pre-nup, but I don't want any of that. I'm naïve enough to believe in trust and Joe and Sandy like and trust her too., That's good enough for me. She works like a Trojan, morning, noon and night and in the heat she has a glow about her. Her eyes sparkle, her smile is infectious and her enthusiasm never stops. She's like a Duracell bunny.

Chapter 10

Julian

Surprised to see me back? I was surprised to get a call from Sandy. I didn't really get to know her. I didn't really get to know Joe but it was nice to hear from the wife. She called me and asked how I was. I told her I was well. Was I taking all my medication, she asked and I said I was. Was I busy, she asked. I said I wasn't and asked her why.

She promised me it had nothing to do with pity or charity on her part, but she was starting a charity with Joe and their daughters and asked if I would like to help. I didn't know what with but she told me there would be jobs to be done, looking after the post, parcels to send, calls to make and take, filing to do, records to keep, plenty, she said.

I asked her if she was sure I could do it and she told me she wasn't but because I had taken a lead, because I had tried, because people did respond there should be plenty that I could do and do well. She was going to pay me a living wage but I had to promise to stay on the meds and appreciate that work was work and I would have responsibilities. This was like the most important thing for her but she said she wanted me to do well and that made me feel I could do well. I said, "yeah, Mrs Quigley, I am well up for it". She said I should call her Sandy but I told her I might feel it was too personal, too friendly for what I thought about work and we agreed Mrs Q.

    Six months in, man, I'm busy, there's so much stuff to do. We've done a few of the schools and we are getting used to doing more. Mrs Q. said I should get myself a passport as they might need me to go abroad. That was massive. I've never been abroad and I would have shit myself if anyone had asked. The girls are great and supportive; they say they couldn't do it without me. I reckon they are pulling my plonker but they say they mean it. I feel good, I feel confident, not with everything and going abroad would be big. But I like what I'm doing and I like myself.

Chapter 11

Joe

We had had the idea for the charity, well Sandy had a better idea than I and it was supposed to find us a purpose but the girls took over. They are such well brought up girls. They work all the hours and set up a crèche in the charity offices to make sure they and any mums that work for us have somewhere to put the kids, see them during the day. There's also a room with a TV and a couple of tablets and a PlayStation for the older kids to drop in and see their folks if they want to.

The sad thing, well, not sad, but a consequence of all this is that Sandy and I didn't have much to do. The girls are quicker off the mark than we are, have smarter ideas, realise them quicker than we could and get the benefit of what we do out to where it is needed sooner than we can. The idea of the distance learning to make the money go further with modular lessons using multi-lingual tutors was fantastic. It means we can get up and running in no time. But we are not needed except as trustees to approve the spends.

Bec has the money earning for the charity and she has put systems in place with Buzz that will grow as the charity grows. The youngsters are doing it all and we're not doing what we wanted. However, what we wanted is being done quicker and better than Sandy or I could do so we can't grumble.

We made a different kind of move. We put Hendrix on the market and, because of its place in the story we got a very good price for it. Charlie reckons there was a premium of a good fifty grand over other house prices in the area. We had so many people come and look at the house and then go away saying "we'll think about it" or "I'll have to talk to the family" or "I've got a few other houses to see". I have a friend who works in car sales and they have something called the "be back bus", which never comes back and all these people are on it and don't have the heart or balls to be upfront about their motivation for wanting to see the house. A bunch of time wasters, if we were short of time or had better things to do. But we sold to a lovely young couple with kids who will use the house as a family home instead of how Sandy and I used it to just slob in front of and shout at the telly and cook indulgent food.

Buon giorno. We're learning Italiano because we have bought a place in Umbria. We have an old farmhouse we are renovating with thirty acres of olive trees and ten acres of oranges and lemons. We got it for the same money as we sold the house in Welwyn Garden because it is a bit run down and out in the middle of nowhere. This is good. We aren't trying to avoid the seriously Catholic Catholics in the country but they would have to drive a good ten or so kilometres to come and protest and I don't think they have cottoned on to who we are. No siamo Giuseppe e Alessandra. Buon giorno, como va. We both have lessons twice a week and Sandy has tapes that she listens to more assiduously than I do. We are busy on the house which needs modernising although it does have one of those big standalone baths we had at the hotel on the Cotswolds and yes, we do share from time to time.

We are trying to renovate the house using materials that are age related and sympathetic however things like the kitchen are getting mod cons as well as flagstone floors, marble surfaces and beautiful cupboards. We are splashing out a bit because we do like cooking and there is so much fresh produce in the market in town as well as butchers, breads and booze, of course.

The only other things we have splashed out on are a pair of shoes, let's call it a tribute to Simon, from Florence, plain brown loafers that cost me seven hundred and fifty euros. And a couple of cars. When we were travelling, Sandy saw an Alfa Spyder and fell in love. I spent ages looking for one, eventually finding a 1967 boat tail, in red with black leather seats and importantly a Nardi steering wheel. Authentic to the last and beautiful to behold. I bought an early sixties Mercedes Ponton Kombi (look it up, it is a very plain old estate car but full of charm and very usable) because I fancied a beaten up old car to use to bring materials to the house that would just go for ever. We have a specialist in classic cars in the town who made sure I wasn't buying a lemon and he keeps them fettled.

I also used the Kombi on our first olive harvest to get the things to the press and the oranges and lemons to the wholesaler. This rural life is wonderful. It isn't too demanding intellectually or physically but it is enough to keep us busy and content. I'd like to thank, especially, the Hare Krishna group for showing up early in the scheme of things and getting the Iman, the Vicar and old Father Corr to react.

I think Sandy, who made this all happen should tell you a little more about what we do here. So, thanks for reading. Addio miei amici.

Chapter 12

Sandy

So, Joe has left it for me to finish up. We are really enjoying life here in Italy. We didn't want to splash cash on indulgences and mainly exist on our pensions and the little income from the olives, lemons and oranges. He will have told you about the cars. My Alfa is a beaut. I imagine myself as an older Audrey Hepburn with a scarf delicately wrapped over my shoulders, wind in my hair; it's a left-hand drive and I love it. Joe's old Merc is better than he makes out but we do use it for what it was intended, a workhorse.

We still get up early. It seems impossible to shake that off, and one of us drives to the village for croissants or some such. We squeeze our own oranges, the coffee is awesome and we do some work on the farm, not much. It gets hot around midday and we have cold meats, olives, anti pasti and salads for lunch and often a large glass of local red. A nap in the afternoon, read, potter, look out for the tradesmen coming to work on the house. What's particularly special though is we have dinner, veal and pasta, or fish and then drive into town for the passagieta. This is great and involves ice cream. You buy an ice cream from one of gelatarias and go for a walk up and down the main road in town. It's very social with lots of nodding and buona sera and we have met, albeit on brief acquaintance, a few couples but for now, while we learn the language and while the fuss dies down, we will keep ourselves to ourselves.

Back to the house after the ice cream to a glass or two of grappa. The terrace at the back of the house has distant views of hills and cypress trees, vines and barley crops and is truly beautiful. We sit and chat or read and pass the time.

Joe has regressed into his late teens and early twenties. His beard is long and grey and unkempt and he has a pair or workman's dungarees, trying to get that old sixties look back, that come down to just above his ankles with a pair of espadrilles and a beaten up straw hat. Ever the peasant but he is such a handsome man now the lines on his face have retreated a little and he has colour in his cheeks.

I should tell you it isn't all about Italy though. We fly home at least once a month to attend meetings at the charity. We are both trustees and we approve the spends and see the girls. It was fun to find George and Julian, who both tried to do so much to keep the peace but failed spectacularly and have them work with us doing things they are happy doing. No pressure. The girls are in their element, Daisy travelling and Bec in charge of the funds. Buzz is happy and looking forward to his wedding.

The flights are a bit of a drag, the local airport is tiny, Luton is a chore but it is all in a good cause and we love it. We're happy. We talk about Steffan when once we might not have done. He has a legacy, in the schools and in mine and Joe's fond, no not fond, loving remembrance. One too many glasses of grappa and one of us will well up. Poor little sod. Well done for giving us so much.

The end.

Printed in Great Britain
by Amazon